A Royalist

The Loyalist's Daughter, or, Tale of the Revolution

A Novel: Vol. II.

A Royalist

The Loyalist's Daughter, or, Tale of the Revolution
A Novel: Vol. II.

ISBN/EAN: 9783337051693

Printed in Europe, USA, Canada, Australia, Japan

Cover: Foto ©Andreas Hilbeck / pixelio.de

More available books at **www.hansebooks.com**

THE

LOYALIST'S DAUGHTER

A Novel

OR

TALE OF THE REVOLUTION

BY

A ROYALIST.

IN FOUR VOLUMES.

Vol. II.

LONDON:

ADAMS & FRANCIS, 59, FLEET STREET, E.C.

1867.

J. SWIFT, Regent Press, 55, King Street, Regent Street, W.

THE LOYALIST'S DAUGHTER.

CHAPTER XVI.

He took a bugle from his side,
He blew both loud and shrill,
And four and twenty belted knights
Came skipping owre the hill.—Old Ballad.

THE gratification of her inquiries was not a greater pleasure to Diana Vine, than the little passages which had passed between herself and the youth. For she was not made of that material which is proof against the language of tenderness or gaiety, whether addressed to herself on her own proper account, or if not for the sake of her mistress, with whom we must leave her, to impart all the wonderful and exciting things, which she had heard and seen, during her short but eventful absence.

Hubert's voyage of discovery with the Oxford men, if boys of fifteen or sixteen years of age may be called such, had inspired them with an

exalted sense of his experience as a navigator,
and of his judgment as a pilot. Their confidence in his guidance was confirmed, both by
his tried sagacity and his age, which by several
years exceeded that of any of the party. His
inferior rank in life too, under such peculiar circumstances, but above everything his local
knowledge of the place and its denizens, induced
them to put themselves under his guidance.
No sooner had they fully realised the extraordinary position of their valued helmsman and
friend, than their impatience and impetuosity
burst all restraint. Hubert's report, coloured as
it naturally was with a thousand blood-stained
atrocities, in which he steeped the character of
the master who had been vile enough to dispense
with his services, increased the young men's
fears for their absent comrade.

It so happened, either by chance or design,
that on their way to The Royal Oak, (which ill-
nature or envy said had once been kept by Peter
Penderel, an uncle of Miss Penderel, whose
loyal association with the Royal Oak was well-
known,) our party fell in with a discontented
band of labourers and tradesmen, who had been
put off from week to week, with a promise of
wages, which they had not yet been paid. They
were in deep sympathy deploring to each other
their ill-treatment and distress. Indeed the
demands on the purse and the attention of Lord
Lovelace had, since the landing of William,

been so exhausting, that his exchequer was reduced to cheques and promises drawn at sight upon the rich future, which was freighted with wealth and honours. His present and available means, his own property, if not a trifle of his ward's, had been ill or well spent, according to the view of conflicting parties, in fights and plans against the Government of James. The poor man's hard earnings were alienated from him, and diverted into channels of politics or ambition. To such, said the discontented, it mattered not what prince, or potentate, or power reigned over them, so long as they obtained food and raiment, and a fair day's pay for a fair day's work.

"'Tis just as he served me," said the crafty huntsman, who had overheard their conversation. " He only makes use of us all, as you use your old pickaxe,—driving us into his earths and throwing us aside when he is done with us. Law and debt, soft solder, and even smiles, will not support your wives and children. While we, like so many moles, have been working under ground, clearing out his choked holes and secret passages, or making his fortune in the fields, the bloody colonel has made use of what is ours and made us toil for his own schemes : he has run rather cunning, but his hounds are now brought to a check. He must try back again. He has once more broken cover, and now is your time. He is to have a chop at the " King's

Head," said Hubert, solemnly, before he returns again to Hurley.

The Oxford men, not having heard of that inn, seriously believed that no less than the head of King James would satisfy the cannibal lord, and shouted, one and all, "Let us have a chop at the traitor first."

Their excitement began to defy Hubert's control, so that when he undeceived them they had attained to such a heat that even a cold evening in December could scarcely cool them. In the mean time the recital of one grievance led to another until the measure of their wrongs was nearly full, when Hubert, improving the opportunity, tempted them into the first of a combination; and partly leading, and partly coalescing with them, went on towards Lady Place, deeply touched with sympathy in their suffering, and burning to avenge, through them, his own grievance. They had not advanced far, when they were met by the peasants, who were returning from the cottage of the gardener where they had been talking over the affairs of the country. They informed Hubert of their desire to obtain by violence that redress which their late employer, Lord Lovelace, refused to their humble entreaties and just demands.

The precise object of their expedition was not very clear to them. Hostility to the Lord of Hurley, rather than any defined advantage to themselves, seemed to insure their co-operation.

The young and popular huntsman now found himself at the head of a dozen stout fellows armed with pickaxes, spades, hammers, or whatever implements their craft required, and which the time and place supplied. The neighbours had seen Hubert perform wonders in the hunting field, and were ready for any excess into which he might lead them. "Only be silent and steady," says he, " in your march."

He told them just enough to answer his purpose, of what was going on in the great house. The young gentlemen, with great respect, he reminded of their high station, and the serious dangers any false or rash step might incur. Their loyalty alone would enlist the household of Lovelace, and perhaps the insurgents of Berkshire against them. " Act in concert, and wait in ambush for a while as a body of reserve," says Hubert. " Let us keep our strength and our cheer for the moment of attack. Indeed," added he, with a foresight and strategy which might have done honour to an older general, "cover always affords a shelter to the old fox who buries his game out of sight, and has always an advantage over the hounds. If possible then, though the old fellow himself is prowling outside, we must try to scent the noble game he has left unearthed, and rescue him from such durance. We will try cunning; if this fail, we must bring all our forces against the garrison. We can effect an entrance into the mansion," says he, " through the windings of the ruins and the east postern gate; which has on former occasions often afforded me and my jolly companions and some of the more audacious domestics a secret passage to nocturnal revelry, and a safe and unobserved return." Saying this with the air of a man who had full confidence in his own resources, and the influence he had over others, he hastened on to the Oxford road, along which four or five stout yeomen farmers and half a dozen of Mr. Morton's tenants were riding in company from Reading Market. They were discussing the important and alarming state of the country, and the probable result of William's arrival, with all those profound, impartial, and convincing arguments peculiar to their class when animated by after-dinner influence.

"Our king," observes a farmer, ruddy, fat, and fortunate, "is a free trader in religion and in corn. No proper tax to keep the foreign grain, ay, and bastes, out of our market."

"The Prince of Orange will promote the interests of the country by his restrictions, and give us a chance to live," cried Master Williams, whose face was like a full moon, beaming in all its fulness through the agricultural distress, which could only be appreciated by the agricultural mind.

The arguments were conflicting, the conclusions unanimous. The farmers were the victims of oppression. They would vote for the farmer's friend.

" Who is that," says a cavalier, who was jogging up to the last speaker, accompanied by some friends of the high church loyalists, who were dissociating prelacy from Popery, and denouncing William as a dissenter, " who would smash the church, and make the nation a Babel of sects and Dutch conventicles ?"

Hubert and his rustic friends held aloof for some time, more alarmed than pleased at the publicity to which they were exposed. They soon moved and marched three abreast. The Oxford men, by some sudden impulse, joined the cavalier and high church party, and fell to the rear of this detachment of cavalry : so that now there were two parties in nearly the same interest, but not incorporated, organised, or reciprocally directed to the same immediate object.

The farmers had recourse to the consolations of the bottle under their distresses, and made an evening of it at The Oak, soothing their discomforts with baccy and brandy-and-water.

The cavalier and his high church associates were more on the alert. They were armed with pistols and swords, and were evidently prepared for offensive and defensive warfare.

The boatmen had discovered much in their expedition which had also been found out by their new acquaintances. The cavalier and high churchmen had been themselves once undergraduates at Oxford, and were deeply imbued

with loyal principles. The young men were un-
suspecting and unreserved. They frankly told
their seniors all which they could learn of Hough,
whose name revived many recollections of happier times at Oxford.

The cavalier and his party expressed their
concurrence in any plan which was practicable to
liberate the young man, and even to punish the
rebel who had dared to confine him.

Hubert, by that intuitive knowledge with
which the illiterate and the shrewd rustic is so
often gifted, soon discovered the communion or
feeling and interests which the elder party had
with the younger; and to serve so valuable a
reinforcement, he respectfully advanced towards
the foremost of the party, the cavalier, whose
hounds he had occasionally hunted since his dis-
missal from Lady Place, intimated his readiness to attend his party, and render them any
assistance in his power. So saying, he turned
to the young gentlemen, and imparted to them
his instructions, which they instantly communicated to their elder companions.

The fact of attacking a nobleman's mansion
sounded stunningly strange in the ears of
scholars and gentlemen, and seemed an unwarrantable aggression. Every Englishman's house
was his castle. But then Hurley House was
the prison of an innocent young gentleman,
and must be opened for his escape. It was
finally arranged to approach the house in two

divisions. Pondering well on the boldness of
the undertaking, Hubert marched his ditchers
and dammers and bargemen to The 'Oak,'
where he halted them, and plied them with
some good October, outside the door. "Now,
comrades," cried he, "let us to this gear, and
the dickens is in it if we cannot get the young
master free. Bear us a hand. Lie under the
west wall of the ruins till I sing a view-holloa."

Entrusting this ambuscade to Gaffer Giles,
the foreman of the gang of labourers, he with
cap in hand offered his guidance and services to
the united forces of the loyalists; including young
Tate who seemed disposed to mutiny, but was
forced forward with the rest. "Should the
postern be made fast," said Hubert, "it would
be easier to make a breach in the wall and storm
the place than to force such a barrier. But if
you will wait a wink, I'll blow my horn as a
signal for your rapid advance to the front,
which is least defended, and where I may want
your commands." He meant their assistance.
"So now having ridden to cover, gentlemen,
only wait a bit behind this clump of trees, till
I see whether the old badger's earth is stopped
against us."

The sportsman cautiously wound his way
under the shelter of evergreens and thick shrubs,
till he reached the postern gate, through which
he hoped to take the place by surprise, or even
to rescue Hough without opposition or disturb-

ance. To his great disappointment, but not to
his dismay, he found the once friendly postern
now secured by bolts' and bars, as immoveable
as a rock. To deliver the steersman from such
a prison, as well as to avenge himself on his
late master, was a task not to be abandoned; he
would sooner be the forlorn hope himself than
shrink from such a magnanimous adventure.
He reconnoitred in silence and solitude all the
well-known weak points of the building. The
result of his cautious observations taught him that
the garrison, whom he intended to surprise, were
prepared for an attack. The sentinel whom we
before noticed, or some other soldier, who had
relieved him, paced the weary self-same beat in
the courtyard, but under a different window, one
which was guarded by bars, and in which was a
flickering light. He supported a gun on his
shoulder of great length and unwieldy weight.

"I'll e'en see what stuff the rebel cuckold of
the son of a bitch is made of," said the huntsman to himself, "before I summon my allies, or
spoil the sport." From all which he could
perceive, a body of armed men, contrary to all
probability was in possession of Lady Place.
To carry out, therefore, his plan, he could not
with any tact or address conceal himself; he
therefore boldly presented himself at the front
of the house, near the hall door, which he
essayed to enter.

"Stand, you rascal, stand," cried the sentinel

on duty for the night, levelling the huge gun at the intruder, as if he were only taking a long aim to make sure of him.

"What do you take me for?" said Hubert, coolly, with an air of indifference. " It is very unsportsmanlike to shoot your quarry, which might afford you good sport in the chase, and you will disturb the game which are asleep at this time of night. There goes an owl," says he, "just rising out of the ruins; try your hand on the bird of night."

" I am too old a bird to be caught by chaff," says the soldier. " You are a dead man unless you tell me at once your business and your name."

Perceiving by his accent that the sentinel was a stranger, Hubert in his turn took up the language of defiance, and expressed with indignation his surprise that a friend and servant of Lord Lovelace's should be treated with suspicion and mistrust.

" The colonel is beforehand with you, cried the sentinel, " he has already supplied the house with a garrison, and we need no additional defence."

" He who offers resistance to the commissioned messenger of the colonel offends his lordship and must pay the penalty of such folly. I only want Master Hough of Oxford, and shall esteem it good service if you will deliver him to me, without any of this ruffle and nonsense."

The sentinel, with his gun still presented, sternly demanded the proper warrant by which Hubert so authoritatively claimed the prisoner.

"I am come, as it would be evident to any but a stranger, like yourself, on the business of those who have a deep interest in Prince William's affairs, with letters for a worshipful gentleman, Mr. St. Aubyn ; only give me time to find them for you," added the huntsman, pretending to rummage his pockets for documents, which, in fact, had never existed.

The man with the firelock became impatient, and actually had his hand on the trigger, when a window just above him opened, and thence came a calm solemn voice, quietly admonishing the soldier, "Take the fellow's word for it ; I have seen him in the service of Lord Lovelace. Let the young gentleman go, and save further peril and this unseemly division in the camp. The country is in arms, and any uproar at this time of night may bring the riotous rabble upon us."

Taking advantage of this diversion in his favour, Hubert spoke the sentinel fair. "Hearken, old musketeer, before your arm is wearied with that 'ere exercise of ' present !' I crave parley with you, my fine fellow, and when you have the authority I give you," holding out a paper, "if it be not signed by your own colonel, shoot me on the spot as a liar and a scoundrel."

During this address, the sentinel's countenance exhibited an incessant play of passion, wrath, hesitation and fear; for the very name of Lovelace struck his ear as a sentence of death. Impressed by the plausible manner and self-possessed confidence of Hubert, the soldier stood motionless and off his guard.

Advancing steadily with the document, which he seemed in the very act of handing to the poor sentinel, and with more of the tiger than the lion in his action, he sprang upon his astonished opponent, seized him by the collar, and whirled him to the ground. He wrested the weapon from the hand of the trooper, placed his foot on his neck, and the muzzle of the musket close to his head. "Only utter one word, and you die the death," whispered Hubert. Scarcely was the last word out of his mouth, than with one loud, long, practised and tuneful blast of his horn, the huntsman awoke the wildest echoes of the ancient ruins and the denizens of the woods from their repose, and quicker than lightning brought the Oxford crew and their new confederates to the spot. The hounds, accustomed to the tones of Hubert's sprightly music, set up one yell and deafening yelp which made the welkin ring. The elder men who brought up the rear of the advanced Demies sent up a shout, "Hurrah! hurrah!" meanwhile the trooper was secured and bound hand and foot.

The first howl of the storm was growing into

a tempest, or as Hubert had it, as if the world, the flesh, and the devil had broken cover and burst away, and were all in full cry. Amid which the house dogs barked fiercely, as if they had some notion of what was going on, mingling their frantic yells with the shouts of the assailants. Such a horrible discord had scarcely been heard since the building of Babel, and might have awakened the slumbers of the dead monks. Women shrieked, cattle bleared, the din of war was mingled with lamentations and woe. The tumult shook Lady Place to its foundations. Amid this bedlam, the clear voice of the stroke oar, Mr. Tate, struck up in measured hexameter, which might have done credit to the lecture room —

"Exorcitur clamorque virum clangorque tubarum."

Tate, who preferred strategy to violence, pointing to the postern described by Hubert, recited mildly—

"Limen erat, cæcæque fores, et pervius usus,
Tectorum inter se Lovlaci postesque relicti."

The hurricane of terrific sounds which made night hideous was sinking into a lull, when the huntsman's view-holloa rose high over wood, water, and glen, in a loud inspiriting shout, never excelled in his palmiest field day in Berkshire. Impatient of each moment's delay, as if possessed with some sudden fury, the bargemen and labourers, the drainers, and bricklayers rushed from their ambuscade like tigers, but soon fell into good order at the east wing of the mansion. The rage and fury of the hounds, who rejoicing in the sound of Hubert's familiar shout, became at this second excitement perfectly beyond all bounds. Even before the actual assault, might be heard most unnaturally and frantically the baying of dogs, the crowing of cocks, and the furious yelping of the fox-hounds, amid the clash of implements and arms.

By this time Hubert found himself at the head of some three score stout fellows, all now formed and ready for action. Lights began to fly from window to window, and figures to flit about, inside, through the front rooms. The night was impenetrably dark, and shrouded the monastic ruins in deeper melancholy. The dense masses of clouds above them, the roaring of the winds through the crevices, the cry of the hounds, which had subsided into a dismal howl, the screech of the owl threw a mystic veil of necromantic horror over the strange scene. To an attentive observer, shadowy figures might be perceived rather by the rustling sound of their movements under the shrubs than by any distinct forms amid encircling darkness. Hubert, like a skilful general, once more reconnoitred the house and all the undefended points with which he was already tolerably familiar. No sooner had he returned to his motley division of besiegers than in reply to his shrill whistle the irregular stragglers who lay under cover ap-

peared in a moment in the rear of the besiegers.

Faircloth, fearful of incurring the charge of
cowardice, now appeared with his head at the
safe side of a strong, mullioned, well-grated
window, and challenged 'the marauders,' as he
called them, to tell him what they meant by disturbing the respose of a peaceful house at that
time of night.

A well-directed shot from the gun which
Hubert had wrested from the sentinel was the
reply. The charge glanced off from the mullions,
and only increased the major domo's courage.

" We are not without a garrison, which my
lord has left to protect the mansion," said he.

" Garrison or no garrison, my fine fellow,"
cried the huntsman, " we will have Mr. Hough.
His crew are gentlemen to the backbone, and
we will stand no nonsense. We have no desire
to disfigure your pretty face, nor to rumple your
ruffles ; we would not hurt a hair of your peri-
wig ; but if you are not the gentleman I take
you for, we will mince your delicate body as you
mince your fashionable words."

His most eloquent reply was a volley of no
vain curses, but telling shots, which poured forth
conviction on the besiegers that Faircloth had
something more efficient than mere insults at
his command. One or two of the outsiders fell,
for the garrison had not taken a line, and the
most forward were falling back to their destruc-

tion, when Hubert in his best voice cried, "Hark forward, hark forward, my mates ! Now, Gaffer Giles," shouted he, "bring up your fellows to the scratch : into the cover we must get, and if the old dog shows no sport, we must e'en unearth him for a run." Once more his bugle sounded to the charge. He rallied his forces. "Let us, my lads, level the rebel lord's stronghold to the ground, and add it to the ancient old ruins."

"If everybody had his own," cried Tom Brown, the head barger, "what he calls hisen isn't hisen. We han't been paid no honest wages, which we earned with the sweat of our brow." This speech had only less effect than a discharge of small artillery from within. One terrific hurrah rebellowed through the ruins, shook the very foundations of the place, and was followed by a tremendous crash of windows.

"Stand back, ye boobies, boors, and brutal bumpkins ; ye clods, ye mucks, ye ill-bred louts, ye rough rascals and pig-headed clowns, ye rake-shells, ye rapscallions, tag, rag, and bobtail, before we make dog's meat of you, for the hounds who are yelling for such a feast." To carry out this doughty threat, Faircloth rushed down stairs towards the hall, out of which, through iron bars that resisted all entrance, the well-dressed gentleman and his most effective followers let fly at random a few shots upon the assailants. Several volleys were soon exchanged, without

much effect on either side ; for in the emergency
the ammunition for fowling purposes had been
substituted for more destructive lead. The
assailants were more excited than seriously
wounded. At a given signal, which passed from
one division to another, the whole assailants,
combining their forces into one main body, concentrated their strength, and were only waiting
the word of command to carry the place, or to
die in the attempt.

Mr. St. Aubyn, who had coolly calculated the
interior weakness, and formed a fair estimate of
the numbers outside, wishing to prevent loss of
life, and destruction of property, which could
only end in the defeat of the defenders, and
entail much misery on both parties, turning
to Mr. Faircloth and the upper servants, thus
slowly and even solemnly spoke :

"As glory awaits the brave, who pour out
their blood in a good cause, even so there is
severe censure in store for the rash and thoughtless combatants, who bring danger on their
comrades and their friends without need and
without a chance of success. From what I have
observed by the dim and unsteady lights of the
place, and the lamp which still is left burning
over the gateway, there is no defence we can
make, which can avail us against such desperate
odds."

"What, Sir ! What !" interrupted Faircloth,
impetuously, nay impertinently, forgetting his

usual respect to Mr. St. Aubyn. "What words
are these?"

"The words of soberness and truth," answered
the unperturbed and serene gentleman. "We
must surrender, or bring destruction on Lady
Place."

To some this advice appeared worse than
treason, to others an insult to their courage and
behaviour.

With unaltered mien, St. Aubyn met their
offensive looks, saying, "I have told you the
only way open to you to save the house and
property of your master, your colonel, soldiers,"
glancing at the few troops near him.

"The first man," cried Faircloth, seeing some
of his subordinates wavering, especially when
the sound of the pickaxes and hammers against
the lower part of the house like battering rams
reached their ears. "The very first hand,"
passionately exclaimed the valorous gentleman,
"that is raised to open the door to such a rabble,
shall never be lifted again." Turning, in a rage
which he could not master, he betook himself to
the soldiers; "my blood," said he, "is ready
to boil at the very thought of surrender;" his
address was cut short by a tremendous wild war-
cry without, and the word "death" three times
reverberated throughout the buildings, and came
up to the inmates like so many hollow echoes
from the vaults below.

"Liberty to young master, or blood and fire."

c 2

The worst oaths of the worst of the cavaliers mingled with the cry and filled the stoutest heart in Lady Place with dismay.

Once more St. Aubyn calmly recommended negociation with the enemy, who were now supported by many just springing into action; and the dense mass of surging humanity, like a compact engine, was dashing against the house. Pickaxes, sledge-hammers, and whatever fury suggested, had effected a breach, which St. Aubyn observing, once more tried to bring them to reason, and said with earnestness and great coolness, "You cannot, my friends, hold out against these men any longer: surrender."

"Slay the traitor, slay the coward," was the savage outcry with which those inside greeted the truly brave man.

"However precious revenge may be," continued he, "we may not imperil the lives of those under our care by vain opposition. The house will be wrecked, many lives lost, if these desperadoes once set a foot inside, and induce the cavaliers to follow. I hear their voices in the distance, we shall pay rather too dear for our foolhardiness."

"Be pleased to inform me, sir," said Faircloth, putting himself into an elegant attitude, with energetic action and eloquent expression, "are you, on your own proper account, prepared to assent to conditions imposed by a discharged servant of my lord's?"

Mistress Di, who had been near the orator, and by smiles and gestures applauding his speech, gradually approached nearer to him as if to encourage him, while she slyly, with a dexterity which might have done honour to a London pickpocket, abstracted a bunch of keys from his pocket, to which was attached that of Hough's cell, and, yawning carelessly, slowly withdrew with her prize to her mistress.

In the meantime, Hubert was too good a sportsman not to observe these movements and turn them to his own advantage.

Assuming a courage which he never felt, the gentleman's gentleman delivered himself with great pomp and dignity, "Are you all mad? Do you think me so mean-spirited as to submit to a fellow who is not good enough to black a gentleman's shoes, or hold a candle to my own attendant? Only let the soldiers fire at once," said the grand man to Mr. St. Aubyn, "and we shall scatter them like chaff before the whirlwind."

While all these oral demonstrations were going on inside the citadel, hostilities outside were of a more martial character. The high church-men, the cavalier, the drainers and barge-men were widening the breach in the most vulnerable part of the edifice. The Magdalen men were the first to fling themselves into the breach, as a forlorn hope, singing, as they entered,

" Moriamur et in media arma ruamus;"

while the cavalier, who had a lingering word of
Virgil left in him, cried out with great spirit,
    "Sic animis juvenum furor additus."

The house was to all intents and purposes
captured. All that remained to be done was to
make a desperate attack on the posts occupied
by the defenders, and if practicable, to take un-
molested possession of the place.

While the conflict was thus raging, or rather
the assailants carrying everything before them,
Hough, who had been startled on the very first
aggression of the assailants from a disturbed
sleep, suffered more from suspense than actual
dread. Quite unconscious that the attack had
anything to do with his liberation, he could only
collect enough by the uproar to guess that some
party hostile to Lord Lovelace had taken the
opportunity of his absence to demolish his
house. Bewildered and dizzy at being thus
aroused from his unrefreshing sleep, and confounded by the effect of the many exciting and
complicated events to which he owed his confinement, he started to the window of his cell,
for he had not divested himself of his clothes,
but he could see or hear nothing to relieve his
perplexity. While he was deploring his hard
fate which locked him up in suspense, and was
looking about for some remote possibility of
escape, the hoarse grating of his prison bolt
suddenly fell on his ear. The key turned back
the bolt, the door opened, and a female figure

in an undress evidently thrown over her in the
moment of alarm—her hair streaming wildly
on her shoulders, her eyes glancing around with
fear, and bearing an aspect of forced resolution
—stood before him, weeping and trembling, in
the very midst of his chamber in the wall. Surprised beyond utterance or recollection, he could
only look on the damsel, whom his wishes and
thoughts transformed into Lily. Nor was it
until he had recovered from the sudden emotion
which overwhelmed him that he was able to dissuade himself from his first belief. The affected
simplicity and studied choice of language which
struggled to rise above her native vulgarity, soon
convinced Mr. Hough that it was no other than
Mistress Di Vine who appeared before him as an
Angel of Hope.

"O sir! what will become of me?" said she,
with her eyes fixed on the ground, and her
apron between her fingers, "the rapparees have
entered the house, and Mr. Faircloth has
savaged them—all is confusion. Oh! my
young mistress. Lawk-a-day! Oh! my goodness! Oh gemini! Lor! Quick, young sir.
O la! How my young mistress is taking on
about you! how she do fear for you! She desires
to see you a moment."

"Where?—when?" asked Hough.

"In her room—now," said the girl, rapidly.
"This is the last moment of our last hour.
They will fire the house, burn Faircloth, empty

the cellar, and gut the mansion. Hasten ! Hasten ! I shall lose my place very near. I shall lose my life. My mistress can't get over it. Come, come. Speed, speed, sir, for your life ! Follow me," she whispered, placing her hand in the folds of his dress, with a sort of gentle violence, which he resisted, remonstrating :

" Gently, my fair apparition,—show me the way. I will follow."

" I will go before you, sir. Oh ! if you did but know !

" Know what ? " said he, impatiently.

" Know how I felt for you. Oh ! oh ! deara me ! But how could I leave such a proper young man—gentleman,—so excellent in growth and presence, and such a real friend to Miss Lily, to be mewed up like a snail in a snail shell, which you couldn't carry on your back, and to be moped to death."

Avoiding the conflicting parties, and all observation, the girl led the way with great speed down the winding stone staircase. Thence she turned through a side door into a corridor, where stood Mr. St. Aubyn, surrounded by a few of the domestics, in the company of Miss Penderel clinging to him, and placing herself between her old friend and a party of the assailants, who mistook him for Faircloth. That worthy, when they entered the house, had concealed himself in the priest's hole. In their mistake they set upon Mr. St. Aubyn with blind fury, as the instigator of their opponents, and their insulting foe.

Never, even when Lily bloomed in her own tranquil bower, adorned in her most becoming attire, which Di had in her happiest taste arranged, was she more lovely, more serene, and more composed. She seemed rooted to the spot; so that " Solomon in all his glory," to the mind of Hough, was not so glorious as that fair flower, whose tendrils of love twined round St. Aubyn. The sight cost Hough a greater pang than fears for the threatened victim. He was amazed and could scarcely believe his eyes: each new conjecture contradicted the last.

She cried, " Oh! welcome, brave youth; you saved my life, now save a life dearer than my own."

Amid the insensate group who horribly scowl vengeance at the very peacemaker himself, Lily looked like some bright cherub from on high, whose mission was to calm the spirit of the storm. Her features contrasting with the grim faces around her, bespoke her an angel of light whose presence awed violence into subjection. That face which could rarely be viewed by any one anywhere without emotion, in such an hour and in such a scene wore an expression almost heavenly and irresistible to a lover. " Miss Penderel," he cried in accents which betrayed his concern; "what means all this? What is the disturbance, the danger? Who is it whom these men would tear from you and slay?"

"Do not ask, do not stay; but if you would serve me and save yourself, help! help!"

Just at this instant, as one rough fellow was forcing his way against the lady, Hough espied his crew emerging from the apartment into which through the breach they had entered. Delighted at seeing him, they rushed forward to join him, and following him, threw themselves into the very heart of the mistaken rabble, and dealing blows right and left as they might in a town and gown row, diverted the attack from Mr. St. Aubyn to themselves. Hough, like a commander-in-chief, now confident in his men and his liberty, kept aloof from the fight, and approached Mr. St. Aubyn and the young lady with great embarrassment.

The scene, the time and the cause of Hough's presence in such company as the lady and her friend, whom he secretly looked upon as his successful rival, all conspired against his utterance. Lily's eyes turned, and beaming with placid delight met his; her lips slightly parted, and heaving a sigh of relief she looked—it was not now a cold look of caution which she gave him, it was one of soft, amicable, speaking gratitude. There was, to say the very least, a

tone of deep interest in the glance. He would
but too willingly have poured out a tale of
tenderness mingled with fears for her safety,
but diffidence mastered his words. He fancied
that in her every gesture he could see a meaning. How little ministers to the hope of the
young heart ! What a shadow of a shade will
feed the young imagination ! At length his
tongue found utterance : "Every motive which
can influence my conduct—every action of my
future life—every thought which sustains me,
must emanate,"—contending emotions would not
suffer him to utter another word. To cover his
confusion, he addressed words of courteous
sympathy to Mr. St. Aubyn. He desired to
learn the cause of the dastardly ruffians' attack,
on a man so inoffensive and benevolent as he
appeared to him under unprovoked insult. Here
Miss Penderel briefly explained the respective
parts, which the valet and Mr. St. Aubyn had
taken, and how shamefully the flunkey slunk
away from that very danger which he had
brought so boastingly on himself and the whole
household. How the assailants had seldom
seen Mr. St. Aubyn, and in their excitement
failed to recognise, and indeed scarcely knew the
gentleman's gentleman, who rarely soiled his
foot outside the door, and the dress of the one
was of the same colour as the dress of the other.
The valet had retired from the fray, when he
was most needed, while Mr. St. Aubyn in

endeavouring to restrain the fury of the besiegers, whom he desired to spare, had been mistaken for the coward who had needlessly insulted and excited the mob.

CHAPTER XVII.

They knew what's what, and that's as high
As agricultural wit can fly.—*Faircloth.*

To Hough's observations, which were more polite than pertinent, Mr. St. Aubyn replied :

" The rude unthinking herd acted but according to their instinct and their kind ; their fury has been excited, and directed towards one object, whom they believe I defended, at the sacrifice of some of their party, and to the detriment of all. In their present anger and resentment they forget the former benefits they have received from Lord Lovelace. Nursed in earthen hovels they are earthy, and with spirits suited to their huts. Unblest by the light of moral, spiritual, or intellectual light, they are incapable of any feeling beyond the wild impulse of the moment. To them the sufferings and wrongs of this hour are everything. No ray of glory from heaven reveals a better or a brighter state, where patience and mercy will have their reward.,'

While Mr. St. Aubyn, Miss Penderel, and Hough were conferring together on the best course to adopt in such unusual and critical circumstances, Hubert found it more difficult to restrain than it had been to arouse the passions of his followers ; by talking to them, and chiding them as if they had been a pack of hounds at fault, he gladly at length brought them to a check, by assuring them of the personal safety of the youth, whom they so laudably came to rescue ; he even asked some of the most ungovernable to depart with a promise of a regular night of it at ' The Oak.'

" Not without a few more cuts at Master Faircloth's head," answered the foremost of those whom he addressed. " Some of our fellows are hurt, and one of our mates, Bob Bolter, the bargee, is shot as dead as a door nail by the conceited jackanapes," said he, pointing to Mr. St. Aubyn. " Only let us have a shot at the buck and leave him for venison and we are off."

They were presenting their fire arms, and only waiting an order to execute their amiable purpose, when Hough, jumping on a table, cried, with an address and energy which concentrated all their notice upon him, " Before you do anything, listen to the young stranger for whom you have risked so much, and whom you have so manfully liberated, at least from his dungeon."

Here there was a cry, " We were ready to lay down our lives for you, because Hubert told us of the lord's cruelty to you ; we have brought ourselves into trouble, and now you want us to spare the upstart who shot at us without cause, and called us clods!"

" Dang it, burn them altogether and roast them alive," muttered a surly fellow, who had a long grudge against Faircloth.

" Let me talk to you, my honest fellows, before you roast me, because a roasted man cannot speechify. Listen to me. Now you are sensible men ; hearken to me first and afterwards, when I have made my last speech and dying confession roast me. Peace, my masters, every one of you, and I'll tell you good news. Keep yourselves under arms ; but act like yourselves, and be Britons."

This last word elicited a thundering shout of applause. A deep silence followed, during which the Demy said, " you shall have my consent and assistance to fight it out, and to slay the buck, if he is in season ; but," cried he, pleasantly, "let me have my say. My tongue, like my limbs, wants exercise."

" Cut it short," says a fellow in a smock-frock, " and don't be so high in yourself, loike."

" You are mistaken in your man, Faircloth was too fair to endure your touch, and has run away and hid himself; that gentleman whom you would shoot is your protector, your friend,

my preserver, and yours—no other than Mr.
St. Aubyn, the friend of the poor man, and
physician of your sick."

Had the house and vaults been blown up, or
had even the departed monks appeared among
them the hearers could not have felt greater surprise than when Mr. St. Aubyn, at that instant,
with his benevolent brow beaming forgiveness
and compassion appeared near Hough.

"I'll stand to what the young gentleman
says," cried Hubert.

They stood uncovered before the good, great
man. No cheer escaped them, but each man
bowed his head in deep and silent respect.
They begged his honour's pardon, and recounted
to each other a few of his latest charities to
them and their families. They then asked for
Miss Penderel, whose generosity and visits of
mercy they had often experienced. Hough
looked to the spot where he had left her, but
she was gone. He then continued, "the
bravery which you have evinced so effectually
for me in this night's good service I shall never
forget." To Hubert, in particular, he addressed
words of admiration and gratitude.

"Warfare," said the huntsman, "is not
exactly my line, seeing the fox always *runs* for
it. The siege was beyond my mastery, I could
not match it but for the gear which my friends
brought to bear upon the man of finery. The
cavaliers gave their voice for stratagem rather

than violence; but they think themselves well
out of the affair : they are gone."

During this colloquy, Hough put his hand in
his pocket for a few silver pieces, to enable the
fellows to drink his health. In pulling out the
purse and handing it to Hubert for this purpose,
he perceived it was a richly embroidered one,
differing from any he had ever possessed. It
was, however, gone, and he could not recall it.
No sooner had Hubert poured out the contents,
than broad pieces of gold rolled in all directions,
covering a great part of the table with caroluses
and jacobuses. The sight of so much money
filled the men with wonder and admiration.
Hubert was proceeding to distribute the smallest
of the pieces to the leaders of each gang, when
perceiving that, even in the coins of the day,
there were hundreds of pounds, he gathered up
nearly the whole of the money and replaced it
in the purse, returning it with its contents to its
new master. Hough only looked his surprise.

In the mean time Hubert asked their honours'
leave to tell his comrades a bit of a story.

He said, "Once upon a time, and a very good
time it was, a great huntsman coming in from
the chase perceived the cradle, wherein he had
left his infant son and heir, covered with gouts
of blood and little morsels of flesh, and close
to the crimsoned cradle Gelert, his favourite
hound. He threw open the covering of his babe,
but found nothing but blood and clotted gore.

In despair he cried, 'O Gelert! you have de-
voured my boy, my life, my all!' and in anger
and revenge plunged his dagger into the animal's
heart. The hound groaned and fawned upon his
frantic master even in the agonies of death, and
licked the hand which slew him. The master in
his wild sorrow tore from the cradle all the
clothing, and there beneath all his darling smiled
in sleep, unconscious of his danger. On further
search a wolf was found still weltering in his
gore—the wolf which faithful Gelert had slain,
after having covered the dear heir out of the
savage beast's sight, and thus saved him from
death. The huntsman's joy with Gelert died.
In the chase he named his dogs. He called
Gelert, but Gelert was not there."

The worst of the intense broil had now subsided, and the cheers of the Oxford crew might
be heard at the close of Hubert's way of telling
his hearers how fortunate they were in not slay-
ing him who had preserved them and those dear
to them.

Having appeased their appetite for vengeance,
the lowest and most riotous of the victors began
to turn their attention to plunder. They had left
the scene just described the first moment the
Oxford men interfered between them and Mr.
St. Aubyn. Their first impulse was to break
into the cellar, but being alive to their more per-
manent interests, they thought it more prudent
to secure some valuables which they could turn

into money. In quest of such precious things as they could carry away they were prowling about the house. They were lost amid its intricacies, but still more in their own stupid admiration of the rich and massive furniture of the rooms. At last, rummaging about in every direction, they found themselves in a large apartment, panelled with oak, on which were wrought most curiously tilts and tournaments and martial scenes, but especially varied landscapes painted freely and broadly, without much reference to perspective; carved arches and lozenges, which a house carpenter was investigating with the eye of an artificer, tracing many of the figures with his finger as if for his own instruction, and with all that artistic curiosity which distinguishes the artisan from the unobserving herd. The inquisitive house carpenter was just bringing his scrutiny to an end, when touching a portion of the curious workmanship precisely in keeping and identified with the general design of the whole panel, to which it seemed attached, it gradually and noiselessly began to slide apart from the left one to which it had previously been fitted, into the opposite panel. He had inadvertently touched a secret spring. A deep, dark aperture was disclosed to the gaze of the astonished artificer: in silent amazement he viewed the mysterious contrivance, when his attention was arrested by a glimmering light inside the aperture, and he was suddenly struck dumb by an apparition. It was

the figure of a gentleman in a mourning dress
and white neck-tie, not unlike the Roman collar
of the period, which was thus revealed to the
curious observer.

At a time when to be reconciled to the
Catholic Church was an act of high treason,
especially during the civil wars, when Catholic
priests were hunted like wild beasts, and
even in later times, hiding places such as our
artisan had discovered were to be found even in
Protestant houses, for the shelter and concealment
of priests, but in the mansions of Catholics they
were quite common. Such was that at Mosely,
which concealed Charles II. in the hiding-place
of Father Huddlestone, of whom James II. said
to his brother when dying, "This good man once
saved your life, he is now come to save your soul."

In such a house as that of the Protestant Lord
Lovelace we can only account for this hiding-
place by the supposition that in accordance with
his temporal interests and intrigues he harboured
Catholic priests, whom his colleagues and Orange
emissaries might make their victims, if exposed
to their vengeance, and whom he might keep as
hostage.

The blood of the inmate of this receptacle was
evidently so much fevered with fear and excitement, that he was unable to speak. The exclamation of the artisan had brought his comrades
to the spot, and with eager curiosity they peered
into the dimly lighted cell. The feeble ray of

the lamp fell upon an enamelled portrait of the
Virgin and the image of her most Holy Son.
The gold crucifix, richly studded with rubies,
also other saintly relics were visible in the
gloom. A missal lay open, as if recently used by
a reader, who had concluded the Gospel; a rosary
lay by the golden-clasped book near the sacred
vestments: all spoke of the hated religion.

" Heaven be around us," cried the foremost of
the marauders, " what have we here ?"

" Look ye !" said a second, who had once seen
a Catholic celebrant surprised and apprehended
in his robes. " Here we have him in his den ;
the black-hearted traitor and Papisher !"

" And worse still," cried a third, " a *priest !*"

" We'll make more out of him by hauling
him to trial, than by all them ere gimcracks,"
meaning the robes, said another. " Lug the
Roman rascal out of his den," cried they all at
once. And yet they hesitated, as it were, awed
by the cabalistic mysteries of Romanism until
they ventured to read the Popish features of
their victim. No sooner had they taken their
lesson out of that book than they looked upon
him with scorn, and dragged him looking like
a dead thing, out of his hole.

Owing, probably, to the priest's hurry of
mind, or anxiety to do all which he was required,
a sort of spasmodic jerk of his arm inflicted a
blow on the foremost of his captors, who returning the same with interest made the blood flow

copiously from the Papist's nose. His features disguised in his own blood, the inmate of the cell was dragged out and carried into the very heart of the contending parties, who had by this time coalesced, forming ' a committee of the whole house ' to debate the terms of an amnesty and the conditions of a truce; for the garrison was not going to incur the risk of the colonel's resentment without some recompense.

No sooner had the blood-stained priest and his escort bearing the symbols of his religion appeared, than all with one voice agreed that Lovelace wore two faces under a hood. Most of them thought that the prisoner, the d—d priest of Baal had some secret. deep design, against the honest Protestants of the mansion. Their first impulse was to commit him, without a hearing, to the dungeon which Hough had vacated, and to have him up for trial, making him liable, in the eye of Justice Toogood, for all the turbulence and damage committed on that eventful night at Lady Place. The sight of the sacred vestments, consisting of a chasuble and cope, confirmed the decision of both conflicting parties, who, by this common object of their hate and fear were united together for the common good.

The feeling of mutual hostility having now in some measure been suspended, the jarring parties mingled in active union against the detected priest.

" A foul plot !" cried a burley bargeman.

" Nor shall it be smothered, though its father was nearly stifled," sneered the carpenter.

" The whole thing," cried a blacksmith, who was the oracle of the village, " is a popish miracle. May the devil blow wind into the plot ; I thought it was dead long ago."

This sally made all parties laugh. At this moment the butler, who had been out of the trouble and regaling himself with the farmers at " The Oak," returning, and finding the rage of the storm had been already quelled, entered the room. That gentleman was quite popular ; he left everybody alone in the present emergency, and, like Gallio, " cared for none of those things."

He was voted into the seat of judgment, to pronounce sentence against the papist. But no sooner was the trembling, dumbfounded culprit placed before him than the butler burst into a laugh, which first shook his sides, and then the very room in which the judicial proceeding was going forward. He soon, however, recovered his gravity, " Where is your evidence?" asked he, sternly.

" Here, my lord," cried a voice, in mock respect, producing the sacred vestments and the missal.

" If you have not more evidence," said the judicious butler, " I must charge the jury."

" You see already the criminal at the bar has had his claret drawn," said another.

" Claret!" said the cellarer, " who dare touch the claret under my care? I shall not take the trouble to go on. I may not be judge and counsel for the prosecution," said he, and flung himself out of his chair in a huff.

A murmur, arose and the low hum of many voices recalled Mr. St. Aubyn from his attendance on Miss Penderel. He took the butler aside, and signed to Hubert, who was near, to join them. The three were soon in close communion, when all the jury began to deal out summary punishment on the terrified captive, who was not allowed even to defend himself.

" The fellow," they shouted, " has hatched a damnable conspiracy which will blow up Lady Place and us with it."

Mr. St. Aubyn, being really alarmed for the fate of the poor man, desired that he should be fairly examined, and, if guilty, that he should be delivered up to Mr. Justice Toogood. An indistinct buzz of consent, and then silence followed.

" What is your charge against this silly fellow?" asked Mr. St. Aubyn.

A farmer, Sam Styles, who had only heard that he was a papist, sagaciously observed, if he was a papist it was his interest to blow up Lady Place, and to massacre every Protestant in Hurley; and if he was a Catholic *priest* it was his duty to instigate others to give him a lift in the business.

" But first, farmer, let us see that he is what you take him for," said Mr. St. Aubyn.

That most of the present company were strangers both to the domestic servants and the economy of Lady Place was evident; old Port, the butler, who never accompanied the colonel on his expeditions was an exception.

" I beg your honour's pardon," said Hubert, " but suppose, as the dog fox is now fairly un-kennelled, we wash away the bloody traces of the hunt."

With the consent of Mr. St. Aubyn, a bucket full of water and a mop were applied to the face of the culprit; when, lo and behold ! Mr. Fair-cloth, whose fairness had been so frightfully dis-figured, stood confessed to all present.

" By the mass," cried an Irish labourer, who had gone to see the sport, as he called it, " it was then after all a rale thrue blue Protestant that did the job for his riverence, in order to give him back his own colour."

One loud roar of laughter convulsed the com-pany (for all particularly disliked Faircloth), and made that gentleman feel as if he wished to sink down into the floor.

" Its all darned loike summat I once seed acted at a fair," said Styles ; " but its droy work, I wants sammat to wet my whistle."

" What do you want ?" said Mr. Port.

" I aint no ways partikler, let's have a little of your old namesake."

The other farmers, who already bore the external evidence of their internal stimulants, seconded the motion.

Before the butler acquiesced he took off his hat and consulted Mr. St. Aubyn, who, in concert with Mr. Hough and Hubert, decided that an amicable negociation should first be entered into. Hough acted as mediator, then throwing a handsome sum of small pieces among his liberators, he thanked them again for their assistance, and begged that they would withdraw quietly to their respective homes. No objection being made, all further discussion was cut short, and off the whole party excepting the farmers decamped, shouting at the top of their voices the song of the "Lillibulero," a satirical ballad against Irishmen and Popery, the gibberish and tune of which had taken the fancy of the nation. The second part had been added after William's landing.

The jovial farmers, indisposed to trouble their heads further in a matter which had lost all the excitement of Popery and promised no gain, had already attained to that stage of absorption which demanded an additional supply, still lingered behind the rest of the reconciled besiegers. They preferred ease to the glory of the triumph. To avoid complications, and to 'do nobody no harm' was, they said, their object. The butler, true to the interests of his master, to whom he desired to attach the yeomanry, made everything snug in his own room. The generous wine, the soothing pipe, the blazing wood fire, were all congenial to the agricultural mind and body, and suited well thoughts, which under the highest inspiration took no greater or more heroic range than their wide tracts of land. Their own interest was their philosophy. Agriculture, they said, was the support of the State; they were therefore licensed to grumble and repine; and he who complained not when such high interests were at stake was unworthy the name of a farmer.

" As for that poor got up thing, Master Faircloth," they all chimed in, he might dress himself up in the finery, the gentility and the vices of his betters, but they were certain to a man that two bottles even of the excellent port they were drinking would leave him under the table. He could, therefore, be no gentleman. " In the servants' hall," cried the farmers, " he was howdacious enough to say, we were only one remove from our own bastes; but the height of his imperence was the assertion to them as know'd no better that the first farmer and the inventor of ploughing was a pig, and that we were all pigs rooting up the clods, to which he compared us.

The butler delighted his guests with the dates of the best vintages. The precise age at which such and such wines might be drunk to perfection. How a man might begin with one bottle at a time, and by carefully cultivating his

talent and his capacity might attain to his three
bottles under his belt in a little time; but what
delighted and amused them most was a Protestant pack of cards, to which Mr. Port invited
their attention, pointing out to them the figures
at the back, and whole representations of all the
tortures, massacres, and other enormities which
had been perpetrated by the Catholics—supposing
the Popish plot to be a reality.

It was drawing towards midnight, yet Hough
was still in conversation with Mr. St. Aubyn,
and though so late, was pleading eloquently with
him for admission to Miss Penderel's presence
once more, before he said farewell for ever to
Lady Place. Mr. St. Aubyn, yielding to his
desires, led him to the young lady's apartment.
"I have brought our young friend, for such we
may now esteem him, to bid you adieu," said
the elder gentleman, taking Hough by the arm;
then turning to him, said, "remember, time
wanes, you have not a moment to spare."

The youth and the maiden had much to say
to each other, but their hearts were too full to
give utterance to their feelings or their thoughts.
At length Harry said, "Our meeting has given
a new and absorbing interest to my existence,
a feeling of love and devotion which neither
time nor separation can obliterate. Indeed, the
pain of parting is more than the joy of our
meeting. Before I leave you allow me to
indulge a hope that I may again meet one to

whom I owe so much happiness. Oh! condemn
me not to a perpetual banishment, to which
death were mercy."

"Indeed, indeed, my generous friend, we
must give up all thoughts of ever meeting
again; it could but afford us regret and sorrow.
My heart is not my own to give," she said
quietly, in a low tone, glancing at Mr. St.
Aubyn. "Even were it not so," she continued,
"I could never give myself to one with whom
I had not the most perfect communion of feeling
and religion. Deep gratitude, the gratitude of
a sister, whose life you have saved, I shall ever
entertain for you."

Arousing himself with a violent effort, Hough
replied, "Had not the superstition, which I
can scarcely think one so wise, so lovely, and so
noble as Miss Penderel can believe, corrupted
the pure stream of life, which flowed from the
original fountain of truth, I would, I would do
anything less than exchange my soul for a pearl
of so great price."

Lily gave him her hand in silent adieu. He
gently pressed it, and in the depth of his grief
said, softly, "Why should not time and prayer,
your good sense, and the history of the Church
bring you to a knowledge of the saving truth
which I enjoy, and thus our faith, our hearts,
our future destiny for earth and heaven, for time
and eternity, would be one—one undivided being
of bliss. Let me beg one favour more; suffer

me only to state the errors of your Church. Let me refer you to the early history of the Gospel purity."

She could not master her emotion at his concern for her good, and could scarcely restrain her tears. She looked into Mr. St. Aubyn's face for her answer. "If you leave me at once and for ever," she cried, "until my conversion is complete, I will comply with your request. Farewell my preserver, my friend!" she added, and vanished from the room. Mr. St. Aubyn at the same instant disappeared by another door, and poor Hough was left alone. In sadness he quitted the room, but was once more destined against his will to overhear a conversation.

The sage farmers, quite inspired by the best wine they had ever tasted, launched out into such political discussions as none but farmers can appreciate or understand. The bucolical intellect and the agricultural mind had at this stage of their potations broken out into practical georgics.

"Be the lord the farmer's friend?" asked farmer Rumbellow.

"The Papists and manufacturers have had it all their own way," cried neighbour Grumbleton.

"The Prince of Orange," says farmer Bags, "will make new tests and keep the foreign corns out of our markets."

"I'll tell you what it is," says farmer Flash; "something must be done to get the corns riz."

"By gar," cried Rufus Rumbellow, " patience is a good mare, but too slow for the times."

" Marry, sir !" says Grumbleton, to the butler, " the fat-kidneyed, red-faced rascals of Tories have had the sun on their side of the hedge too long by half. They talk about England's true anointed king; but gie I the prince that'll do his duty to the nation, and keep up the price of agricultural produce of bastes and seds ; and I be blow'd if we care if he be Papist or Pagan, Tory or Whig."

" But," says farmer Jolly, " the king, though less extravagant than him as is dead, has put new dooties on wines, on tobacco, on sugar, and on linen. Now, barrin' this pure port, I ain't tasted no wine since harvest ; but a little sugar to sweeten one's grog, and a pipe full of the weed to make we poor farmers forget the bad times ; and cheap sheets to lie betunes when we are awearied at night, are no more than our due."

" The Prince of Orange is a rebel," said Master Holdfast, who was less disaffected than the rest.

" He is a good sorted un," says Bags, " and a prince every inch on un. He will bring plenty of gin, and hollands, and schiedam into the country."

" So much the worse," says Mr. Holdfast ; " and bring down the price of malt."

" The only good the Dutchman will do is to kill the priest varmint," said a Puritan.

" Better still, said his next neighbour, " he'll do for all the attorneys. Luke Lattitat served me with a notice to quit because I was in arrear."

" And the parsons?" asked the butler.

" They bees no good, only to take tithes and eat up our produce like locuses," said Bags; " a prelatist aint no better nor a papist."

" None of your cuckold craw thumpers and papishers, such as the king," cried Grumbleton, " sent to eat up the forage all about Reading. The troopers, I tell thee, man, haent left not a morsel of food for man or baste."

" But where is the prince all this time?"

" Marry, Master Holdfast, they be bringing him to Windsor, and this very evening he must have passed near our neighbourhood."

" I hope the lord," says Farmer Freeman, " will now, after all his scrimmaging, be rewarded with a situation under the new Government, and be able to lower our rents."

" His lordship is a brave warrior, and merits promotion," replied the butler.

" My Lord John is the veriest Whig in Christendom," says Mr. Port; " he has been arrested six times for political offences; the last crime laid to his charge, however, was a shame: merely that he had denied the validity of a warrant, signed by a Roman Catholic justice of the peace."

" But I have heard as how he were apprehended and put in quod," said Mr. Flash.

"Sarve him right too; he placed a blasted bumbailiff in all the housen, when the 'olders could not pay their rent," said Grumbleton.

"Never mind," says the butler, "he is a valiant soldier. The colonel, with seventy followers well armed and mounted, left Hurley about a month ago in order to join the Prince of Orange, and make him King of England. But a strong party of the enemy had been posted at Cirencester; my lord would brook no delay, so resolved to force a passage; his friends and tenants, you know, stood by him like men."

"We didn't ought to know so much about it," broke in farmer Grumbleton, "for our poor boys paid dearly for their bravery."

"Yes, but," continued the faithful butler, "his lordship was taken prisoner, and sent to Gloucester Castle by Beaufort's troops. The people of Gloucester rose and delivered his lordship from prison, he collected his horsemen, and with halters for bridles, and some irregular infantry armed only with clubs, is marching unopposed through counties once devoted to the house of Stuart, and will soon enter Oxford in triumph.

"The Tory University is converted to the Whig interest, and will receive him as well as the Prince of Orange with honours.

"If his lordship had only waited here till the Oxford man, whom he, in his turn, imprisoned, had been set free, Lady Place might have been

spared this peril. The Oxonian was given in
charge to Mr. Faircloth, but the fellows so
frightened him that he hid himself, and they
took him for a Popish priest, and gave him some
rough handling. If you *must* be going, gentlemen," abruptly added Port, rising, " I wish you
a very good night. I have much still to arrange
after this terrible work."

In passing out they saw Hubert waiting on
Mr. Hough, who had a word for each of them.

Most of the farmers present had relations and
friends at Oxford, where, during the preceding
year, mass had been celebrated in more than one
college. No sooner did they observe Hough
than they asked him about Obadiah Walker, who
had turned University College into a Popish
abomination. Hough took no notice of them.
The farmers, however, nothing abashed by his
silence, in their present merry mood, sang a
ballad then popular in Oxford, the burden of
which was—

> " Old Obadiah
> Sings Ave Maria,"

and thus they all decamped full of the good
times which were coming.

CHAPTER XVIII.

I can no other answer make, but Thanks,
And Thanks, and ever Thanks.—*Shakespeare.*

A grandam's name is little less in love
Than is the doting title of a mother.—*Shakespeare.*

HUBERT and Hough seeing that the company
had taken their final departure, and that there
was no further commotion or restraint, determined to make their way out of the house as
speedily as possible. The doors, however, had
been locked, and, according to the rule of the
house, the keys carried to the valiant and now
recruited Mr. Faircloth for safe keeping. That
gentleman had retired for the night, so that
Hough and Hubert remained prisoners still in
Hurley House. While wandering through the
corridors, in hopes of finding some mode of
egress, they heard the merry voices of the rest
of the crew, and followed the sound until they
entered an apartment at a distant part of the
house, where they found them regaling themselves with a good supper, which Miss Penderel
had ordered to be laid out for them. Hough
was only too glad once more to join his young

E 2

friends, and they all sat down, inviting Hubert
to join them, after their evening's work, as
merry as crickets.

Hough eagerly asked what news they had
acquired, and what perils they had escaped.

The Right Reverend Colonel Compton, they
remarked satirically, had once more bristled up
his courage into all the military ardour he had
felt twenty-eight years ago in the Life Guards.
The figure which he made in the progress of the
Princess Anne had been the talk of the county.

Next to the Prince of Wales, the king's chief
object of anxiety was the great seal, which he
feared would be fished up out of the Thames—
such were the powers this talisman possessed.
The grand jury of Middlesex had found a bill
against the Earl of Salisbury for turning Papist.
They had also heard that while the Prince lay at
Hungerford, a sharp encounter took place between two hundred and fifty troops, and six
hundred Irish who were posted at Reading.
The king's troops fled with the loss of their
colours and of fifty men.

Most of the young men called this civil war,
and an attack of the foreigners on England;
but Mr. Tate thought far otherwise; the Dutch
had only assisted an English town to free itself
from the dominion of the Irish. So late as the
eighth of that month the commissioners, two of
whom Hough had overheard at Lady Place, had
been received by the Prince's body guard with

great military respect. Halifax was spokesman. Hough inquired if they knew where the Prince was gone.

The Prince's original intention, it was reported, had been to proceed from Hungerford to Oxford, but the arrival of the deputation from Guildhall induced him to change his route and hasten on directly to the capital. When William found that Lord Faversham had dismissed the royal army, he exclaimed with bitterness, "I am not thus to be dealt with, and that my Lord Faversham shall find."

"And so he will," cried Tate.

The Irish soldiers had seized a richly laden East Indiaman, which had just arrived in the Thames, but not being able to find a pilot soon ran their ship aground, and were compelled to lay down their arms. James had travelled along the shore of the Thames.

"I cannot make out that Halifax," said Hough.

"We heard," says one of the crew, "he hoped to mediate between the king and the Prince without exposing the country to the risk of a new dynasty and a disputed succession."

"But," said Tate, "it must be clear to you that Halifax's mission to Hungerford has been a fool's errand, a mere mock embassy, alike insulting to such a refined politician and delicately minded statesman, and unworthy of a monarch. James, we must all admit, never meant to abide by the terms which he had instructed the commissioners to propose.

"For," continued the stroke oar, "it seems certain that the king is expected to arrive in London next Sunday evening, and if we hope to see his majesty by Monday we must work our way at once up the Thames."

"So far as I am concerned I feel that we have tarried too long already in the house which has been my prison," said Hough.

This sentiment jumped with the humour of the whole party, who readily rose to depart. But Mr. Faircloth had retired, and the keys were not to be had.

"I wish," cried Hough, "the confounded ass had kept himself awake till his execution, which he richly deserves, and had slept afterwards."

"Has he not been condemned?" interrogated the rest of the crew.

"Mr. St. Aubyn, whom he abuses so shamefully, saved the cowardly caitiff from the punishment he merited," was the reply.

Does it seem strange that among the natural subjects of the Oxford men's apprehension they had no suspicion of Faircloth's treachery or ingratitude? They were young, is the answer.

A few words between the exulting confederates determined them in adopting the plan Hubert recommended,—to make good their retreat by the obscure passages leading through the postern door, which he knew was only bolted on the inside. Mr. Port refused to take any share in promoting an escape which might be less agreeable to his master than the flight of King James would be to the Prince of Orange. He refrained however from any decisive opposition.

Hough was as brave as he was sensible of real danger, but his recent experience of certain devious labyrinths in subterranean regions promised him no door of hope or deliverance at the end of such long dusky passages. In the joyful company of his comrades, and confidence in the faithfulness of their guide, he was inspirited to make the attempt.

All followed their leader through the various windings of the intricate labyrinths, threading their uncertain way with difficulty where Hubert felt perfectly at home. At length the whole of the party emerged into the open frosty night air, feeling as if they had just come up from the bottom to the surface of the water. The fresh breeze breathed into them a new existence. All slackened their paces, feeling secure of liberty. Hough stepped aside, and paused under what he believed to be Lily's window. He looked up wistfully to the case-ment. He soon heard, or thought he heard, a female voice trembling between joy and grief; nor was he mistaken. The exclamation was distinct, though plaintive: " My friend—my brother—my noble preserver,—I shall not be happy until I can make you sensible of my gratitude." Nothing was visible but a small hand, distinguished in the grey dawn by its delicate whiteness, which was scarcely less snowy than the handkerchief which streamed from it, and which it suddenly let fall, heavily weighed down by something which brought it directly to the ground. Quickly picking it up, Hough raised his eyes to the casement, but it was deserted. "It is, perhaps," said he, folding the dear token to his breast, "the heart's first, best, fond gift of a sister's love." And he went on his way soothed, if not rejoicing, at the happy omen.

The Demy could neither conceal from himself nor Miss Penderel, nor, indeed, from Mr. St. Aubyn, that he had allowed himself to form an attachment, for the moment at least—a devoted attachment to a girl who could only in return give her gratitude, or the affection of a sister. "I have," thought he, "opened my heart to a hopeless affection; whatever may be the still concealed expression of interest wrapped up in the treasured handkerchief, her last words were simply words of friendship. Oh! why have I been guilty of such weakness for one who can never be more to me than a sister? I have, thank heaven, taken no undue advantage of our position." He fondly pressed the treasured gift which had come down upon him, to his heart;

he recalled the words of the giver; he gave to both the token and the words the colouring of his own feelings. The very difficulties of his position hurried him on the faster to entertain new hopes to urge his suit. His was no common claim to affection. His whole being was more resolutely bent than ever in weal or woe to link his future with that of Lily Penderel. He once more hastily replaced the valued memento in his bosom, as hastily drew it forth again, and with it inadvertently the embroidered purse, which came so mysteriously into his possession, and of which he had no knowledge—which, however, he could not in his own mind but attribute to the generosity of Miss Penderel, through the agency of the gushing and demonstrative Di Vine.

The fact is, young Hough's sentiments for one of whom he knew so little, were due to the accident which placed him in such an extraordinary position, and to the inexperience of his years. Lily was the first young woman who had made an impression on his heart; this he felt, but there was no help for it. The maiden's unaffected kindness, the high-minded, fearless sympathy with which she met him on equal terms at their last interview, appealed right to his heart of hearts, and only tended to increase those sentiments which he felt were hopeless. He would, however, subdue his feelings. Her appeal to his honour and his courage, her desire that he should think only of her as his debtor,

should be obeyed. He would at least win her esteem and respect. "After all," thought he, "Lily
Penderel may be the betrothed of another. Her
friend, though my senior, is evidently in her confidence; to him she looked for her answer to me."
The last thought went like a poisoned arrow to
his heart. The dead leaves at his feet were not
whirled around and about him by the midwinter
wind more effectually than were his hopes
scattered by such recollections. "Whether she is
betrothed or not," said the infatuated youth, "her
erroneous creed, her notions of heresy and
schism, place a great gulf between us." All he
could be certain of was this, that no man ever
did or ever could love her as he did. An older
though less devoted man had already gained
what to Hough was worth more than the whole
world and all its glories.

While thus musing, he was suddenly recalled
to himself and his real situation, by the voices
of his companions reminding the youth of his
own former admonition, to hasten their departure.

He cast one more fond, lingering look at the
enchanted casement of Lady Place mansion.
Never than by that imperfect light did it seem
so interesting to the lover; and certainly, if we
may credit the history of the time, it must even at
the dawn of a winter day have been very beautiful.

Beneath the slopes and pleasure grounds of
Hurley, down which our party are now descend-
ing, the Thames rolled classically under woods

of beech. Here, in a sheltered cove, they found their boat.

The small pulse of earliest light trembled in the eastern heaven. The breeze awoke with the peeping day and greeted its return; the leaves rustled in the morning air; the deer, startled from their beds of fern, bounded across the avenue. In short, every sight and sound of that sequestered scene contrasted with the disturbance of the past night. There was a soft hazy harmony with its own wintry hues which hovered over the scene, imparting a soothing influence to the anxious mind of Hough.

But still all was partially obscured in twilight beneath the arching branches of the trees where their boat lay, made fast to a stump.

Hubert was the first to jump in that he might shove her along side the bank for the convenience of the young gentlemen. "All right," says he, and in an instant the whole crew passed by him into the boat.

While they were looking anxiously around to see if any one were stirring in the neighbourhood, Hough on his way to the stern stumbled over something in the bottom of the boat. It was rolled up in a bundle, apparently of rough homespun cloth or frieze. It might have been a living creature, but it seemed to have no life nor motion; but when a second of the crew, not being aware of the obstacle, kicked his foot against it, it began to shuffle off its coil, and after an effort or two gained an erect posture. The under drapery in which it was swathed was the colour of the grey dawn and scarcely perceptible.

The young men could not but shrewdly suspect at this moment, that after all Faircloth had been at the bottom of some treachery, and had employed some wretch to betray them; but a shrill, trembling, and peculiar tone assured them of their mistake.

"Hubert," screamed this mysterious sound, "my darling boy! What is the meaning of this? What has old grandame done to offend you—to send you from her, my grandson,—the dead image of his father? You shall not leave me." She crept stealthily up to Hubert, clasped him in her skinny arms, and hugged him so closely in her wiry grasp that he could not extricate himself from the poor old woman's embrace. He tried to separate himself from her with tenderness, but with a gentle violence; she clung to him and mingled her tears with his and covered him with kisses. She bowed down the strong man's heart and changed his resolution, but not before she had sunk down exhausted at his feet. He carried her in his arms out of the boat: affection mastered patriotism, love of adventure, and every other feeling.

His adieus were mingled with regrets, which the crew could fully appreciate and understand, for they too had home pictures in their minds, and the poor words which the huntsman uttered awakened sensations in his new friends which had either been lulled to sleep by the spirit of romance or banished by excitement.

"God speed you, gentlemen," were the last words of the huntsman that reached the receding crew, as, propelled with steady sweep, the Oxford boat, in the increasing light of day and into the placid water of the Thames, glided on her course.

CHAPTER XIX.

A soul exasperated in ills, falls out
With everything, its friend, itself.—*Addison.*

Ev'n to the dullest peasant standing by,
Who fastened still on him a wondering eye,
He seem'd the master spirit of the land.—*Joanna Baillie.*

CONGRATULATING our young Oxford friends on their escape from Lady Place, and wishing them a prosperous course, we must commit them to their decisions, while we return once more to the king, from whom our new acquaintances have diverted our attention, since we left his Majesty and faithful comrades in the hands of the rabble.

The varied romantic region through which we have travelled from the immediate subject of our story seems long, but the time is short, for between the monarch's capture and his departure from Faversham, in which we now rejoin him, hardly three full days have elapsed.

In resuming the thread of our narrative, we crave leave to remind our readers of the state of the country on the eve of the British Revolution.

The news of James's flight passed like lightning from the galleries of Whitehall to the streets,

and the whole capital was in commotion. The
king was gone.—The Prince had not arrived.
—No regency had been appointed.

The lords had sent for the two secretaries of
state. Middleton refused to submit to an
usurped authority; but Preston, astounded by
his master's flight, and not knowing what to
expect, or what course to adopt, obeyed the
summons.

Rochester had till that day adhered to the
royal cause, but now saw only one way of avert-
ing the general confusion. " Call your troops
of guards together," he said to Northumberland,
" and declare for the Prince of Orange."

The principal officers of the army were inclined
to William, and resolved to assist the civil power
to keep order. " When our king commands
what is unlawful, we must obey him passively,"
concluded they ; " in no extremity are we justified in withstanding our lawful Sovereign by
force ; but if he resign his office, his authority
over us is at an end."

In the mean time, the evil passions of the people
having been freed from control, what Macaulay
calls the " human vermin," being neglected itself
by ministers of the Church and of the State,
burst from the cellars and garrets of the civilised
Christian metropolis, and rose into terrible importance. Every den of vice poured out its
scum, every bear garden its savages. The gin
palace and brothels, the refuse of humanity—

housebreakers, highwaymen, cutpurses and cut-throats; with these were mingled idle apprentices, for whom the excitement of the riot had a charm. Even honest men of peaceable habits were impelled by religious animosity to join the lawless mob, to swell the cry of "No Popery!"—a cry which has more than once endangered the existence of London, changed dynasties, secured the election of senators, and which on the present occasion was the prelude to outrage and rapine.

Before the king leaves Faversham the report that the country is without a Government, that London is in an uproar, travels fast down the Thames, and spreads confusion and misrule in all directions.

The houses of many Catholic gentlemen were attacked. Parks were ravaged. Deer slain and stolen. Ecclesiastical and domestic architecture bear to this day marks of the popular violence of the terrible time.

The roads were traversed by a self-appointed police, which stopped every traveller, till he proved that he was not a Papist. The Thames was infested by a set of pirates, who under pretence of searching for arms or delinquents rummaged every boat that passed. Many persons, anxious to avoid the insults of those who hustled and detained them, were glad to ransom their persons and effects by flinging gold pieces to the zealous Protestants, who had assumed the office of inquisitors.

Even during the short stay of the royal captive at Faversham Mr. Justice Jenner, Burton, and Graham, the king's solicitors, Giffard and Leyburn; two of the Vicars Apostolic, Obadiah Walker, and several others, were brought prisoners into town. But the trial most painful to royalty, was the rough corporal usage, which James himself had for the first time undergone, and which seems to have discomposed him more than all the indignities he had yet endured. No treatment afflicted him so miserably as that which he received on board the hoy. Indeed, the rude and savage attack upon his royal person at Faversham was never forgotten, and, we fear, not for many years forgiven, by the king. The poor monarch, however, had not only himself been shamefully treated, but had seen his faithful friends and followers insulted and pillaged. Yet to James, with all his faults, so deep and loyal was their attachment, that many of them, including various ranks, ever since the flight of their beloved monarch had become known, had been attempting to follow him; and the roads towards the sea coast were covered with fugitives endeavouring to escape, as well as with persons on the watch to arrest every stranger proceeding in that direction. There was a mad panic abroad. Men suspected each other. They feared to walk soberly, as in the day, without the protecting mantle of the Crown extended over them.

This seemed rent from the top to the bottom by two conflicting potentates. The barriers of shame were broken down by the extent of corruption and treachery in high places. The examples of infamy were so many and so sudden that several were reconciled to the ignominy of their crimes by their associates in rebellion.

That in such general confusion of right and wrong the judgment and feelings of humanity should both have been bribed by gold is no wonder. The influence of filthy lucre had naturally descended from the upper to the lower classes.

In such times of popular excitement, when the enthusiasm of the masses is both rife and rude, the tide of passions rushes over all moderate opinions.

All which James had ever achieved for the nation, all the hostages to good faith, years of unimpeached honour granted to him in his early life as a sailor and a soldier, in his advanced years as a tolerant sovereign, were forgotten in a moment. Nay, there was an exciting pleasure now in the detection of any real or supposed lapse in the once esteemed monarch. The root of all evil, even worse than witchcraft, was at the bottom of the worst misfortunes which overtook the king at Faversham. It would seem through the length and breadth of England, society was disorganised, honourable feeling perverted: a cry of exultation over the great and the fallen shook the land, and pierced the monarch's heart with a poisoned barb, which none, perhaps, but himself could understand.

Notwithstanding the outer marble of cold indifference which has been polished by statesmen and varnished by practice to conceal the interior heart, there are moments, even in the lives of statesmen and kings, when levelling misfortunes and the personal calamities of life, not only fill them with deeper sufferings, but evoke louder lamentations than the peasant would express; especially in such constitutions as that of James, which grief had so impaired, that the body, wearied and worn, weighed down the mind to its own level. Under this state every little accidental obstacle which as a younger and less afflicted man with a ready jest or a graceful indulgence he would have passed over, he now felt as an intentional insult. The gossiping even of the sailors, to whom he had always extended such a royal freedom, he was more disposed to repel than to acknowledge. Their conduct, however respectful, seemed to the mighty fallen as impertinent. So fearfully had the sudden stroke turned friendship into wormwood, and steeped the royal mind in sorrowful suspicion. To say that his soul was insensible to such a malady were to assert that he was more or less than a man. It was this feeling which deprived him of right reason. And which

of us, who has passed through painful reverses
and been thrown out of our sphere upon a heartless world who mocks at our calamity, has not
some time or other felt that he were the subject
of contempt which is the mere creation of his
own morbid sensibility. Unconscious of our
own altered sentiments and seeing everything
through a melancholy light, that makes darkness visible, we can only read in each well-
known face a lesson of our own humiliation,
which has no existence but in the clouded fancy.

The state of the country which we have
described and the feelings it was calculated
to induce must be borne in mind to make some
of the most stirring events of our narrative in-
telligible to the reader, who has accompanied
us back to Faversham.

The old sailor to whom the early part of our
history has introduced us, evidently felt such a
strong interest in the prisoners, for such, in fact,
they were, on board the hoy, that he was ready
to risk his life in their service. Thrusting
himself between Ames and the king, lest the
beastly ruffian should profane his sacred Majesty
by the foul touch of a traitor, the brave old
fellow did his best to bring the rascal to terms.
The truth, however, is, that honour had been
violated among thieves, each of whom seemed
equally entitled to his reward. Amid the dead
of night motley groups and scattered knots of
the lowest of mankind were studding the beach

of Faversham. These gradually formed together into a sullen mob. The loudly avowed object of their meeting was "Death to the Papists." " Shame, shame, to the man who aids their escape!" "Down with the traitors!" " Tear them to pieces!" were the cries heard on all sides.

The confused din from the outside soon penetrated the cabin. The mingled crowd, with mingled voices, put up one fierce huzza, and all pressed down in one body towards the boat. The word for which they waited was not given, therefore, no violence was committed. The venerable sailor inspired the crew with a better feeling, and kept back the crowd until it was arranged by mutual consent that the king and his party were to disembark. In ten minutes his Majesty, supported by Hales and Strickland with pistols in their hands, and followed by Ames no longer backed by his friends, who had mutinied against him, and the old man; was seated in a coach drawn by four stout horses, which the ancient mariner's son had, during the parley, secretly, and in concert with Hale's coachman, placed in readiness for the emergency. Strickland was supplied with a horse from the same stables, while Hales entered the carriage with his Majesty. The post boys fixed themselves in their saddles, cracked their whips, and dashed off towards the principal inn, while the mob splitting into a dozen

channels, fled on every side with roars of terror,
or of laughter, according to their distance or
danger from the heavy vehicle. The yells of
disappointed rage drowned the cries of merriment
or alarm.

The spirited guardsman had enough to do to
keep off the fastest of the pursuers. " We are
not without means of defence," cried he. His
horse, as if proud of his duty and his rider,
cleared the way about the carriage, but " Whoop
Papist!" "Whoop 'Ales !" "D——n the Pope
and his crew!" resounded through the dull
night air.

" There they go in a hand gallop tantivy to
Rome !"   " Vengeance on Petre !"   " The
hatchet-faced oyster-eyed priest!"   Such were
the elegant greetings which welcomed the poor
king, who was mistaken for Father Petre, or the
chaplain of Sir Edward Hales.

This was the third night of agitation and distress which his Majesty had passed with little,
or very disturbed sleep since his sorrowful separation from his wife and child.   Scarcely,
therefore, had the fatigued monarch, in a quiet
chamber of the inn, betaken himself to the
repose which his worn mind and body required,
when a deep long slumber came over him, from
which he did not awake until broad daylight
streamed through his window, under which,
there was a Babel of confused sounds that
aroused him to a sense of his situation.

Already was the valiant cornet, refreshed by rest, standing by the bed and waiting the wishes of his Sovereign, to whom he had fully made himself known the preceding evening in the cabin of the hoy.

James, though aroused by the sounds under his window, could scarcely clearly understand where he was; he looked wildly around him, and was starting from his bed, when the young soldier presented himself to his king, and, going down on his knee, besought him to be calm, consoling his Majesty with the reflection that many of the people, though hostile to his cause, were affectionately attached to his person.

"Be of good courage, my liege," said the youth, with that tact, taste, delicacy, and address which might have done credit to an elder man; assuring the king with a cheerfulness, which he himself assumed, that they had passed through the worst.

That system of good breeding which represses all selfish indulgence of grief and cheerfully meets the claims of an emergency demands the greatest self-command,—a self-command and fortitude which never obtrude the sorrows of the afflicted on his neighbour in adversity. There is, perhaps, no Christian forbearance more courteous than that which merges private wrongs and distresses into the over-mastering desire to make others forget their sufferings, or at least reconcile them to their lot.

In no instance could this high tone of noble bearing be more beautifully and practically illustrated than in the conduct of the immediate comrades of the unhappy James. The gay but gentle attempt of young Strickland to sustain the spirits of the little party showed a noble and high-souled courage which alleviated the sadness it could not avert. He assured his Majesty that the senseless fury of the rabble was not directed against the King of England, but against a few imaginary and supposed priests.

"I fear your sword arm has been hurt in our defence," were the first words of the king, "and sadly neglected."

"My arm is scarcely worth a thought," cried the young man. "My only regret is that it had not finished the hog Ames before the accident rendered it useless. I never was better in my life."

"Good Heaven!" mourned James; "why did I ever become a king; only to become the sport of rebels—the wreck of the noble and the loyal? What can be done to stop the ruin which is falling on our friends?" His looks were even more melancholy than his words; for sorrow and suffering had set their profaning marks on the face of his sacred Majesty.

Before Strickland could divert the monarch from his grief a knock was heard at the chamber door, and Sir Edward Hales entered; but not before he had stumbled over some animal which lay like a bear in a shaggy covering at the door, and sprang upon him fiercely. It was one of the ringleaders of the rabble who lay there to guard the monarch lest he should escape. No sooner had the human savage started to his feet to pounce upon Sir Edward than a huge staghound, hearing the scuffle, came in two bounds to the spot.

Edwards, the landlord of the inn, rushing to the spot, and trusting to his dog's sagacity, cried out, "Take him, Topham; at him, Topham; well done, Topham!" But Topham, more true to his own noble instincts than to the character of Topham, after whom he was called, sprang upon the sneaking skulker.

Charles Topham was an officer of the Commons of England who had been empowered to put down "the hellish and damnable plot" within the bowels of the kingdom. But mine host only saw the dog's nature through Protestant spectacles, while the noble animal, not perceiving the mark of the beast on the Papists, defended those whom he was urged to attack. The third spring brought his teeth to the brutal watcher's throat, on which he fastened as if true to some canine instinct of loyalty and hospitality even in the house of his master the innkeeper.

Hales, being thus wonderfully rescued from the ruffian, appeared before the king, calmly observing, with a profound reverence, that his Majesty had, after all, a Popish dog left to defend him. Nor was it till Edwards, his master, used all his threats and entreaties, and even bit the dog's tail severely with his own teeth, that the enraged animal would desist from his loyal purpose, and let go his hold.

The very fellow who had stationed the night watcher to keep the king in custody was now the first to laugh at master Prowler, and thus made an unexpected diversion in the king's favour, during which the faithful baronet assisted his Majesty to dress in order to show himself to the people. All this time James shuddered, and declared that the only thing which could speedily recover his shattered nerves would be a release from the retinue with which his Kentish subjects had honoured him.

" Your fears are groundless, my liege," said Hales. " There is more than one who makes a shrewd guess at your rank, and as many as recognise their sovereign will protect him."

" There are certainly," observed Strickland, " those in the crowd who claim the honour of serving under your Majesty when Duke of York, and not a few have discovered in me, your devoted servant, a kinsman of Sir Roger Strickland. There are," concurred both attendants, "men in the mixed multitude, who would not only rejoice in your Majesty's escape, but lay down their lives in your defence." These soothing words brought a gleam of hope to the king's countenance and quelled his most anxious fears.

Mine host of the King's Head prepared the best breakfast which the hopes of his gains could supply and the place and time afford. No delicacies of toast and tea, varied sorts of bread, buttered rolls and coffee graced the table; but such old English fare and solid viands as did duty for the occasion. A round of beef, ham, and capons, which an hour earlier had cackled and crowed with the rabble, and last, but by no means the least, a huge venison pasty, as savoury as it was huge,—the contents of which Sir Edward knew to his cost had been stolen from his park. Indeed, Sir Edward was but too well known as a Catholic loyalist.

At the very moment he was consoling his sovereign, his park in the neighbourhood was at the mercy of a band of rioters, who were employed in shooting his deer and pillaging his mansion : so that probably the very best part of the breakfast, for which he paid so magnificently that morning, came out of his own well stored supplies. Though served up somewhat roughly, with mantling old ale foaming in pewter flagons, yet the royal party swallowed down the morning meal and their annoyance. Even the royal appetite itself made no objection to the plain substantial food, for the hard fare and scanty commons of the three companions since their departure from London made the welcome exercise of their jaws no mere nibbling at a dainty.

Right glad were the faithful attendants to see the cates finding such a hearty reception into the royal capacity; earnest and cordial was their co-operation upon the rich fabric of venison, which shared even a worse fate than Sir Edward's grander edifice of Hales Hall, which was only partially demolished. The drink, which was from the cellars of the latter, was such as might be expected, and washed down everything unpleasant for the moment, while it was silently but mentally quaffed to the honour and safe return of their sovereign.

The repast ended, James called for writing materials,—wrote, re-wrote, tore what he had written—wrote, tore, and wrote again; and at length to his satisfaction penned a note, which he handed to Strickland, who immediately called for a horse, which was already at his service, and galloped through the crowd, to whom he waved his hand.

"A Strickland for ever!" rent the air, and followed him till he was out of sight. In the meantime Sir Edward Hales induced the anxious monarch to take the air, and thus by his uncon-cern and confidence win the goodwill of the people, or, at least, disarm them of their hostility. Sir Edward Hales was accosted by some with respect, by others he was passed in sullen silence, while by one or two miscreants he was openly insulted.

That the seamen and peasantry, who had

reassembled at such an early hour about the temporary residence of the new arrivals, were actuated by some motive of interest or curiosity was evident. The precise object of their meeting was apparently scarcely known to themselves. Every eye was watching the two companions, who had not proceeded many yards, when an old seaman, the same ancient mariner who had already befriended Strickland's efforts in defence of King James, now came out from the crowd, and falling on his knees before the monarch, recognised him, and reverentially uncovered, begged to kiss his hand, which the king held out to him. The old man watered it plentifully with his tears.

"When your most gracious Majesty," observed the old man, "was Duke of York and Lord High Admiral of England, when our navy triumphed over the Dutch fleet, the chief slaughter, you remember, was on our ship, around your royal person, for the friends who loved you best were standing by your side, and we," says the enthusiastic old man, "were covered with their blood."

"About a quarter of a century ago," said the king, as all the memorable events of that glorious day rushed at once through his mind. A gleam of happier and brighter days passed over his face at the thought, but left it in an instant more clouded than before. "My brave old comrade," continued he, "I remember it well. You were

between me and Lord Muskerry when he fell at
the same instant with Charles Berkeley. You
covered me with your own body, and thus saved
me. But how are the friends of our house
rewarded? How is it that you are still without
promotion? Oh! my friend," cried the king,
" would to God I could show you my gratitude,
or repay such loyalty and love !" He burst
into an agony of tears, which almost mingled
with those of the veteran sailor, who, in his
turn, went on—" If your sacred Majesty owed
your life to me, and if my life was endangered
by my having sheltered so great and good a
king, I only did my duty. Oh! that I had a
dozen lives to put between you and danger!
But what has brought the hero of so many fights,
the great sailor king, to such a plight as this ?"
The old man's heart throbbed, his speech
faltered, he could say no more. His son, a
stalwart, handsome, active young sailor came to
his support, and made his obeisance to his
monarch. The tone of the old man as well as
his words, his devotion, and that of his son,
attracted the attention, and softened the rude
asperity of the unthinking swarm of gazers into
sympathy; the tumultuous and yet tender feelings of the moment were too much for the spirits
of the monarch after their recent depression.

"This is too much, Sir Edward," said he,
regretfully, " can we find no means of rewarding
such fidelity ?"

It was, indeed, a touching sight to behold the father and the son throw themselves, in spite of prejudice and party feeling, at the feet of outraged majesty. A few of the spectators who witnessed the scene shed tears. The hiss and the jeer of last night had subsided into the sigh of sorrow the next morning. There was a low moaning as of men who felt remorse. There were those who even wept aloud.

While the mind of James was occupied in reflecting on the sudden change in his favour, he noticed not the approach of a young woman, apparently in the garb of an upper servant or of a lady's maid; a sort of muffler or veil partly concealed her countenance. She was running with the speed of a deer through the amazed throng, when one, out of respect to the king, held her back; "Odd zooks!" says he, "the wench is mad."

She, speaking with hurried but decided accents, observed, "They cannot, they shall not prevent me: I will speak to his Majesty. They may kill me, but they shall not hurt a hair of his sacred head."

The young sailor, who was still with his father, uncovered in the presence of the king and Hales, was startled at the sound of a female voice, which was evidently familiar to him, for he instantly sought the spot whence the sound proceeded, and rescued the young woman from the well-intentioned restraint of the bystanders;

and after an embrace, to which she offered no
violent resistance, so far at least as the eye
could glance beneath her hood, which concealed
her features, she threw herself in a transport
of grief and concern at the feet of the king, who
motioned her to rise.

"Oh! my poor lassie, say, what brings you
here?" In an under tone, he said, "the queen
and the prince are safe."

"What does this foolery mean!" cried some
in the crowd; but she heeded not their words.

"I am distressed, my liege; I scarce know
what I would say, or how to speak to one so
grand as the king of England, our master,"
cried she. "Ruin yawns before your Majesty.
O! mighty majesty, do not rush on death, and
be your own ruin. Think of the beloved queen,
whom I, among the lowest of her servants,
adore; think of the prince; think of yourself.
Come back again; bring back to us here again
our queen."

Should this outburst of feeling in a household
servant in the presence of the monarch be considered unnatural or presumptive by the reader,
let him remember that this young woman is the
same who lamented so feelingly the supposed
loss of the prince at Whitehall, and loudly
praised Lady Strickland for her spirited conduct.
She was also the favourite chambermaid of the
queen, for though not more than twenty-one
years old, she only remained to take care of her

Majesty on the alarming illness of the prince a few hours after his birth. The Countess of Sunderland was Lady of the Bed that night, and ought to have been in attendance.

The poor girl bitterly regretted that she had not been allowed to share the adversity of her royal mistress, and on the first intimation of the king's departure from London had hastened towards the Kentish coast in the hope of being able to follow her beloved queen.

The Earl of Winchelsea, a loyal Protestant, who had been Groom of the Bedchamber to his Majesty, had married the accomplished Anne Kingsmill, favourite maid of honour to the queen. The earl and his lady were now residing at their mansion in Kent, not far from the scene at Faversham. Thither the maiden repaired in the first moment of her bereavement and desolation.

The tidings of all which had happened to James flew with a celerity worthy of the steam-engine or the telegraph of our day, and almost beyond the power of credibility, preceding the more uncertain intelligence of the absurd and contradictory reports of the newspapers of the time; as though the birds of the air had carried the tidings; or, as if coming events had cast their shadows before them. The fact that carrier pigeons then, and for thousands of years before, were swifter than our present steam .speed, and truer, perhaps, than the telegraph, for the exchange of thought, or the medium of correct information, is as well authenticated as it is lightly considered; so that the faithful maiden might easily have received tidings of the king even without the aid of Lady Winchelsea.

The whole scene in which this maiden took a part passed in half the time it has taken to explain it. Overpowered by such touching and loyal devotion from his loyal liegemen and domestic servants, James rejoiced as a king, but wept as a man. The instinctive and involuntary acts of homage performed by the faithful old mariner, by his son, and by his son's sweetheart, betrayed very generally the rank of the object of their devotion.

"The very ruffians," says the accomplished and very erudite Miss Strickland, "who plundered and insulted him, when they saw his tears were awed and melted; they fell on their knees and offered to return their pillage. The seamen threw their hats in the air, and gave three cheers for their own lawful king. 'God bless him,' cried the crew of the hoy, and all around re-echoed the shout. 'The king shall have his own again! No foreign prince! No Dutch Billy—ruffian!' The seamen joined their forces and formed round his person, and challenged the whole world to touch a hair of his royal head."

"Thank God," cheerfully responded the king, "even at Faversham there are hearts as loyal as they are brave."

The very voices who cried, " Down with him !" last night, were now raised in loud and loving acclamations in the monarch's favour. A new light, with the new day, had evidently broken in upon them. Their horror of the Pope had given way to their homage of the king. They saw and knew their Sovereign, and it is just within the wide field of probabilities, that the free gift of so many coins which bore his royal image may have endeared them to the original.

Availing himself of the lull which followed, and taking a scrap of paper from the same pocket book which enclosed the receipt for the £300 of Jacobuses, with such materials as were at hand he wrote a few words on it, and with some trepidation entrusted the paper with secret directions to the young sailor, Ben Brown, who at the instant was saying something mutually interesting in a whisper to his lover. Edwards, who kept a close look out on all that was passing, fearing that the hope of his gains was gone, or going, rushed out of the inn, followed by the very scum of the rabble, whom he had excited to sedition by strong drink, which found vent in party cries ; he turned suddenly on Ben Brown to intercept him, and secure the paper on which so much might depend. The wary and active young loyalist, however, perceived the design, and, recognising an agricultural labourer mounted on a cart horse entrusted

to him the royal express, roaring into his ear,
"Whitehall, haste." Sir Edward Hales, on
whose business the man was at Faversham,
reiterating the word, "Whitehall," cried, "for
your life, ride."

The horse was clumsy, but powerful, and,
urged by the peculiar language and action of
the rider, broke into a rough gallop—a series
of jumps, which astonished the weak minds of
the drunken rebels, whom he left prostrate,
clinging to the ground lest they should fall
lower. The old sailor, with a loud laugh, which
shot his quid of baccy from under his jaw almost
into the face of royalty, declared the craft was
under weigh and had run down the landlubbers.
The sailors thought it a capital practical joke,
and laughed, after which there was a dead
silence; when Edwards, seeing the sailors off
their guard, collected his mustered clods, and
brought them forward, all charging in a body,
like a bull with his eyes shut. The seamen
pressed closer about their monarch, and formed
a living wall. Brickbats and stones fled from
all points against them, but they kept their
ground so firmly, placing those outside who
had fire-arms, that the missiles did but little
damage. Indeed, so complete was the defence
that he for whom it was made was unconcious
of the assault.

At one moment the king cried, "What evil
have I done ? What crime have I committed ?"

At another he spoke incoherently of many things. Now provoking the rabble with his censure; and now conciliating the sailors with his praise. " Make ready a boat, my men, put me on board, get her head well to the sea, lest the blood of your admiral be on your heads."

In vain did Sir Edward endeavour to restrain the paroxysm of the crushed and distracted monarch, and to soothe his anguish. To no purpose did old Brown and his son supplicate his Majesty to rely on the sailors while there was one drop of blood in their veins. Every allusion to the painful circumstances of their late misfortune the baronet carefully avoided, adroitly turning the conversation to their approaching journey back to London and their welcome reception at Whitehall.

So cruel did the decrees of fate seem to James that he felt himself a victim sacrificed by those he had loved, most loved, while vice, meanness, and treachery prospered on the side of his ungrateful children.

In the broken state of his mind and body he could not realise the consolation that virtue itself has no more sublime attribute than its power of bearing cheerfully unmerited affliction; and that in the destiny of the good and the great man there is nothing more noble than his patient resignation to the will of Him who " has borne our sorrows and carried our griefs."

Immersed in the gloomy thoughts which had

shrouded his mind, he wandered from one theme to another, feeding, as it were, his morbid appetite for sorrow. He had sunk into a reverie on the borders of despair, from which he was startled by a shrill exclamation of wild joy from Kate Colemore announcing at the top of her voice the rapid approach of a body of horsemen, whom she evidently expected. "And in the van," cried the ecstatic girl, "I see the handsome young red coat whom I met on my way from Lord Winchelsea's."

At that instant Lord Winchelsea, escorted by a body of well mounted yeomen and tenants, galloped into the space where the king was surrounded by friends and foes, just in time to meet the shock of the hostile party, before which the sailors, who had so long kept their ground, were beginning to give way. The king was all but in the power of the rabble once more, when one shout of exultation burst from the seamen. And Strickland was with Hales by the side of his Sovereign, followed by the earl and his troop, who, without any formal attack, sent the cowardly mob from the presence of the king, on whose ransom they had calculated as their certain prize.

CHAPTER XX.

Have I not had my brain sear'd, my heart riven,
Hopes snpp'd, name blighted, life's life lied away ?—*Byron*.

He that can endure
To follow with allegiance a fallen lord,
Does conquer him that did his master conquer,
And earns a place i' the story.—*Shakespeare*.

No sooner had Lord Winchelsea made his way
to his Majesty, and finished his first greetings,
which were mingled with regrets at his situation,
than the monarch demanded to be conducted to
the house of the mayor. The rabble, excited by
the base publican Edwards, whose show of hospitality was only to cover an unfathomable depth
of treachery, fearing that the hopes of his gain
would go with the king, opposed the removal of
James. The seamen, however, supported by a
few of the Earl's followers, and led on by Strickland, bore down the dull, dogged dastards, and
carried their point, though not without a struggle.
This bout, of which the king seemed unconscious,
lasted about ten minutes, but in it Strickland
earned for himself the character of a hero, breast-
ing the opposing stream which rushed against
him, scattering the mob in all directions with

his charger, while he refrained from actual combat. He was one of the king's own, and identified with the sailors. The tide was turned, and
a good English cheer announced the victory.
The king, and even Sir Edward, who was by no
means popular in the neighbourhood, and no
prophet in his own country, came in, as well as
Lord Winchelsea, for a share of applause.

Nothing could exceed the generous and disinterested cordiality of the loyal welcome which
the mayor, who seemed to act on his own unaided
judgment, gave the poor king, destitute as he
was on the world, without a country or a home.

This generous personage, unlike the pampered
magistrates of other towns, paid all the respect
in his power to James, and what the royal guest
valued most, treated the sailors, with whom
Strickland chose to remain outside the house,
most sumptuously, affording them oceans of grog
to drink the health of their Sovereign—a bold
toast on that occasion.

The open-hearted and generous valour, but
above all the unaffected identity of the guardsman, both in danger and in revelry with themselves, raised Mr. Strickland so high in their
estimation, that Ben Brown, as their spokesman,
declared the young blade was made of the real
stuff—a chip of the old block. Young Brown
could not repress his admiration at the height of
this good fellowship, which seemed to attach him
closer to the young soldier, whose horse he patted

on his arching neck, and caressed him with such
words as were more expressive of endearment to
a ship than an animal. Then raising his attention above the steed to the rider, with his hat in
one hand and a front curl of his hair in the
other, he looked the cornet bashfully in the face,
as if he had something to tell or to ask about
his Majesty.

"What's the matter, my man?" said the
officer.

"Did your honour meet the wench?" asked
the sailor, while a colour mantled to his bronzed
cheek, which might better have become the
maiden for whom he timidly inquired.

"What wench?" demanded the other.

"Why her what went on her marrow-bones
to the king, God bless him," answered young
Brown.

"I met a buxom wench as I was going to
Lord Winchelsea's; light-footed and light-hearted
she tripped along, scarcely bending the grass
under her feet, and disappeared in a path through
yonder copse, but not without a word between us."

"But she ben't light o' love, sir," rejoined the
sailor.

"She will be safe and happy with my Lady
Winchelsea's servants," said Strickland, with a
look of sympathy.

"The wench when I seed her, before she left
this here place for Lunnon, her did say as how
she could never be happy without her Joe."

The truth is that Brown and Kate had fallen in love in the natural way. They had lived in the same village, and been playmates together. Such love, like the small-pox without vaccination, is most dangerous.

"Make yourself easy, my good fellow, about the buxom damsel until you see her again."

"How can I see her?" was the question, "for my Kate says a grand lady is to take her to the queen in France. She has a right to her taste to be sure, but d—n me if I part with that ere gal for all the world."

"With what lady?" asked the soldier, carelessly.

"I can't rightly remember her name, but 'twern't no grand title, but summat like Plowman or Farmer."

"Was it Plowden?" said the guardsman, with some trepidation, which he could scarcely conceal.

"I'll be danged if that baint it. Her who is expected by Lady Winchelsea. And when I think on her in her place with the great folk, how much snugger it be than the cot of a poor sailor lad, I fear me she will better hersel, and lave I for a d—d frog-eater," muttered he, sorrowfully.

Whatever else the cornet might have inferred from this expression of feeling, there was one thing certain, the sailor's devotion to Kate Colemore was not less than his attachment to the royal family.

" The base-minded wretch Edwards, who pretended friendship for our party," whispered the sailor in Strickland's ear, " has sent to the Prince of Orange for directions about the king."

" The dog !" cried the other, " we will arrest him for high treason."

At this moment Strickland was summoned to wait on his Majesty. And both young men parted with mutual feelings of sympathy and good will.

Strickland found the Earl of Winchelsea striving with great respect and gentleness to soothe the king's alarm, and to persuade him to return to London.

" You are no longer in custody, my liege ; my brave followers have possession of the town." Hales corroborated the Earl's statement, and Strickland's entrance and report of the general feeling of the crowd in favour of the king, gave an influence to the advice, which his Majesty could hardly resist.

Moved by the united entreaties of his friends, he took a few rapid turns through the apartment. At length he spoke. " My return to London may involve the country in civil war and all the misery which it entails, and may not only endanger my son's accession to the throne, but may vest the invader with the rights he so unnaturally usurps."

" You are right, my liege," says the earl, " but your appearance in the field, at the head

of your people, who only want the signal to
flock to your royal standard, will prevent that
effusion of blood which you so justly deprecate,
and preserve to your dear country the sovereign
whom at heart it reveres. Our swords are impatient to jump from their scabbards in defence
of your birthright and your throne, which the
heartless usurper, first creeping in through the
prejudices of your subjects, then boldly bursting
through the law of nations, of nature, and of
God, seeks to make his own. Only sound the
loud trumpet, the fife, and the drum, and the
flower of the English and Irish armies, the
military force of your own native Scotch, all
as loyal as they are brave, will secure to you
the crowns which are now a glittering tempta-
tion to the mercenary and the faithless. Let
the disbanded army be recalled,—let us form
in columns of march,—let your majesty take
your place in the centre: and we shall invite
our Dutch friends to an entertainment for which
they have no appetite."

"What you say, earl," rejoined the king,
with anxious indecision in his countenance,
"what you say seems reasonable enough; but
I long for peace."

"But, my liege," said Winchelsea, "there
is a false peace, like the lull of the weather
which precedes the storm. The object of all
just war is peace, which cannot be purchased
by compromise."

"I am well aware of the fidelity of the Finch family, and of your cousin, the Earl of Nottingham, and the rest of my Protestant zealous loyalists ; and of the noble spirit of the Kentish gentlemen, for whose intervention at this miserable moment I am grateful. I am, however, painfully sensible that those who have been the most strenuous of my opponents are now high in the ascendant. On them mainly your counsel would throw me for support. How can I rely on that allegiance in my adversaries which has been denied me by the creatures of my bounty? How then can I return to my capital, the very centre of the despotic power of Britain's sovereign,—a suppliant, or a prisoner, even at the best, a monarch at the mercy of his opponents? Is it come to this! and must the House of Stuart submit to such conditions as a mob, deluded by a foreign potentate, can impose?"

Weary and oppressed by a bodily malady which mastered his spirit, the wretched monarch sank down on his seat in despondency, and could remonstrate no more. A thousand fancies of horrors and dread humiliations took possession of him, and completely unmanned him. "Their object," thought poor James, "after all, may be to hand me over to the invader." So fatal is the treachery of the few in whom we have confided, to our trust in the thousands who have never deceived us, and so vividly and terribly impressed on the feelings are some horrors, that they are a deathless terror to the person who has once been scared by their frightfulness. James had been betrayed by the friends of his bosom, the children of his prayers and of his love. He had seen the swelling, giddy surge of the restless rabble sweeping madly against his very palace, bursting every barrier, ·rolling onwards, and daring to approach him as unawed and as defiant as the waves that washed the feet of the Great Canute. The fevered pulse of the vexed throng had been felt by him in London. The flaming fireflood, streaming through all which he deemed most sacred, still glared in his eye. The false chime of stunning sounds and jarring wrongs still rung in his sickened. ear. The king suspected everybody—feared everything. He seemed amazed at the tranquil faces and serene quietude of those around him, and could scarcely acquit them of indifference or insensibility.

Strickland, who was more zealous for the honour than even the life of the monarch, could restrain himself no longer, but most suppliantly falling on one knee, made an appeal to chivalry rather than to the infatuated monarch, addressing him with such gentle violence and natural eloquence that his Majesty was not unmoved by the touching speech of the youth. Seizing his advantage the guardsman brought new motives and fresh arguments as reinforcements to his aid. "Oh! that I had under the sanction of your

great name an order to take the very lowest
place in any service of danger or toil! Oh! that
I had but an order to reconnoitre the outposts of
the insurgent army; to examine their strength;
to explore the nature and extent of the obstacles
between them and London or Windsor!"

How far he might have ventured to press his
arguments it is impossible to say had he not been
abruptly stopped by the king.

"We must try fair means first. My object
is to reconcile my actions with my duty. There
is a terrible conflict between the great purpose
which you have at heart and the nature of him
whom you address. I have just been thinking
over my varied fortunes, which bring to my
mind at this moment the pious sayings of St.
Francis of Sales." Then, turning to Winchelsea, James said, "Earl, have you seen his
'Introduction to a Devout Life?'"

The nobleman, at the time having more confidence in the defence of the sword than the
consolations of religion, declared that the Saint's
works had not come under his notice, but that
he had heard of his love letters to a gay lady
called Philothea, which were not, he believed,
generally read by Protestants.

"By Protestants and Catholics," rejoined the
patristic monarch. "My grandfather, James I.
of England, was as good a Protestant as I am
a Catholic, and as much opposed to Rome as I
am to Geneva; well, he was wonderfully taken

with it, and asked his bishops why none of them could write with such unction and feeling."

Some of the party suggested that the book must have been dedicated to King James; others presumed that it was richly adorned, and dedicated to Henry IV. of France, or to his queen, Mary of Medicis. But the king, somewhat impatiently, assured them that it was dedicated formally to the Divine Majesty of Heaven,— the Prince of Peace, whose birth was peace, whose legacy was peace,—a peace which neither time nor eternity could give or take away. Such was the peace he coveted next to the crown of glory, which fadeth not away. His three crowns, compared to that crown, were nothing. " The true servants of God," he continued, " use their riches like their garments, which they put on and off at pleasure ; but, as St. Francis hath it, ' false Christians hold to what they possess, like animals to their skin.' "

" It is fortunate," broke in the mayor, " that there are some thrifty families, who, by their saving industry, have risen to affluence and wealth. Their independence neither apes the bowing equality of the Frenchman nor the offensive licence of the Republican. I know that we, who hold our estates from certain guilds, are looked upon as mushrooms. Our titles in the records of peerage are a parody upon gentle breeding."

" But," rejoined the king, " the traits which

conciliate in the first instance so slowly the
aristocrat in his prosperity, have won their way
to nearer intimacy, and demand gratitude from
the men of high degree in the hour of need,
such as that which afflicts your worship's royal
guest.   Let cautious and prosaic noblemen
spend their fortunes in prudent extravagance
and display, or even, in revolution ; the
merchants of England, in a crisis, are our
glory and our strength.   But no interest can
save us from the changes and reverses of our
lot."   In this vein the king ran on, while his
hearers, though anxious to indulge his humour,
were at the same time impatient of the delay
which kept them from the busy and stirring
preparations for the king's journey back to
London.

"Whatever may be the future destiny of
James Stuart," said his Majesty, " your conduct,
earl, to our loyal friends, and your noble response
to our call, convince me that I am still king of
England."   Then, after a silent pause, looking
earnestly at Winchelsea, he appointed him in due
form Lord-Lieutenant of the County of Kent, and
Governor of Dover Castle.   "Now," added he,
" having performed at least one act dictated by
my duty and sanctioned by my conscience, I
feel more resigned to my return to my metropolis,
which, perhaps, I ought never to have abandoned.
' Fidens animi in utrumque paratus.'   I commit
myself to the protection of the King of Kings."

"Blessed be God," said Hales, who himself was, however, by no means confident in his sovereign's cause, "I will arrange everything for your journey."

James retired early to bed, apparently more composed in mind, trusting to the loyalty of those who surrounded him.

While young Strickland slept soundly, not a dream disturbing the healthful calmness of his rest, Hales and his elder associates were full of care and sleepless thought. As for the king, notwithstanding his outward signs of resignation, he past the live long night in restless excitement. It was not, indeed, that he had no plans, but rather that he had many; and such conflicting ones that they marred and contradicted each other. His head wandered wildly through the past, the present, and the future. Unmitigated and incessant was the pressure of thought; the safety and succession of his infant son, apprehension for the queen, at one moment, sentiments of affection, at the next, a feeling of vengeance would rise uppermost; every attempt at calm judgment was defeated by the wretched state of his physical health and the flow of blood to his distracted head. In the cry of the night wind the spirit of heaviness was talking to his heart. Exhausted nature had not yet fortified herself by even a short tranquil repose, against the assaults of trouble. Nor is that sensibility, morbid as it may appear in a great sovereign, an imputation on the character of James ; for experience will show us that it is not the strongest natures who can endure grief the longest, or shake off misfortunes the soonest. The reed shaken with the wind, or the bending twig, will more easily recover its elasticity than the noble oak its stately majesty from the shock of the tempest. The full unmeasured extent of his ruin unfolded itself gradually before the sleepless 'eyes of the misguided monarch, until, at length, the accumulation of his griefs, and at last bodily fatigue wearied him into a sleep, just before daybreak, from which he was aroused at a late hour in the morning by the measured tramp of infantry, martial music, and the word of command.

It was the militia, under Sir James Oxendon, taking up their position in front of the mayor's house, which awoke James and attracted the notice of his friends, who had been up and stirring many hours. They evidently suspected Sir James of base treachery, under the mask of loyalty.

" To what fortunate event are we indebted for so early a visit from Sir James Oxendon with his loyal guard of volunteers?" politely asked the Earl of Winchelsea, from the window of a room adjoining that of the king.

" We have heard of your inability to protect his most gracious Majesty, and we are come to guard him from the rabble who have so shamefully assaulted him," replied the colonel of militia.

Winchelsea shook his head indignantly. A smile of bitter meaning passed between his lordship and Sir Edward Hales, who was with him.

The manly beauty of Strickland's face was rendered still more striking by the air of defiance and disdain which' was just breaking forth from him into utterance, when Sir Edward restrained him.

"His Majesty doubtless will give you the credit for this proof of devotion which it deserves," said Lord Winchelsea to Oxendon. "Your unsolicited assistance must, of course, be as disinterested as it is needless; for we cannot dispense with the Coldstream Guards, who will be in attendance."

Sir James sneered a sneer of withering incredulity.

"Men under arms," said Winchelsea, "commanded by a loyalist like Sir James Oxendon, enlisted in such an honourable cause, crazy though they be, cannot fail to appreciate the merit of their officer. They are not yet, however, familiar with the sound of the royal drums and trumpets, and may possibly, in their present state of discipline, mistake them for the martial music of the insurgent band. However this may prove, you will not be responsible for his Majesty's safety. The highest destination to which you can aspire is your self-sacrifice to your country's good. You will in due time, doubtless, be canonized among the martyrs of patriotism ; for, a victim you will be to your disinterested policy. Your honoured name will be eulogised in letters of gold by the rising generation, who will be proud to recount the coronets you declined, the places you honourably rejected, the proffered dignities you could not conscienciously accept, and the unpurchased rank which still holds you a true friend to the king. The step on which you have ventured, sir," continued Winchelsea," " is directed by a spirit which is independent and high above the vulgar bigotry of party feeling."

The gallant commander of the militia, perhaps irritated more by the bitter sarcasm of the speaker's tone, countenance, and manner, even than his words, became pale with passion, and, trembling with rage, lost his self-possession. He bit his lip, then in an accent he could not subdue replied, " I will not insult your own judgment by saying, that I feel it as unnecessary as I do offensive to my brave soldiers, to make any reply to your insinuations. This is not the time nor the place for me to notice such liberties as you have allowed your tongue to utter."

Hales then took up the strain where Winchelsea had left off, without seeming to hear a single word which had dropped from the considerate officer. " My good neighbour, your fellows prefer the rural felicity of their homes to the crown of martyrdom. If they cannot rise to the ambition of the gallant knight who leads them to glory, let them return to their occupations, which poets and philosophers have celebrated. Let them turn again 'their swords into plowshares and their spears into pruning-hooks.'"

"Their swords have a duty to perform, and they are ready," cried Sir James. Scarcely had these ungraceful words been uttered, when the king joined his faithful adherents, and fully entered into their suspicions of the officious colonel.

The window was closed, and a confidential conversation passed between those inside. Above the rest might be heard the voice of Winchelsea, saying "The double-dyed villain, does he suppose we cannot fathom the shallows of falseness?"

Strickland, himself the very soul of honour, was breaking out into a fiery burst of indignation against the proffered aid of a traitor, at the same time grasping the hilt of his sword, when the sound of wheels, the clatter of horses' feet, and the heavy roll of state carriages interrupted the youth, and thus saved him the rebuke of his elder comrades.

Sir James Oxendon, believing what he desired and expected, took the splendid equipage and glittering escort for the retinue of the Prince of Orange, or at the very least, for the brilliant display of his commissioners, and therefore gave the

new arrivals a military salute. After his first
gracious greetings he addressed the four noblemen, arrayed in all the glowing attire of their
rank, as follows:—"We are only waiting the
pleasure of his Highness, or his orders, as our
king, that we may consult his wishes with regard to the gentlemen who have taken shelter
under the wing of the misguided mayor of this
town."

"Indeed?" said Lord Middleton, who was accompanied by Lords Aylesbury, Litchfield, and
Yarmouth.

The diplomatic secretary and successor to
Sunderland, who saw at a glance the little game
of Sir James Oxendon, gravely replied, "So you
are keeping his Majesty in safe custody."

"Just so, my lord."

"But have you any reason to believe that his
mighty Highness will thank you for this gratui-
tous piece of service?" asked Lord Middleton.

The traitor hung his head abashed, while the
four lords cast upon him those cold, cutting looks
of withering contempt, which said, "You intended to sell your king, but you have sold yourself for a sneer of the usurper."

Oxendon was covered with confusion; the
truth began to dawn upon his anxious mind.
He was actually advancing to bend his knee
before the king, who had again appeared at the
window, and thus made himself the laughing-
stock of the loyalists and the greater part of the

spectators. The scene seemed even to rally the spirits of James, and bring him to himself.

"This visit is unexpected, sir," said James, with his former dignity. "To what do we owe the unusual and extraordinary advantage of your company?" The convicted wretch could only back out of the royal presence, until his horse fell on his haunches.

"Having paid your homage to the king, you would, perhaps, as a military man, wish to be introduced to the commander of his forces," said Lord Aylesbury, as he turned to enter the house. This was enough; the militia and their leader were in full retreat before the deputation from Whitehall could enter the house.

"Welcome, my lords," exclaimed the king, with the most unaffected cordiality. "My heart in its sorrow told me that you would not consign me to exile, and enable an invader to undermine my throne."

"Your information reached us by the hand of the peasant that your Majesty has been insulted and delayed," said Lord Aylesbury, "and from what we see all around, your account of the insolence of the mob and of the dastardly impertinence of their leaders has not been exaggerated. Your Majesty will not find us wanting in the hour of danger to your royal person; in the day of your prosperity we kept aloof, for we could not sanction all the proceedings of your ministry, nor promote the interests of that faith which we have been taught to think error."

A deep flush mantled over the king's careworn cheek. Turning his eye quickly on the nobleman, to whom he presented Hales, Winchelsea, and Strickland, with a word in favour of each, he scrutinised the deputation with a look full of anxious inquiry.

"Take your seats, my Lord Secretary Middleton, and you my lords; no men can better advise us what to do in this emergency; take your seats then beside me, and let me have the benefit of your counsel, and your tidings from Whitehall."

With deep obeisance and some diffident reluctance they seated themselves near the king.

"First of all, my liege," said Earl Middleton, "without any conditions or guarantee on the part of your Majesty, your own loyal guards are on their way to Sittingbourne, thence to escort you, as our Sovereign, on your return to London."

"Good, very good, my loyal friends," cried James, as a faint smile of joy rippled over his furrowed face. "This is the very step my old and tried friend Winchelsea has been so strongly recommending. But what says my Lord Godolphin, who tried to dissuade us from ever quitting London?"

"He is scarcely now in a position to invite your return," said Middleton, with a look of deep meaning, which banished the lingering smile from the features of James.

"You have been in the debates of the last three months, Earl Middleton, and must have heard many measures proposed, rejected, or approved, since my unfortunate departure from my capital. What is your own opinion in concurrence with that of your associates in this mission of mercy?"

"You will be welcome, sire, to the heart of your dominions, without any pledge on your part; but if you would continue to rule over a willing and affectionate people," replied the secretary, "you will, in your good sense and sounder judgment, no longer hesitate to adopt such a modified course of policy as may strengthen your Government, yet not compromise your character as a man, or your dignity as a Sovereign."

"We cannot undo what we have done; we cannot make white black, or right wrong," said the monarch.

"Since you condescend to ask my opinion," said Middleton, "I will give it, or rather the result of the general feeling which pervades England. First, we would submit to your Majesty the necessity for conciliating the Protestant Church."

"All which is essential to its preservation I have done; nay, my Lords, more than my conscience approved," said the king. "Indeed, in my proclamation of last month I conceded all which could be reasonably demanded by any but a conqueror." Then turning an affectionate look on Sir Edward Hales, he continued : " Did I not even remove my own faithful friend here from the command of the Tower, because he is guilty in common with myself of being a Catholic ?"

" We are charged, my liege," rejoined Earl Middleton, " with no extraordinary mission ; we are clothed with no authority ; we are uninstructed and ignorant of everything but our message, and the invitation which we have humbly presented to your Majesty. On obtaining your loyal permission to withdraw we will depart."

" No, no," cried the king, turning paler than he was before, " accident saved me from the treachery of Churchill, and now I am unwilling to fall into the hands of a nephew who is seeking to place my Crown on his own head. I have read the history of Richard II. But you will stand by me, my lords," said the unfortunate monarch. " We shall not be offended by your honest freedom."

CHAPTER XXI.

Conscience, what art thou? thou tremendous power
Who dost inhabit us without our leave;
And art within ourselves, another self,
A master self that loves to domineer,
And treat the monarch frankly as the slave:
How dost thou light a torch to distant deeds?—*Young*.

THE four noblemen wore a grave look, while Middleton, addressing the king with the most profound reverence, said,—

"It would, under any circumstances, be presumption in us to intrude into the domain of the spiritual peers, or to approach your Majesty either with arguments against the faith of your religious convictions, or in favour of the religion of the land as by law established. But, craving the indulgence which you so graciously promise, we will venture, in the spirit of that candour which you yourself evince, to state the opinion of the Archbishop of Canterbury, who seems to have no sympathy with the Prince of Orange. We will even incur your displeasure by telling you the truth, rather than by a false courtesy risk your happiness and your kingdom.

" The Church and her ministers—the Church for which your august father suffered martyrdom

—the fond mother from whose bosom you have been torn—the bulwark of your throne, now calls upon you to return to her embrace, to recant the creed which your subjects dread and detest."

"Oh! your Majesty," supplicated Winchelsea, on his knees, "I entreat you to return to those from whom you have gone out. Avert from us a religious war—make your peace with heaven, your people, and yourself."

"I know, my dear earl, your advice is given in kindness," said the King, greatly affected, taking Winchelsea by both hands and raising him, "but my heart is fixed; my faith is anchored to that Rock against which the storms of sixteen centuries have broken themselves in vain. I am resolved to live and die in the religion which Ethelbert embraced a thousand years ago, when he reigned over the very county to which you are appointed; the religion of Edward the Confessor, and of all the kings of England till the reign of Henry VIII.; the religion of Archbishop Theodore, St. Thomas of Canterbury, and all the Christian bishops of the ecclesiastical capital of England, since the very introduction of the faith into the island which I am called to govern."

The Lord Middleton without any direct notice of the declaration, said if it were true that his predecessor in office and other noblemen abandoned the Protestant for the Catholic faith in the service of the king, he did not see why, under such peculiar circumstances, his Majesty should not, for the good of the state, return to the Protestant Church.

"But what," asked the king, "was Sunderland's real opinion, my lord?"

"He believed," replied Middleton, "with us, that human judgment is fallible, and that wise princes have not only consulted their own consciences, but the interests of their people. Thus your Majesty's maternal grandfather, Henry IV. of France, though he had fought the battles of the Huguenots, conformed prudently to Popery; and, to come nearer home, your Majesty's royal brother, though a Catholic at heart, never obtruded his religion on the institutions of the country, nor did he avow himself a Catholic till the hour of his death, and that at the instance of your Majesty."

"And after all," chimed in the rest of the lords, "there is not such a vast difference between the ancient and the modern faith."

"Suppose, my lords," replied James, with some spirit, for theology seemed his element, "I were to comply with your advice, would the convert statesmen and hereditary Catholics of Great Britain follow my example?"

"Doubtless," replied Winchelsea, drily; "a new light would break in upon them, reflected by the greater luminary. The royal conversion would open the eyes of many."

" There is much to be said for that pure and Apostolic branch planted in these realms," broke in Yarmouth.

" The branch cut off from the trunk I fear must wither," cried James, plaintively. " You acknowledge that my separation from the ancient stem, and my union with the severed branch, would make others follow my example, and thus cut themselves off from the true vine, which alone can give them life. Thus, by so doing, I should not only imperil my own soul but should be a scandal to Europe, leading to perdition those for whom I would sooner lay down my life, and sacrifice not only three crowns, but all the kingdoms of the world and their fading glories."

Sir Edward Hales, feeling that some reason of the hope of the faith that was in him might be expected, declared that he fully concurred with the king, and adhered indissolubly to the noble sentiments of his royal master. " Besides, my lords, I would humbly submit that the instances which you have recited in favour of the conversion of the supreme magistrate to the religion of the people over whom he is called to preside, especially in hereditary succession, are not parallel to the case of our Sovereign, whose restoration to Catholicism is absolutely religious, not political and social. To him the Church which was always in communion with Rome, is the true ark, out of which he believes that neither himself nor his people can be saved. While to those royal converts or professors whom you mention, the Church, or what they maintained as such, was in their hands a mere state engine, which they used for temporal interests."

"Of course," observed Winchelsea, with an arch smile, "as England invariably recognises the dynasty in power, so we always believe that the dominant religion is right. In this event, the popular faith must be the creed of the Sovereign."

"True," said Litchfield, meekly, "your Majesty's ministers are always prepared to pray for the party in power."

"If Heaven keeps the favoured party in high office," devoutly observed Yarmouth, "we must conclude they deserve it."

"If earth were the only scene of rewards and punishments, your conclusion, my lord, would be correct," rejoined James, solemnly. "But merit is not always success, and even when crowned, is in danger."

The oak which proudly rises on the mountain top is riven by the thunderbolt, while the lowly lily of the valley breathes fragrance in peaceful security at the bottom.

"High birth is an accident, but you," he said, looking at Middleton, "have risen by your talents to the first charges of the state. Yet in our times and especially so now, as things are in England, both dignities of birth and merit may lead to shame and disgrace. Thrones totter on the edge of precipices ; crowns fit not the heads which wear them. Supremacy is too often the target for seditious shafts. The glory is departed ; the road to sovereignty is the way to prison and to the scaffold. The warning cry, ' There is treachery, O Ahaziah !' both night and day, is ever ringing in my ears. I hear it in the morning wind ; I hear it in the sad sea wave. It comes in every sound. It startles me." Before he could indulge further in this strain the door of the room suddenly opened, and young Strickland, who had, unobserved, left the apartment to mingle freely with the sailors, and even the freebooters and the rabble, re-entered, followed by a messenger, bearing the marks of a hard ride through dirty roads. Strickland ushered the horseman into the presence of his Majesty with as much form and homage as if all were in state at the palace of Whitehall.

Prostrating himself before James : " I have the honour to be the bearer of a message from Lord Faversham to your Majesty," said the horseman. "His lordship is at Sittingbourne with two hundred of your Horse Guards, where he awaits your Majesty's commands."

In reply to the anxious looks which the king turned on his lords, they answered, "Your Majesty may rely upon their fidelity and devotion."

" Then," said James, " inform the commander of the forces that we shall repair to him where he is without delay, and put ourselves under his escort to London."

No sooner had the trusty messenger gone, and the four lords taken their departure from Faversham to rejoin the peers by whom they were commissioned, than Strickland approached his Majesty with the assurance that all classes of his subjects at Faversham were favourably inclined towards him. " They are as firmly attached to the King of England to-day as they were hostile to the priest, for whom they mistook your Majesty, yesterday," added the cornet.

" Doubtless," said Hales, " we are in a degree indebted to your influence with the crowd."

" True," exclaimed the king, " though, young sir, your prudence is only exceeded by your valour. As a proof of our unreserved confidence and esteem we order you at once to prepare the way for our homeward progress. Reconnoitre the neighbourhood through which we must pass, and send us warning of any traps or surprises designed for us which you may possibly detect."

" There are already emissaries sent along the road," said Strickland, " who will refute the slanderous reports raised by the enemies of your Majesty. We will soon disabuse the public mind, and when the real state of the case is known there will be a reaction which will make the usurper retreat to his bogs and frogs amid the viewless fens of his own country."

"If you should not find quite so sudden a reversion in our favour as you anticipate, young sir," cried Lord Winchelsea, " a few dragoons will restore order; as for my own fellows, they desire no greater sport than a brush with the detached parties of William."

Having taken an affectionate farewell of his Majesty, the earl, at the head of his yeomanry, left Faversham, and went on his new duties, which were regulated by his anxiety for the king.

The young guardsman, having in the interim refreshed himself with some viands and a draught of wine, mounted a splendid horse, which he found in readiness for him at the door, and preceded the king and Hales on the road to Sittingbourne.

The young officer of the Life Guards had not advanced far before he was astonished at the large portions of the population which he met, on their way to the sea : at first scattered thinly along the road at long intervals, but as he advanced the stragglers were more frequent, and grouped into little parties of both sexes and all ages. Here and there were the large lumbering coaches of the period, containing families certainly of the richer, if not the higher classes, with their domestic servants in attendance. All were hastening towards the sea; some evidently from the city, others streamed from the country through

rural lanes and pathways ending in the high
road.

The retreat of the fugitives, for such they
were, had, however, none of the appearances of
hurry or disorderly flight. Each family who was
not favoured with a conveyance, walked on foot
or rode on horseback, forming a separate company distinct from the rest, without confusion.
In the centre of one of these little groups might
be seen a fond mother, weeping as she toiled
along; the infirm grandfather, with his hoary
locks, leaning on her, his daughter, for support;
while her young children, crying with weariness,
if not hunger, are hanging about her, and an
infant at her breast; the elder ones toiling
behind her, under the burden of bedding and
such moveables as they could carry away.

Group after group flowed on, and some few
carts, carriages, and heavy vehicles, in a tide
which appeared to Strickland unceasing and
interminable.

It was not without a feeling of peculiar
emotion that Strickland beheld so many of the
king's subjects wandering as exiles from their
loved fields and homes, to share the fortunes or
the fate of their king. The imagination affected
by the scenes and circumstances in which he
himself was called to act imposed on the cornet
the idea of a multitude. Their numbers, which
in a wide plain would be but a handful, were
multiplied and increased to his eye as they

passed in succession through a narrow road. His extreme difficulty was to evade questions which he was not authorised to answer without giving pain or offence to those who already had more than enough to distress them.

While reflecting on the best means to avoid all parties between Faversham and Sittingbourne, a coach, drawn by four horses, with two out-riders, swept round a turning of the road, and burst suddenly on his view before he could escape the observation of the occupants of the huge and cumbrous conveyance.

Very few in these days of rude rough roads and comparatively simple habits pretended to wheeled carriages, which were at best large weighty concerns, bedizened with tarnished gilding and gaudy colours. The enormous moving mansion which now hove in sight was canopied and chiefly made up of leather. A coachman, who wore a tie wig with three tails, and two postilions, who wore short swords and pistols at their saddle bows, conducted this grand equipage. On the footboard behind stood two lackeys in rich liveries, armed according to the fashion of the day, or, perhaps, of the late reign, with a blunderbuss slung behind each. The insides were a middle-aged lady and two or three children. A sort of recess in a projection at the door of the coach, even then called the boot, was stuffed as full of missals, breviaries, and Catholic books, and emblems of

the ancient religion as is now, or was then, the
boot of Italy.   In an opposite recess, cor-
responding with that already noticed, was
ensconced the gentlewoman's gentlewoman.   On
its nearer approach our young hero recognised
the vehicle by its arms and livery.   It belonged
to a family attached to the royal household.

Adjusting himself in the saddle, and gracefully
showing off his beautiful steed in the best style
of a cavalry officer, the young cavalier was
hastening his speed to pay that attention to the
loyalists which courtesy strictly demands, when
he exclaimed in a transport of joy and surprise,
" Is it possible, or do my senses deceive me ! "
In a moment he was at the door of the carriage,
and after a word of hearty greeting, his eyes
made a rapid tour round the inside of the moving
mansion ; at length, in accents of thrilling
anxiety, which no fear for himself, or even the
Stuarts, could inspire, he cried, " But where is
she ?"   A few soothing replies to a torrent of
hasty inquiries recalled to the hero's mind that
calm composure for which he was so remarkable.

" I had hoped, madam," said he, with a voice
still tremulous with apprehension, " to see her
with you since you are on your way to join the
queen."

His words and manner seemed to strike a
chord in the heart of her to whom they were
addressed.

"I am, indeed, only compensated for the absence of my beloved girl from my side in this hour of exile and distress by the belief that she is beyond peril under the hospitable roof of Lord and Lady Winchelsea." This intelligence was imparted in her usual placid manner, but her voice quivered, her cheek was pale, and her whole presence spoke of an agitation which aroused the fears of our hero and suggested his anxious inquiries.

"What," asked he, "has hastened your retreat? What impels your rapid flight from London without any suitable escort, and unaccompanied by Mr. Plowden? Have you had any unwelcome visitors or alarming intimations?"

"Mr. Plowden," replied the lady, is "detained on business. We have no good news. We have had but too many visitors of late, and among them Lord Spenser, whom you may have met. He spoke much of his recent conversion to the Catholic faith, and declared there was one lady whom he adored only less than the Blessed Virgin. It so happened that our dearest Mary was painting your likeness from recollection; for you cannot, my dear Robert, escape from our memory as easily as you can from our sight. You know the courteous address and infallible tact of the noble scapegrace is equal to an emergency. He approached Mary with diffidence and profound respect, but she was absorbed in the painting, which she desired to complete, and heeded him not.

" ' The true picture of a soldier and a guardsman,' he cried; ' so handsome—so brave, but not more noble and manly than the original, whom I recognise at a glance.'

"Now, you know, there is nothing which wins so much sympathy from us poor women as the admiration which one young man expresses for another, whom we esteem more highly than the eulogist. Mistaking our pleasure at my lord's just estimate of our dear, dear Robert, for civility to himself, his unwelcome lordship honoured us with a second visit before we left London. But our beloved Mary was too evil disposed, and saw him not; and the very next day with our sanction, she said, she would take advantage of our old friend Lady Winchelsea's invitation, and set out on horseback, attended by the servants whom we have dispensed with on our journey. She joined Lord and Lady Winchelsea at Canterbury, and is now with them. A favourite maid of the queen's, who is pining after her Majesty, attends my Mary, and will accompany her to France."

During this recital, Strickland changed colour more than once. "This," cried he " confirms the truth of a rambling story, which I had from a young sailor at Faversham."

"Oh ! Robert," exclaimed the lady, "you have been to us, as a son, and I exult like a

mother in your promotion in the esteem and
and confidence of our Sovereign ; but I shudder
at the thought of civil war. Stain not, my
boy, that bright unsullied sword, with English
blood."

"Believe me, dear madam," replied the
youth with deep feeling ; " I would more
willingly be the bearer of the olive branch
between our dear master the king and that
portion of his subjects, who seduced by the
arch-hypocrite, are now in arms. To prepare
the people for his Majesty's return, to regain
their loyalty, to encourage the timid, to confirm the wavering, to win back the hearts
which have been stolen from him, is no mean
part of my mission. But time is success," he
added. Then stooping down over his horse's
neck he kissed and caressed the children, who
called him Robert. Then a mutual, affectionate,
but hasty farewell was uttered. The carriage
rolled rapidly towards the sea, and the thoughtful horseman resumed his solitary way to London.

In this iron age of railroad velocity, when
everybody sees everybody everywhere, and knows
everything, it would be impertinent to record
any fact at which we might arrive by steam.
But as we cannot be shunted off the present
into the past and vapoured back against the
stream of time, we may, perhaps, be permitted
to note things not generally known to the whole
world. Amongst these there is no more signi-

ficant fact than this,—that the men who took the most active part in the execution of the laws existing against heresy in the reign of Queen Mary were no other than those who a few years before had been foremost in their support of the royal supremacy—holders of the abbey lands. They were as zealous under the Protector Somerset as they were afterwards under Mary. On the other hand, those Catholic bishops who had never shared the national apostacy courageously refused to obey the orders of the persecuting council, and in their dioceses scarcely a conviction took place. Indeed, this severity, so far from being approved by Catholics in general, met with a firm opposition from those who best deserved the name. Thirty-seven members seceded from the House of Commons rather than be involved in these proceedings; and among them was Francis Plowden, a man to whom in the succeeding reign Elizabeth offered the dignity of the Chancellorship, on condition that he would abjure the Catholic faith. He firmly, conscientiously, and with much dignity rejected the proposal.

Of this faithful and unwavering adherent to the ancient religion the husband of the lady in the carriage and the father of the lovely girl, in whom Strickland felt such an affectionate interest, was a direct descendant, and the head of a family who have never fallen from their first estate of the old, old faith. But to return to the young gentleman whose early and fond associations with the Plowdens have carried us out of the era of our tale.

This sudden meeting and unexpected intelligence struck Strickland with such a surprise, mingled with pleasure and pain, that the young lover had forgotten all about his purpose to avoid the public roads to which the interests of the king did not confine him. Occasional travellers, however, and inquisitive fugitives, soon reminded him of his former intention. The roads which even at the best, in the height of summer, were scarcely passable for wheeled carriages, were now cut into deep ruts and full of sloughs. To avoid them and yet continue his resolution, the cornet determined to gallop on the greensward across the country towards Sittingbourne. He cleared a quickset hedge as if he had been taking a flying leap over a bristling wall of bayonets into a hollow square of infantry. He then took to the fields, stopping at nothing, and for the interests of truth we must admit more in the spirit of a foxhunter than a soldier.

The horse and his rider were well suited to each other, and enjoyed mutually the exhilarating exercise, clearing hedge and ditch and rushing through the clear frosty air of the afternoon. Never for a moment, however, did pleasure or recreation, though welcome to him, carry him beyond the limits of prudence. He soon pulled up as if some sudden thought struck him.   Dismounting, he took a careful survey of his steed and his accoutrements, which were spattered with mud, and covered with sweat and foam. Invited by the sound of a neighbouring stream which came babbling down a dingle, covered with hawthorn trees and copsewood, he hastened to the welcome water, in which he washed away the froth from his horse's mouth and bridle. He then allowed him to take a slight refreshing draught of the stream, through which he walked him.   He was no despicable groom, and had nearly succeeded in whisping down the animal with dry fern and withered grass, when his attention was arrested by an indistinct and distant wail.   " Hist," he said to the steed, now champing his bit with pleasure.   " Gently, old fellow; I hear a distant noise."   He listened. " It is only the noise of the brook over the pebbles," thought he to himself.   Still he heard, or fancied he heard, a human voice.   He hearkened attentively for a moment, but heard nothing but the sough of the wind in the copse.

He feared that the loneliness of the place, associated with the agitating scenes through which he had recently passed, was deceiving his ears, and conjuring up images of woe.   Then concentrating, as it were, all his senses in one intense effort of listening, with that anxious strain which goes through our very being, when we hope or fear the near approach of a coming

friend or foe, he placed his ear near the bank of
the brook, and heard nothing but its gurgling in
the dingle. Accusing himself with the sickly
sensibility of hearing sounds which were never
uttered, he walked his horse away in the direction of Sittingbourne, nearly parallel to the high
road, when once more the noise startled his ear.
It was not this time the dismal cry which he
thought he heard at first. He paused. " It is
the galloping of horses," said Strickland to
himself, his sense of hearing rendered more
acute by the solitude of the scene, and the
anxiety of his situation as the confidential
servant of the king. " God grant," says the
youth, " they may not cut his Majesty off before
he can join his guard. The horses approached
rapidly ; near, and still more near, they came.
" It is the sound of horses," said he, and immediately a thick trampling and rough voices were
heard on the road.

As soon as he had satisfied himself that his
first impression had not deceived him, the cornet
examined his arms, tightened his saddle girths,
and, hastily mounting his steed, now in high
spirit, he took up his station behind the thick
copse which intervened between him and the
road. Scarcely had he taken up his post when
other sounds fell upon his ear above the tramp
of the horses and the clank of armour,—the
plaintive accents of a female in deep distress.
At this, the beauteous glow of manly youth

faded into a pallid hue, not with fear for himself,
for that was a thing unknown to the heart of
Strickland. A secret fear for the fate of others
hovered near him. A vague sense of impending
danger filled every breeze that wailed, with a
warning. Every leaf that fluttered thrilled
through the hero. There was a terrible fore-
boding which he could not banish. A sudden
pang of horror shot across his mind as the young
soldier looked around, but saw no help from any
quarter which could aid his single arm to rescue
a captive from, what appeared to him, a troop of
horse !

CHAPTER XXII.

I do not think a braver gentleman,
More active, valiant, or more valiant young;
More daring or more bold, is now alive,
To grace this latter age with noble deeds.—*Shakespeare.*

HIS honour as a knight, not less than his own feelings, urged the young officer to succour the helpless in distress, especially a woman, who seemed to supplicate protection ; but above all a countrywoman, and she, perhaps, attached to the interests of his master and Sovereign. At the same time his mission and confidential employment to reconnoitre and prepare the way before his Majesty, forbade him to loiter or expose himself to any danger not incurred in the immediate defence of his royal master. The mental struggle which he had thus to undergo, might be read in his countenance. It was not a conflict between feeling and duty, but the difficulty of a just decision, which for a moment distracted him. Of one thing he was certain, that as the party drew nearer, the voice of an agonised maiden was lamenting her terrible situation. A cry at once indignant and mournful rose through that winter evening. At first

in one long, swelling note, then broken as if by
sobs, it trembled, sank and rose again, higher
but sadder ; then to the ear of Strickland came,
as it were, the chorus of demons, calling to each
other through the air in hellish laughter, at the
woe, which they were inflicting on their captive.
But still above all, came in accents fervent and
clear, " O Father of Mercy, come to my aid.
O Holy Mother of God, my own dearest mother,
pray for thy child at this hour, worse than death.
Oh ! deliver me purissima mater.   O Jesu, send
me help, before it is too late.   Oh ! brother !
Oh ! friend of my childhood !   Oh ! my dear
father ! Will nobody help me ? Oh ! save me !"

The voice he could not recognise, yet it had
something in its wailing accents that went to
his heart.   He no longer hesitated.   In an
instant he was in the saddle, giving the spurs to
his horse.   He hastily made his way over every
obstacle, and rode forth upon the open London
road, and soon found himself a little in advance
of four horsemen, who were proceeding along at a
rapid pace towards Sittingbourne, and who, by
their accoutrements and the caparison of their
steeds seemed to be English troopers ; though
upon a nearer view he perceived that the fourth
though in dress and appearance not differing
materially from the rest, was a foreigner.

A thrilling sense of early manhood, and the
power which makes the boy a man in his highest
daring and his pride, nerved the arm of Strick-

land; yet the stout, square figure, the stern features, and sullen, nay, morose, savage air and resolved manner of his opponent, while it made him look the most formidable of the party, warned our young hero of the fearful odds. He appeared to Strickland to be a Dutchman, and this opinion was quite justified by the ruffian's spluttering ribaldry and coarse replies to a young lady, who now, for the first time, caught our hero's eye. She sat, or, rather, was held on a horse. Her dishevelled hair and terrified appearance, not to mention the heart-rending exclamations which burst from her lips, indicated but too plainly what at first Strickland had suspected, that she was an unwilling, if not, indeed, a resisting captive, in the hands of the horsemen, who were, with the exception of pistols, armed to the teeth.

With steady eye and firm purpose the cornet surveyed the ruffians and their prize. He backed his horse out of their sight round a turn in the road, retreated unobserved behind the nearest shelter of the copse where he had first retired. Here, as if debating in his mind the fearful odds against him, and calling stratagem as a reinforcement to his assistance, he resolved on victory or death. Suddenly darting from his ambush into the road, he awaited them sword in hand. The insurgents, for such they were, no sooner beheld the unlooked-for opponent than they reined in their horses, and regarded the young guardsman with looks of wonder, mingled with fear. His sudden apparition and manœuvre gave the notion of men in reserve behind the copse, at his command.

He who seemed to be the chief of the escort advanced to the front, and called out in a loud voice, "Out of our way rash boy, or we ride over you!"

"Stand, false traitor! dishonourable soldier!" was the answer. "Stand; let go that lady, coward; deliver her to me, or you will have to settle your account."

"Forward; down with the fool-hardy youth who courts death!" cried the leader to his men.

But the brave cornet gave them no time to make their onset. Imparting to his charger the spirit which animated the rider, he dashed like lightning in full career upon the astonished rebels, and in an instant one of them fell from his saddle mortally wounded by Strickland's sword. The rest were meantime falling upon him with their drawn swords, and the ruffian who was at the head of the party felt his disdain change into fury. He rushed at Strickland as if, at one stroke to master his foe; but he had before him a man of such surprising skill, that he was more than a match for the matured strength of the rude rebel. Seeing himself thus beset, our young hero, feigning a retreat, drew the powerful adversary after him some distance from the other assailants, then whirled round with the greatest rapidity, making his horse, which had the activity of a racer with the power of a charger, perform the boldest curvets. Attacking the broadset Dutchman incessantly and skilfully with the point or edge of his sword, he bounded gracefully, as if it were a mere exercise, out of the reach of the heavy counter blows. The strong man exhausted himself and his heavy horse in vain against the expert life-guardsman. The perspiration that cold evening stood in beads on his forehead. The third horseman seeing the issue of the duel must be fatal to his chief, spurred to the scene of action. The youth dropped his sword as if disabled, turned his horse's head in full retreat, snatched a pistol from his holster, and while the Dutch-man, supported by his assistant, was pursuing the hero with a savage laugh of joy, Strickland turned his well-trained horse half way round, and with a steady aim, cried, " Die, wretch ! die," at the same instant discharging his pistol. The shot took effect in the chest of the horse, which, now streaming with blood, fell down heavily in the agonies of death on his rider, and rolled convulsively over him. He gasped, as he went under, " Ply your spurs ; slay the young devil incarnate ;" then turning to the trooper who had the care of the lady, he cried out, " Make good your escape with your charge ; as you value your life, deliver her to his lordship ;" for he now saw that the issue of the uneven contest was no longer doubtful. But the cornet was as vigilant as he was valiant, and as active as he was cool. By a sudden movement he stopped the way, dexterously parrying the blows which were now aimed at him by the two troopers.

" For your lives give her up to me," cried the young man, with a voice of thunder, and with the spirit of all the Stricklands. Nothing was easier at this stage of the conflict, than to shoot the miserable man who clung to the horse on which he held down his fainting captive, whose sight was troubled, and who seemed unconscious of what was passing around her; but so close to her side did the ruffian ride, that to discharge his pistol at him, were to imperil her. He, therefore, collected his strength which had been already severely taxed, avoiding the disengaged dragoon, a muscular man, who was attempting to lay hands on him; concentrating, as it were, all his energies in his raised right arm, with his trusty sword he cleft the ruffian through the crown of the head down to the teeth. In two red streams, the blood gushed from the unhappy man, dyeing red the drapery of the young girl, and bedabbling her lovely figure all over with gore. For a moment the slain soldier spasmodically retained his hold, then reluctantly in death relinquished his grasp. The lady, pale as a corpse, partially secured to her horse, sat almost breathless with ineffable horror; no feature

moved ; she was insensible and silent as death.
Maddened by the fray, and feeling no longer any
restraint, her swift steed ' from the slaughter fled
frantic away.' Her deliverer could but gaze
upon her, as, like a spectre, she evaded his
anxious grasp. He gazed upon the receding
figure, faint and bending over the steed's neck
in helpless weakness. There was not, however,
a moment for critical scrutiny in his glance.
Breathless with awe and rivetted to the spot
with surprise, for the first time, perhaps, in his
short life he was unmanned and overcome by
the shock. A restless motion of his horse
aroused him to thought and to action. He
debated with himself the best means to save
the poor lady the peril, which still attended her,
at every bound of her steed. To pursue her
would be to increase her fear and her speed; to
accelerate the death which he would avert, to be
the ruin of her, whoever she was, for whom he
would lay down his life. His horse once more
pricked up his ears, snorted, tore up the earth
with his feet. His bewildered rider looked round
for the cause of such excitement, and beheld
the only surviving enemy who was still free,
extricating the Dutchman from the carcase of
his horse, which had nearly crushed him. It
was not the work of a second to mount the
liberated scoundrel on a riderless horse, and
to charge with him upon the Cornet, who had
barely time to collect himself and prepare for

defence. The black veins of the bull-headed
Dutchman stood out like cordage, while he
scowled with the malignity of a demon. He
advanced in a hand gallop towards the young
hero and close to his companion, who was more
disposed to a parley than to a renewal of the
combat.

" Holloa," cried he, in a gruff cranky croak,
placing himself in the way, as Strickland was
retiring to await his opportunity. " No such
haste, young sir. Art Whig or Tory, man or
tyfel ? under vat king, James or, William?"

" I acknowledge but one king," cried Strickland, indignantly.

" Say vat king: speak, or die ! Tam tyffel !"

" Treason ! treason !" cried Strickland, as
if to bring his body of reserve to his assistance,
then, confronting the two men. " Have a care,
gentlemen," says he, " unless you would like
to rejoin your friends in their bloody bath and
share their fate."

" Down with him !" cried the Englishman to
his Dutch comrade, " he is the king's popish
friend."

" If you will only wait," cried the youth, " I
will introduce you to the king and his guards,
they are close at hand," trusting that the
announcement of this fact and the view of their
dead companions in treachery would intimidate
the fellows. But, under the influence of political
bias and religious duty, the patriot rushed in

advance of the Dutchman in that amiable fury which distinguishes all true lovers of their country. The Dutchman, wishing to finish the business, cried out to the trooper to fire his carbine at the "tam tyffel." While, however, the man was preparing to execute the little order, Strickland, whose horse had been rested by the parley, cleared a hedge, and was lost to their sight. The trooper attempted to follow, but in vain. The Orangeman, in desperation, charged the hedge and burst through it, and as he did so received the contents of the cornet's second pistol in his head. The fellow reeled in his saddle and fell from his horse, this time a corpse. The only surviving combatant, astonished at such execution by one arm in so short a time, attributed the feat to the supernatural witchings of popery; and, swearing a terrible oath, rushed forward in blind rage, but in that desperation which gave the cornet more trouble than all the rest. The guardsman had the advantage in three things—coolness, dexterity in using his sword, and the management of his horse. He fearlessly threw himself across the able-bodied trooper's way. Both were redoubted swordsmen. Considering all things, the combatants were well matched, and they themselves seemed to think so, for no sooner . had two or three cuts and pushes been interchanged than they paused, as if by mutual consent, to recover breath, and to gain strength for a duel in which each seemed but too well satisfied that he had met his match.

"You murdering young dog!" said the trooper, grasping his sword firmly, and setting his teeth. "You have escaped my companions, and let loose the papist wench, but,"—here he swore an oath too tremendous even for a trooper— "I will lay thee where thy bloody hand has laid those who ought to have crushed thee. I will empty thy saddle for thee, and send thee to a place peopled with papists."

The cornet's eye rather than his ear was engaged. He parried and returned with quick interest the blows of the boasting trooper. There was a pause. The younger officer's object, we fear, was to provoke to rashness the older and stronger soldier. "Thy villany," cried he, "taints the very air."

Determined and unrelenting courage was common to both; and nothing could withdraw the attention of the combatants from each other. The trooper fought with the inveterate instinct of a thorough bred bull-dog, the Cornet, like a man on whose victory depended the safety and liberty of the captive, and even of the sovereign, whose servant he was. It was now the short critical point on which the hesitating fate of the duel trembled, ere it decided for this side or that, amid the scene of death and carnage. It was the thought of the captive and the king which gave effect and energy to so slight a figure and so

young an arm. It was a wonderful thing how
his determined spirit kept him up. He fought
like a lion, but his strength could not hold out
for ever. Still, however, he maintained the
contest, hoping and expecting some assistance
from the king's party. He felt that if once the
hardy trooper, now impatient with mortal hate,
grappled with him, all were lost. When a man
has beaten three, there is no shame in flying;
so thinking he put spurs to his horse. But
inspired by the spirit of a hundred Stricklands
he thought his flight a disgrace. He resolved
to gain time and rest, and then once more
resume the uneven contest. His retreat drew
the trooper after him. The Cornet rallied
behind the copse—suddenly burst upon the
trooper, who in his pursuit was off his guard
redoubled his thrusts with greater address, and,
before the trooper could recover his surprise, he
was transfixed by Strickland's sword. Collecting
the last effort of respiration, grim in death, he
uttered a fearful oath, and as soon as it was
spoken, expired weltering in mud and gore.

The vicissitudes of this contest, which have
taken so many words to describe, were crowded
into a few rapid moments. The result which
ensued is less usual perhaps in real history than
in romance.

The unhappy event which so unexpectedly
delayed Strickland's progress left on him a deep
and anxious impression. The first burst of

triumph over, the high, beating hope, the buoyant spirit which carried him through the unequal fight, had passed away from the heart of the conqueror, and were succeeded by that deep, depressing reaction which is the result of such overwrought excitement and exertion. His object was not vengeance but mercy; and it was attained. Before the libertine lip of the coward, who had employed his bravoes, could invade the spotless sanctity of a maiden's cheek his miserable myrmidons had kissed the dust, and Strickland devoutly hoped that their profligate master might soon share the same fate. His eye now searched anxiously for the liberated captive, but she was nowhere to be seen. To follow her horse's footsteps were fruitless. "And," said he to himself, "even were I to pursue her, in the agitated state of her feelings she will fly from me as from an enemy." He could only call to his aid the reflection that she was safe, at least from the worst peril which could afflict her, and that she might fall in with the royal party. However this might really prove, "To delay longer," thought he, "is to abuse the king's confidence, if not to endanger his person. There is no stain on the maiden's fair fame, the designs of her persecutor are already defeated."

From thoughts like these, as he resumed his journey, he was startled by the distant neighing of a horse, to which his own steed replied, while in a hunting gallop he eagerly bounded along the turf. Every stride in the direction of Sittingbourne brought him nearer to the spot from which the reiterated and returned whinnyings came, until nothing but a high, thick, holly fence, interlaced with wild rosebriars and woodbine, bearing red berries, with furze at the bottom, forming a complete screen to that very glade through which, by another entrance, Strickland had commenced his gallop, making his horse gaily keep time to the tune which he whistled about an hour earlier, when he pulled up to refresh and prepare his nag for a respectable arrival at the village of Sittingbourne.

He had no sooner passed through an opening in the fence than he beheld a noble steed, a dark bay with a black mane and tail, richly caparisoned, bearing a side saddle laced with silver and gold, and all the gayest trappings of the period, but now bespattered and bedabbled with blood and mire. The beautiful animal's head bent over some object at the far side, which for a second the cornet did not perceive, but when the noble steed, greeting the new comers, raised his stretched-out neck, what was our young hero's astonishment and horror at the sight which greeted his eyes ! A damsel lay lifeless close to her palfrey's feet. Failing strength and fear, conspiring, had evidently made the fainting maiden relinquish her seat. She had fallen senseless to the ground, but was still attached to the saddle by a strap, which had only relaxed but not given way. The gentle and sagacious animal seemed conscious of what had happened; he stirred not a limb, and looked as if he would say, " Extricate my poor young mistress."

The soldier sprang from his horse. To cut the treacherous strap with his sword, to raise the afflicted maiden up to a sitting posture, was the work of a second.

In the well-trained, well-bred, patient animal he could not be mistaken, for that beautiful creature had often carried by his side her whom he loved. The young lady was habited in a velvet skirt of Lincoln green ; beside her lay on the greensward a riding hat with its graceful feather of sable hue. The clustering profusion of golden ringlets, no longer confined by a riband of royal plaid, were now streaming wildly over her shoulders. Her cast of features was soft and feminine, yet not without the expression of a thoughtful mind, which redeemed their mild beauty from the charge of that unmeaning statue-like look peculiar to beautiful blonds and blue-eyed damsels of the Saxon stamp. They were too susceptible of change to be placidly perfect.

To recognise the prostrate maiden, even to him, was not such an easy task. Her elegant riding dress was splashed with mire mingled with the dark blood of her slain captor. The loathsome gore, contrasted with the snowy brow which it partly disguised, had desecrated the

angelic face of the pure maiden ; and yet, combined as it was with those soft wailing accents
which he thought he heard at first, and associated
in his thoughts with all which he had learnt from
Mrs. Plowden, in that mild, mournful countenance
there was something which pierced and agonised
his heart. The whole truth flashed vividly upon
the youth and filled him with apprehension and
alarm. He sickens at the dreadful recollections
of the evening which crowd over him. They at
once sweep through his mind in tumultuous
succession, with a sorrowful meaning—murky
and dark are they as the dusky approach of
the December night coming down on that scene
of silence and solitude. His tears fall not, but
they reach the very brink of the eyelid ere he
can turn them back again to the fountain of the
broken up deep.

He had been wary and cool in the very whirlwind of the furious fight. He had now that
prize in possession ; nay more, his heart's
fondest treasure, which had eluded the villain's
desperate clutch. Action, not mere helpless,
hopeless sympathy, was he felt what the hour
demanded ; yet still he gazed, and could not
withdraw his gaze from the dear face of her
whom he supported. Her complexion, through
which the fresh young blood was wont to blush
as loveliest leaves of early roses moved by the
breath of summer, was now blanched into the
hues of death. The youth's eyes were fastened

on the disfigured girl, over whom his heart was
bowed low in a mysterious sympathy and sorrow.
He at length marked some wonderful change
passing over her countenance ; something which,
to his wishes at least, spoke of returning life.
Her eyes had lost their fixed and glassy expression of death.

A sensible tremor passed over the young man,
not of grief for the dead, but the conflict of hope
and fear, but soon the convulsive thrill of
ecstatic joy. The maiden faintly breathed, but
before she could open her lips she was again
lifeless, leaning her head upon her lover's arms.

A wreath of smoke eddying above the trees
soon caught his eye as he turned to look for
aid. It arose from a sequestered cottage, to
which he hastened with his helpless burden.
But at the rustic gate he hesitated. He
mentally debated : " The chill evening air is,
perhaps, more merciful than man when his hand
is raised against his brother." How could he
explain all the strange circumstances of the
case ? Might not the cottager be an enemy to
the king and the loyalists ? Revolving such
anxious thoughts, he looked through the now
uncertain light for some safer refuge, when he
perceived closer to the high road the top of some
building, lifting its head above the wood, at a
little distance. The building, which peeped
above the leafless trees, on near inspection,
turned out to be a ruinous church, standing on

an elevated curvature, almost surrounded by the winding stream. It nestled among beech trees, in about the centre of the vale which first seduced Strickland into that pleasant gallop which terminated in such an important result.

The hallowed edifice was of dimensions less spacious than the usual Gothic structures of this sort which form such frequent and venerable features in the rich landscapes of old England. Its open stone work tower invited his approach. Time and old memories had thrown a sanctity around it which man had not been able to destroy. Aged elms, weeping ash trees, and monumental yews, had survived the religious works of art beneath their melancholy shade. Tracery of wild creepers, stunted shrubs, wall-flowers, scattered through the ivy mantle, wreathed the ruinous walls in a garland as if in pity to their nakedness. The rude effigies of saints torn from their destined niches during the great rebellion lay prostrate and disfigured. A rude stone crucifix and ancient font of rare design, and other material emblems of the old faith, lay mutilated and half concealed beneath the rank herbage and withered nettles under which they were buried. The winter wind was piping through the almost roofless aisles. In one of the most sheltered of the deep recesses of the edifice, probably a side chapel, lay trampled such forage as the churchyard itself supplied, and which seemed to indicate that the sacred building had upon some late emergency been made the temporary quarters of a troop of horse.

Already the sun had gone down, but his last light lingered faintly in the doorway of the west wing, and in the portals through which he passed away, making the monastic seclusion of the place more solemn. A mysterious melancholy stole over the soldier as he held the soft hand of the maiden in his, and bore her in his arms; her head leaned on his shoulder, while masses of long glossy hair fell round his neck and veiled his bosom.

Two kindred hearts more fond and pure never pressed each other,—like two young separate branches grafted into one. The young man, with the holy fondness of a brother and the noblest feelings of a lover, in her unconscious embrace was forgetful of all else—even of the king; aware of nothing but her presence and her situation. A word was trembling on his lip; but the heart lent the tongue no utterance. To him it seemed as though there were but two human beings in all the world: the girl whom he loved, and the man who loved her; yet they were but one. All had as it were passed away from earth, and these two beings were left alone with nature and with God—the source of life and love. All seemed hushed to silence and repose. The whisper of the night wind through the crevices of the church, the busy murmur of the rivulet, the robin-redbreast's last note, dying

with the dying day, all softened and harmonized
themselves into unison with the cold sad still-
ness of that evening scene.

No sooner had he entered this little chapel
than, laying her gently down, he made for her
a couch of the best of the fodder which he
could collect, covering it with dry leaves which
had fallen from the trees. Here, with delicate
and anxious care, he laid her; this done, from
his firelock he struck a light and kindled a fire.
He then cautiously satisfied himself that her
spirit had not fled, and that the blood, which
had left unsightly marks upon her, was not her
own. He was in the act of noiselessly spreading
over her his military cloak when a fresh alarm
made him shudder for her safety.

The clatter of more than one horse at full
speed broke the silence of the time and place.
It could not be the royal party, for the sound
came not from the direction of Faversham. It
could scarcely be the flight of fugitives still
towards the sea, for none would venture to be
out so late. He could only believe that his ear
had deceived him; and, consoling himself with
this reflection, he was soon lost in a romantic
reverie, and took no further heed to the noise.
His thoughts were occupied in tracing the links
of the chain of events which bound the present
to the past, and connected him and Mary
Plowden together so mysteriously.

He took the girl by the hand, covering it with

kisses, saying, tenderly, "Fear nothing, my dear sister—my Mary."

To his horror, she motioned him to leave her, and turned upon him a look of loathing and hatred. His cheek was flushed, then at once he turned ashy pale; a cold shudder ran all through him. His very blood seemed to freeze in his veins.

"You traitor!" she cried; "your touch profanes a Christian. How dare you thus approach a virtuous and honourable lady of a loyal house? Begone! leave me here to die; but spare me this insult. Your heartless audacity drives me out of my senses. But you vile coward and caitiff, you have me, you think, a helpless victim in your power, and you exult in my misery. Neither fear, nor pity, nor honour can influence such a ruffian. I never injured you nor yours; and yet you have torn me from all whom I love: my father and mother, my friend dearer than a brother. Oh! that he were near! he would smite you to the earth, as he smote your guilty comrades. But God watches over me, and is my Protector. Your punishment is in store. The lightning—Heaven's thunder and dire vengeance—the tempest of God's wrath, will whirl you to destruction. Begone, sirrah; begone! out of my sight! Your foul presence sickens me."

In vain the young man tried to soothe her anguish, and to bring her to herself; to make himself known to her. But in the delirious paroxysm of the shock which she had undergone she heard nought, she saw nought, but the wretch who had surprised her in her ride during her visit to Lord Winchelsea; the hired ruffian, whose only object was filthy lucre.

"Oh! my dear Miss Plowden—Oh! my Mary, be your own dear self again, and hear me," he said, imploringly.

She again signed him from her. She wore a shocking smile of triumph, quite alien to her nature, while words of deprecation escaped her lips, and agonised the heart of Strickland.

"May fear kill thee, and seize upon thy dastard heart and slay thee! How dar'st thou take my name upon thy vile lips? And how didst thou find it out? But my dear brother, the companion of my youth, will avenge me. My father cannot be far off; he will not leave me behind. To me he will bring safety and release; to you, wretch, despair and death.—But, back! Hush! coward, I hear my father's step.—Release me, father!—brother!—help! help!—father, help thy poor afflicted child!" Scarcely had she uttered the last word, when Strickland was startled by a rustling noise, which drew his attention to a window, whence the sound descended.

The window commanded a view of the interior of the chapel, now the chamber of the affrighted maiden. The apparition of a middle-aged man,

in a riding dress, attracted the cornet's notice.
The unwelcome intruder with difficulty let himself down into the church.

The last part of Miss Plowden's wild wanderings, addressed to the ruffian, whom in her delusion
she still thought was in her presence, must have
reached his ear; for, rushing up to Strickland,
who stood in darkness only made more obscure
by the flickering and fitful blaze of the fire, he
cried, " Stay! for your life stay! you unmanly
rascal—base caitiff that you are. Lay not your
coward hand on the daughter of a loyalist; for
such I am sure she is, from the words which I
overheard." Already he unsheathed his sword to
slay him to whom the maiden's words appeared
to be addressed.

CHAPTER XXIII.

She speaks poniards, and every word stabs;
Is all the counsel that we two have shared,
The sister's vows, the hours that we have spent,
When we have chid the hasty-footed time
For parting us,—O, is all forgot ?—*Shakespeare.*

ALL the strange visitor could imagine in the
agitation of the moment was a lady bitterly
remonstrating with some hired ruffian who had
her in his charge. Under this natural delusion,
boiling with righteous rage at the ill-treatment
of an innocent damsel, he drew his sword and
was about to bury it in the heart of his own
child's deliverer and preserver, saying sternly
as he advanced, "Yes, you will merit all and
more than the young lady said." And, for the
interests of truth, we cannot deny that Mr.
Plowden, for he it was, could not help bestowing
an execration upon the poor-spirited rascal who
had taken such a vile and dastardly course to
gratify some wretch tenfold more the child of
hell than himself.

"You coward traitor ! how you shrink from
a fair fight ! your conscience cries guilty."

He was astonished at the unresisting patience

and high-minded forbearance of the young man, who stood still with his arms folded.

"Swear not, sir," cried the youth. "A curse is like a stone flung upwards, and may return on the man who sends it."

Before Mr. Plowden could execute his threat he began to recognise in the voice and language of the speaker that of an acquaintance, if not of a friend, whose face and figure, dimly displayed by the light of the glimmering fire, confirmed this impression.

"Thrust me through the body, and bathe your impatient sword in my life's blood! but never, never will the hand of Robert Strickland be raised against the protector of our beloved Mary."

Had a voice from one of the surrounding graves struck his ear it could scarcely have amazed him more than that which arrested his attack. Could he really believe his senses? However this might be, the words of him, whom he a moment before had determined to slay, brought a mysterious, strange, and discordant music to the memory of the mistaken bewildered assailant. They carried him back to other times, to all he loved, to all for whom he lived. The well-known accents, so painfully out of unison with everything around, filled him with an indescribable sensation of mystical awe, not unmingled with resignation. Happier thoughts of other times, like holier spirits, amid the desolation of the desecrated house of God, came to him and called up earlier feelings: home endearments and home joys. Everything took a hue more sombre even than reality. He felt that since his family circle had been broken up there was no dear devoted inmate waiting for his coming, and longing for his expected return.

The darkness and gloom of the place reminded him that already he had entered on his pilgrimage of exile through scenes of confusion and domestic distress.

Strickland's words and voice had struck upon the right key; all doubts of his identity vanished. The arm which but a moment before was raised to slay him, now pressed him to his heart; the father and the lover of the dear sufferer, who lay before them, were locked in each other's arms. A mutual transport of manly sympathy bound them in one long embrace of friendship, too deep, too hallowed for description. As a performer on the lute sounds all the strings to tune it, so some heavenly agency had touched a chord and regulated the travellers' hearts, and tuned them in sweet accordance with God's will, and to his greater glory.

Mr. Plowden was now composed—resigned, though he looked haggard and careworn.

To look upon Strickland without admiration was impossible. His personal graces and noble bearing under every influence were natural to him. At this affecting crisis, however, to a

strict observer, the manly beauty of his countenance, though impressed with an air of the
most decisive resolution, was softened and
subdued to a cast of almost feminine tenderness,
which but ill-assorted with his military appearance. His solicitude for her whom he loved,
and who truly loved him, was open in his face.

" But my brave knight-errant," said the elder
gentleman, and his voice, which slightly faltered
at first, calmed down to firmness as he went on,
" what poor maiden have you here in this
region of romance! Her voice has in it something like the voice of our Mary. But she is
safe under the protection of Lord Winchelsea,
to whose mansion she repaired on her favourite
steed, on whose gentleness and sagacity you
know we all rely, escorted by two grooms who
have my confidence. Besides, even had it been
possible for her to be here, it is not in her
nature to repulse the man whom she loves as
her brother and her friend, nor would she require
any proofs of your devotion to give her confidence
in your protection. However reluctant she
might be under ordinary circumstances to incur
a debt of obligation to any other young man to
whom it would afford a great advantage over her,
to you her debt of gratitude would be repaid
by affection. The very words of the distracted
girl whom we have just heard belie the sentiments of our own dear Mary towards her brother
and her early friend."

After a moment's anxious pause the cornet laid his hand on the shoulder of Mr. Plowden, who was still unconscious that in that afflicted maiden he beheld his dear daughter.

" Be composed," said he, " and be yourself; only listen and trust your ear, for the words I utter are true and faithful. It is our Mary." The senior traveller heard no more; one intense and overwhelming emotion mastered him; heart, mind, soul, strength—all the rays of life's bright light centred in that one poor object. His deep affections turned to her, and claimed her for their own. His lips pressed hers; he covered her pale face with kisses. The fond father fixed his eyes upon his child; then, like a pent-up torrent breaking forth, the warm tears gushed out; and with the heart's loving cry, " My own girl," he fell upon her neck, and wept tears of joy mingled with grief. Endearing words which the heart lent the tongue rushed to his lips; but alas! alike insensible of his presence and fatherly endearments, she made no sign. Turning from her, in a paroxysm of grief and amazement, to his young friend, he poured forth a rapid, full tide of inquiry, to which Strickland's reply was, with little variation, a brief statement of the events which have been already narrated in this faithful history.

By the time he had ended, Mr. Plowden seemed to have recovered from the first bitter pang of grief, and soon resumed his own quiet,

tranquil state of mind, of which the young
soldier availing himself, now in his turn asked
a hundred questions, one jostling the other
before it could get out of his mouth ; now in
quick, but measured, succession, like wave upon
wave, but yet distinct and full of meaning.   Mr.
Plowden's story was soon told.   It was plain
and concise, such as the time, place, and circumstances demanded.

He had been detained in town by family
affairs of great importance.   He had been
naturally anxious to preserve his ancestral
house and hereditary domains for his now
exiled family, and had nearly concluded a
legal transfer of all his landed property to a
neighbour and his assigns, from whom it
might revert some brighter day to the Plowdens
of Plowden, in Shropshire.   But in order to
render the conveyance valid, and secure the
estates from confiscation by the probable future
dynasty, many technical precautions were indispensable ; nor was it till he thought the arrangement formal and complete that certain allega-
tions were brought forward which must be refuted.
Suspicions affecting the parties to whom the
said property had been made over were advanced
and still must be removed.   To establish the
characters of the purchasers as honest Protestants and safe subjects of a Protestant
monarch, direct proofs and concurrent testimony, not mere presumptive or circumstantial

evidence, must be produced ; nothing less, indeed, would satisfy the judgment of the Catholic Mr. Lovelaw, who had already legally anticipated the true interpretation of the statutes and righteous decision of the law courts under the apprehended sway of the invader, from whose grasp the faithful conveyancer was desirous eventually to rescue the aforesaid estates to the heir, executors, administrators, and assigns of the family. " Having at length overcome every obstacle and floored every ob= jection," said Mr. Plowden, " I was hastening rapidly towards the sea to rejoin Mrs. Plowden, intending on my way to call at Lord Winchelsea's and bid adieu to our beloved Mary, who is speedily to follow us to the Continent."

He continued to explain to his young companion that he had not encountered any opposition on the road ; that he, followed by his groom, a shrewd lad. and a quick discerner of men's motives and the little games which each played, and whose skill in horsemanship was only exceeded by his loyalty, was proceeding at full trot, in anxious anticipation of a happy reunion, when his horse snorted, and resisted every effort of his rider to urge him forward. He stood rivetted to the spot, trembled nervously in every limb, under the impulse of the spur made a fearful lounge, and at the same instant stumbled over some object in the road, which, to the rider's horror, turned out to be the dead carcase of a

horse, which, with the trooper who had ridden
him, lay weltering in mud and gore. So scared
at the sight or smell of his slain fellow creature
was the horse, that he frantically rushed away
from the spot, defying all control, and became
quite unmanageable. It was a most trying
moment for Mr. Plowden, whose servant, some
distance behind, was now separated by the sudden
flight of the horse from his master; and as the
closing evening wore on, he could discover no
trace of the beaten track, nor any return to the
high road. In the mean time accident effected
for the benighted rider what all his strength and
address could not achieve. The unrestrained
animal had in his mad career sprained one of
his legs at the fetlock so seriously, that he suddenly fell from the top of his speed into a limp,
which threatened a downfall. Perplexed and dis-
heartened by the disaster, the rider dismounted,
and found himself in a lonely, open country,
unguided and really unable to proceed in any
fixed direction, for as yet neither moon nor stars
in the heavens had succeeded the sun which had
gone down. While revolving the painful par-
ticulars of the accident which had placed him in
this terrible uncertainty, its appalling cause and
the possible consequences of this dismal delay,
his attention was suddenly diverted from such
gloomy reflections to a distant light, glowing
brightly amid encircling darkness. At first it
flashed upon his eye like a will-o'-the-wisp in

the swampy fields, but as he made his way towards it, it remained stationary, and thus encouraged hope. Sad and troublous as were the country and the times, in his present emergency our traveller thought it better to fall into the hands of men than to expose himself further to the perils of the night. He therefore made the best of his way on foot for the guiding beacon, concluding that it shone from some human habitation, where he might at least inquire his way to the main road, from which he had so far and so unfortunately been carried by his frightened horse.

The first words which he heard, while he paused on the window-sill of the old church, thrilled through his heart with that sort of mysterious recognition which disturbs us when we dream that we are in a dream, in which prospect and retrospect, anticipation and memory, are all confused into one inextricable labyrinth of wandering fancies.

Mental anguish and bodily exhaustion had so changed the accents and the voice of his child that they only struck the father with an undefined and unintelligible horror. The whole scene which at the same instant he witnessed gave the virtuous and withering rebuke of the distracted but unconquered and afflicted girl a terrible meaning, which nerved his arm and urged his impetuous assault on Strickland, to whom he imagined they were addressed.

At the close of this recital the veil was rent

away; the father and the lover saw clearly the guidance of Divine Providence, which had thus brought them together. Once more the grateful and now enlightened senior folded to his bosom the brave youth in silent admiration and affection, then both turning their fond attention to the subject of their united solicitude, found to their great joy that she had fallen into a tranquil sleep, and was breathing regularly but almost imperceptibly with a motion merely expressive of life.

Both were fervently offering up the heart's fond prayer for the maiden's restoration to herself and to them, when they were disturbed by the irregular tread of horses' feet. Before they could form any idea of the character or object of the new arrival, Mr. Plowden's servant stood before them hat in hand, and in breathless palpitation.

He had, it appeared, from his account of himself, been for some time directed in his course over field and flood, and hedge and ditch, in the dusky twilight by the retreating footsteps of his master's runaway horse, now muffled in the mire, now beating softly on the greensward; and again, when the feet had altogether died away, the clatter of the headlong gallop down some stony lane took up the guiding sounds, until at length the groom, in the very heat of what he called the steeplechase, which it certainly was, fell in with the riderless horse, that

at first seemed unable to stir, but, encouraged by
the sight of his fellow steed, he pricked up his
ears and made a desperate struggle to keep up
with him. "But," added he, "lame as he
was he did me good service; for just as I had
taken him by the bridle and caught a gleam of
the light which brought me to this old church,
two horsemen, who seemed to be stragglers
from a detachment of Whig cavalry, and apparently in pursuit of some party, hearing two
horses neighing, and myself talking loudly to
several troopers of my own party whom I con-
jured up, they took alarm and went in a different
direction."

From all which the gentleman could collect
from the account of the groom, it appeared that
some unworthy lord, who had earned for himself
the unenviable distinction of a man of intrigue and
pleasure about town, was in the present instance
less anxious by the hand of his bravoes to revenge
his quarrels, than to effect the abduction of some
pure and beautiful lady who had rejected his
addresses. Under the mask of political intrigue
and hostility, his real object was the possession
of the fair being whose wealth, not her merits, he
appreciated.

The deep silence which followed this recital
was broken by a rustling noise in the recess
where the poor damsel had been laid on her
temporary couch. Towards her all eyes were
turned. The entrance of Harry Horseman had

evidently disturbed her. The story of his adventure had induced a relapse into her former delusion, and the noise was caused by her removal of the embroidered cloak which covered her. She was sitting up staring wildly about her dreary chamber. "Where am I?" she exclaimed. "The wretches have buried me alive! But look! their vile blood is on my garments—disloyal, brutal blood!—see how black it is! Their hands still press me down—and oh! they have torn me from my beautiful Kitty, and robbed me of my dearest pet!" Then shuddering, and making an effort as if to extricate herself, she sobbed out piteously, "Their arms are like serpents wreathing their loathsome coils miserably around me. Relieve me, relieve me—oh! relieve me!! Help! help! For heaven's sake save me! 'Libera me Domine!'" She sank down in helpless and hopeless exhaustion.

By her side sat her father, and him to whom she was no less dear. Their sensation of unutterable anguish touched the heart of the servant, who stood aloof, as though he heard not, saw not anything.

To a parent, a friend, or indeed to any one not utterly depraved, there could be nothing so terrible as to see an intellect like that of Miss Plowden scared into a gloomy chaos, peopled by fiends, and so disordered by the ruthless hand of profligacy. Still in her aspect there was now and then a glimpse of brightness and beauty which dispelled the melancholy haze spread over the beholders. The detested spots of blood were soon washed away by the father's hand, with water conveyed in a helmet by Horseman from a neighbouring stream. The servant brought a fresh supply, cool and clear, at the bidding of his master, who with it moistened the pale lips and bathed the marble temples of the lovely girl. She slowly opened her eyes.

" The stain is wiped away," she murmured. A faint ray of returning reason passed gradually over her features and spoke of interior light, but still as the fitful blaze of the feeble fire to the old church, so the glimmering of her mind made its own darkness more visible to herself.

" Oh ! Strickland," said Mr. Plowden, in a transport of joy, " her senses are coming back to her, like the dawn of a happier day."

The long-loved and familiar voice of her father —the endeared and welcome name of her brother and playfellow came to her ear, and arose to her memory and her heart like the soothing sounds of a well-tuned, well-remembered instrument ; or like the sweet singing of birds in the sylvan solitude, when the winter is past and gone.

" I think I feel my loved father's hand upon my head as he was wont to press it when fond words of comfort fell from his loved lips into my infant heart. The blood, I see, is washed away. My ears drink in the name of my dearest, earliest friend. Oh ! where is he ?"

The young man approached her gently, and
in those sweet natural accents, which were
music to her soul, said, " Mary, I am by your
rude couch. Accident apprised me of your
peril, and Heaven and the Blessed Mother of
our Most Holy Lord have brought us once
more together. You are safe, and I am
happy."

" Yes," said Plowden, as if interpreting what
was passing in the minds of those at his side;
" about as near to human happiness as life and
its vicissitudes allow us to approach."

" My own dearest father," said Mary, as in
an ecstasy of ineffable delight and restored
reason ; she threw her arms around him ; " how
happy your presence makes me! What a world
of agonising torture do your words remove from
my heart! You are, then, really with me. I
am free. My honour and fair fame are in safe
guardianship."

" Beyond danger, and secure in your innocence, and in your father's protection," said
Strickland.

" Then," she observed, with a smile border-
ing on playfulness, " you are a prophet of good,
Robert. Your mantle which has descended
upon me must leave me a portion of your pro-
phetic spirit and your valour. But as for this
blood-stained garment, spotted in human puddle,
I tear it from me, and cast it away as a filthy
slough." And with this she cast her riding

dress from her with disgust, and felt lightened, as if rid of a weight of woe.

No sooner had she done so, than a beautiful little crucifix, suspended from her neck, was displayed to the eye of her gentle brother. She kissed it. The sacred emblem was his own parting gift. Her pure, clear complexion, though ashy pale, was serene; the bright blue speaking eye had ceased to glare, and was assuming its native loveliness; the rich auburn hair waved loosely in natural curls, streaming over her fair face like summer's golden clouds veiling the placid moon. Her figure was in keeping with her countenance, slender, graceful, elegant, meet temple for the soul which it enshrined. She was truly a favourite child of Nature and of Heaven. She had been called the Bluebell of Whitehall. To Strickland she was a flower of Paradise. Over her he shed a tear of joyful love. It was to her a pearl of great price, and mingled with a kindred tear of hers.

While from her mother she inherited the gentle delicacy which appeared in every lineament of her face, from her father her very nature and her being imbibed the animation and yet thoughtfulness which beautifully mingled and adorned her countenance. To him the likeness of mind bore evidence in her face which closely resembled her father's features.

So tender and overwhelming was the sympathy

M 2

and affection which the father and the youth, who was loved as a brother, had felt for each other, that they could only be silent. There was a deep pause, amid which the steady tramp of horses was heard.

"It is the advance of the king and his friends," cried the soldier. "They are now," added he, listening, "at the point of the London road, nearest to this spot." Saying this, to avoid suspense, he took up a position on the broken wall, which would enable him to see, or rather to hear, any one approaching. He soon discerned a horseman, and before he could descend, a dashing rider on a lofty horse, bounding over every obstacle as if in the noonday, was close to the doorway. The rider had flung himself from the saddle in order to enter, when he was challenged by our young hero.

"Thunder and 'ouns," says the stranger; "sure 'tisn't your mother's son that stands before me! But in the name of the Holy Virgin, St. Michael, St. Patrick, all the saints in the calendar, and twice as many more, what brought you here at this time of the evening?"

"And if I may be so bold," rejoined our hero, "let me ask what brought you, the gay Honourable Clare of ours, to this haunted rendezvous?"

"By the Lord Harry its the thruth I am telling you, 'tis my good steed, Faugh-a-ballagh, that carried me here. Whisht! hearken to him how irreverently he paws the graves. 'Tis no right thing he sees. Its clean and clever, in elegant style from Henley-on-Thames to London, from London to Faversham, where I found the king, from Faversham here, he carried me safe and sound. 'Tis as fresh as a daisy he is after it all, and wanting more exercise. But I'm making a long story of it. I'll tell you how it was. I was hunting in Berkshire, and came across a boat's crew from Oxford; hearty fellows, considering they were made of Saxon stuff. I had often met them at college. The steersman fell into the water after a girl whom he was anxious to save; he pulled her out, then fell in love, and next fell into the hands of her guardian, who made him a prisoner for his pains. A devilish handsome young woman they say she was, but not to be named on the same day with her maid, who was called Di something—Diana of the Ephesians. By twilight I met her alone, and worshipped her; God forgive me."

Successfully suppressing all appearance of the impatience which afflicted him, Strickland said: "But, my brave fellow, how does all this interesting adventure account for your welcome presence here?"

"Sure, it's that same I was going to tell you when you halted me, and I in such haste—upon my sacred honour I am; and now I am forgetting where I was. We must try back. Her mistress, the water nymph, was in concert with mistress Di Vine to get the youth out of prison who got her out of the river.

"I was by the same token intrusted with a note to the Oxford men, with whom I had intended to co-operate in the liberation. After delivering the note, I was riding old Faugh to the "Royal Oak" stables to put him up. In the meantime, a skirmishing detachment of the insurgents from Reading, perceiving that I was one of the Royal Body Guard, gave me full chase, for flight was my only chance against so many, and was in my case the better part of valour. I slackened my speed after a time, as if my horse were breathed, and let the fellows come up all but within shot of me; I then entertained them with a gallop of two miles over a stiff country, and wished the devil would take the hindermost of them, for I was up to a wrinkle or so; I reined in a bit; got my horse on a sound sod, and waited for my attendants; making sure of their game, they came helter-skelter like murdering devils as they are. 'Take it asy, Faugh-a-ballagh,' says I; then, in a canter, we tempted the bull dogs down to a wide deep inlet of the Thames, concealed from their view, which no horse between this and that, barrin' Faugh, would attempt. On we went. The Irish horse measured every stretch, gathered himself up at the bank: 'Now or never,' says I, putting a wild Irish screech and a cut of the whip under him, which lifted him up into the

air. The animal bounded from the green sod
like a stag, and soared over the deep wide creek,
coming down, more like a bird than a horse, on
the other side ; I settled down elegantly in my
saddle, looked behind, and to my heart's delight
saw the whole posse of the spalpeen spawn of
Old Nick twirling about in the midst of the
depth, crawling like water snakes and hissing
like red-hot demons in the stream. There they
were, sprawling and floundering about : it would
have done your serious heart good to have seen
them. They swam and they sank, they shouted,
they spurred, they swore, they sputtered, and
splashed, and spattered, but all in vain. ' Keep
your powder dry,' cried I, bursting my sides
with laughing, when whiz comes a shot, which
was nearly making a vacancy in the Life Guards;
but here I am. And why, and how am I here ?
Well, as I was riding along the road Faugh-a-
ballagh snorted and sniffed and apprised me of
some nuisance in our way, which I found to be a
brace of insurgent dragoons and their horses ; a
little further my horse swerved from a third, and
behind a high hedge, my dear fellow, fornent
this spot on which we are standing, some dogs
fighting for the carrion fare were feeding on a
man and horse. This revolting sight, where not
a royalist seemed wounded or slain, coupled
with your vestal light there in the church,
brought me to this spot, in the hope of finding
a remnant of the loyalists ; and one I see at

least. And now, my lad, let me have your report of the affray, before his Majesty stumbles over the slain."

Briefly, modestly, and with deep emotion, Strickland related the events of the evening, which had involved such vicissitudes of sorrow and rejoicing. A thrill of horror and grief shot through the other; for beneath that gay, thoughtless outside there was an unfathomable depth of feeling sacred to sympathy and affection; a hearty good nature lived under his Irish buoyancy.

He was a singularly handsome man for his age, which, though it exceeded that of Strickland, yet had not attained to the perfection of manhood. A glorious forehead, high, broad, and as white as it was majestic, surmounted a pair of as joyous, large, blue eyes as ever animated the countenance of youth. His complexion wore that beautiful colouring of health which nothing but exercise in the open air can bestow.

The contrast between the young men was only equalled by their mutual friendship. That quality of the one which the other did not possess was reciprocally appreciated by each.

Robert Strickland was not only cool by natural temperament, but subdued by education, training, and, above all, by that self-control which the stricter discipline of the Catholic Church enforces.

O'Brian Clare was a plain type of a thorough-going Irishman, fond of field sports, unschooled, and as free as the air he breathed. His world was yesterday and to-day, without a thought for to-morrow. This meeting with Strickland brought back pleasant memories;—the painful facts of his recital tinged the present with melancholy. Action was Clare's forte.

"The Mother of Heaven be near us!" cried he. "Sure something must be done."

"First of all," said the other, "we must send Mr. Plowden's man to apprise the king of what has taken place, and to relieve him from unnecessary solicitude at my absence." With this Strickland, under the sanction of Mr. Plowden, despatched the groom with a line, written by the light of the fire, to Sir Edward Hales; he then presented his brother officer of the Guards to Mr. Plowden, who had all this time been watching the sufferer while she slept.

The three men, now together under such extraordinary circumstances, were at home in the desolation of their present lot. Their first, if not their only care was for the safety of the poor young lady; for Clare's report of the straggling insurgents and their apparent design fearfully confirmed that of the groom. Apprehension was bringing the poor father low; but the spirit and invention of the young men rose with their difficulties and dangers.

"Upon my sacred honour," says the Irish-man, "I have just hit upon a plan to throw them off their scent."

"Then out with it, my boy," says the other, "and don't be periphrastic."

"We must achieve by clever scheming," says Clare, regardless of the admonition, "what we can't effect by strength.   That's the fact of it."

"There you are again," interrupted Strick-land, with an impatience which he could not suppress.   "To the point, man, at once."

"Let me alone for that," cried the other. "How can you put an English head on Irish shoulders; and if you could, the devil a better you'd be, for the Celtic genius could make no use of your Saxon brains."

"You have a vulgar prejudice against the Saxon.   Go on."

"Yes, and you have always a hard word to fling at our heads; and yet Ireland has been the field from which the great intellect of England has been transplanted."

"Enough, my dear fellow," says the English-man; grasping his hand, shaking it affection-ately.

"Where's the young lady's riding toggery? It must, after all the blood and carnage, be unfit for such a wearer."

"Here it is," said Strickland, holding up between his fingers the riding dress, all be-spattered and bloodstained.

"Devil a better I want," says Clare, with enthusiasm, vainly trying at the same time to insert himself into the garment. "Bloody wars!" cried the youth, in desperation, "sure its myself that's too big for it entirely. Still there is genius in the idea. Don't be meddling with me, but let me have my own way."

Strickland assented, not indeed that he had any great confidence in his friend's stratagems or resources; but at this interval his strength was to sit still, and he longed for quiet. He accordingly humoured his companion's mood, and therefore stole noiselessly away to gratify his own mind—we need not say where. After a few minutes he quitted the interior of the building, but started with no very agreeable surprise, while a faint blush bespoke his astonishment, to find at the entrance the jennet, for which with the other horses the groom had so laboriously provided "extra muros," already saddled, and perfectly equipped and mounted by the apparition of a lady of the size and symmetry of the accomplished and now prostrate rider.

The Irishman had taken a wooden cross from one of the graves, broken the arms so as to seem quite natural in the sleeves in which he placed them, then binding rubbish round the upright piece to the proper bulk of a figure, he made the whole a capital fit. Having drawn the body and skirt of the riding habit over it, and gracefully surmounted the top with the lady's hat and feather, which he took the liberty to appropriate to what he believed her interests, he mounted it on the jennet. The effigy only wanted life to be a perfect horsewoman.

"Trust me, Strickland!" cries the youth, in an ecstacy at his own handiwork, "William's sleuth hounds will be thrown off the scent, and when they come to a check, my Lord Spenser may try back for the fair vixen, who has at present escaped him. Your own dear Mary Macree shall not be cut down like a daisy in May by such a heartless villain."

Strickland coloured, his eye flashed.

"Yes, my lady," continued O'Brian to the image which he had set up, "off and away." He was just raising his whip to send the jennet toward the road, when the other arrested his hand, and taking him by the arm, pulled him with the horse and rider back again. Before, however, they could re-enter the church, the king's physician, who had joined his Majesty on the road, and a messenger of Sir Edward Hales accosted them, but not before they had taken off their hats and bowed gracefully to the lady on horseback.

CHAPTER XXVI.

Persons of Genius, and those who are most capable of Art, are always most fond of Nature: as such are chiefly sensible that all Art consists in the imitation and study of Nature.—*Pope.*

Intrepidity is an extraordinary strength of mind, which raises it above the troubles, the disorders, the emotions which the sight of great perils is calcuted to excite.—*La Rochefoucauld.*

THE night had come down on this dreary abode, and the young cold pale moon shed but a dubious light, making the deep shadows darker, so that the physician had naturally enough mistaken the effigy for the young lady. The young men with all their efforts were unable to repress a smile.

The newly arrived doctor was a grave, stern man, conscious of his high position, and dignified in his manners. He was proceeding to congratulate the young men on the extraordinary and surprising recovery of the patient, for whom even his Majesty was so unnecessarily alarmed, when the Honourable O'Brian burst out into a fit of uncontrollable laughter.

With an accent calm and unmoved the man of medicine said, "Gentlemen, here must be some mistake," and was riding away, annoyed

and perplexed, when Strickland cried out, " It
will be the greatest affliction of my life should
my young friend's unruly laughter deprive the
young lady of your inestimable aid. Let me
beg that you will hear my explanation, and my
brother officer will satisfy you with any apology
you may demand."

" By heaven !" cried Clare, when the doctor,
yielding to Strickland's entreaty, returned, " I
could not help it, even had St. Patrick or the
Pope been present. It's not the lady but her
effigy you see," pointing to the figure on the
jennet. " And now the murther's out. Give
me your hand, and at a more convenient season
I'll tell you why and how I managed it."

Strickland now conducted the doctor to Mr.
Plowden, and then rejoined the Irishman, whose
laughter still overcame him. At the same
moment Harry Horseman suddenly made his
appearance, splashed from head to foot, and
in much agitation, declaring that he had seen
a labouring man, who seemed startled at his
presence, and who cautioned him that the old
church was haunted. " There," said the old
man to him, " what is that before us," pointing
to the doctor, " see how they can't rest in their
graves, but must be disturbing the night," pointing to the light, " with their unholy fires about
them. That man will be spectre-smitten," says
he, " if he go further."

" We parted only two hundred yards away,"

said Horseman, with a sort of " Lord-deliver-us " look which by no means soberized Mr. Clare.

"But, gentlemen," said the groom, "what are you up to? Here is my horse covered with filth, and my boot tops and saddle stained with wet and mire, and the poor jennet could not rest in his shelter, cold comfort that it was. What would our young mistress say? And then to make such a guy of her ladyship!—a tattidooly to scare away the birds!" Horsman's eye was too practised to be deceived even in the dark. "By your leave, gentlemen, I must take the jennet with my own horses to his poor bed again."

Clare hesitated, but yielded to Strickland's compliance with Horseman's reasonable wish.

While a silent calm now prevailed within, the singular idea that first crossed Clare's brain, again recurred to his mind. He suggested to Strickland that, that, or some similar stratagem should be tried. Now, whether it were a love of adventure, or a desire to master the difficulty by a triumph of genius over apparent defeat, at this period we know not. Strickland's was that unaffected, almost cold courage, which resides in all great geniuses, and imposes on masses of humanity. That of O'Brian's was an impetuous neck-or-nothing daring, which made a dash at danger. The Englishman, therefore, could not feel confidence in his friend's stratagery. Still, he was convinced that the aspect of affairs

demanded some manœuvre more conducive to
the safety of the young lady than any force of
arms which they could command; especially as
both the young men must rejoin his Majesty
that evening at Rochester, where he was to
sleep.

" But, my dear fellow," remarked Strickland,
" even if we could squeeze a broad-shouldered
officer of the Guards, six feet high, into the
dress, how would your brogue and voice of
thunder do duty for the soft and gentle accents
of a timid damsel ?"

" Yours is the logic of love, my friend," says
the open-hearted descendant of an Irish king.
" Love rules the camp," but, interrupting himself, cried out, " I have it, by Jove ! Upon my
word of honour, it's the sprightly notion I have.
Take my word for it, the ulterior result will
alter your notion of my generalship. Here's
Horseman. He's a fine little fellow, as delicate
as any lady, nearly the height of his young
mistress, and in her riding habit would be the
model of her."

The recollection of the groom's address, and
management of the jennet, how gracefully he
rode him in female attire, to break him in—how
from constant attendance on riding parties, he
had caught so much of the manner and gentleness of the higher classes, that his fellow servants
called him Miss Horseman. All this rushed to
Strickland's memory. It was his youth alone

which had exempted him from attendance on his young lady, on this sad journey.

"Your idea, I think, might answer," said Strickland. "Now I think of it, the fellow is an excellent actor; and in our little amateur performances acquits himself to perfection."

A deep pang shot through our hero's heart at the terrible contrast between the sunny past and this dreary night.

O'Brian gazed at his friend for a few seconds, then exclaimed, "I know you are thinking about hair-brained risks and rashness; but it's in earnest I am, upon my faith!" And he felt his hand affectionately pressed by Strickland, who said,

"You are, after all, right, perhaps. I yield, but we have only our own consent. That of the master, as well as the chief actor, must be obtained."

Before O'Brian could reply, the physician appeared, and took Strickland aside and talked gravely to him; then, bidding them farewell, made the best of his way to the high road again. The groom re-appearing at the same time, asked respectfully—"Did you call me, gentlemen?" He was impatient to learn his orders. But the hero's whole soul was now steeped in one delicious reverie, wherein nothing but the figure of his Mary moved.

Throughout the whole livelong winter night he would have kept a silent watch—lingering near her, whispering words of love: but action was her safety, and too late, too long, had they already loitered there. His countenance since his interview with the doctor had resumed its wonted cheerful aspect. The words of Clare reverberated in his ear—they were hackneyed words, but had a real meaning. "Something must be done."

The stratagem was worthy of Clare's abilities, which were truly great. Resolving the plan of action methodically, yet rapidly arranging every detail of preparation in his own mind, Strickland hastened to Mr. Plowden: first, to see the object of his solicitude; and, secondly, with the sanction of her father, to co-operate for her safety with O'Brian in gaining over Horseman to the plan, from which his friend anticipated such a grand issue. To his great joy, Strickland found the lady, thanks to a reviving draught from the doctor, in a degree, convalescent; he obtained her father's sanction of Clare's stratagem, and returned to his waiting friend in a few minutes, to whom his absence had appeared an age. The groom not only undertook the part assigned him, but rejoiced in having the charge of the beautiful favourite of Miss Plowden, whom, with her father, he was to join at Lord Winchelsea's, where he hoped to learn something of his fellow-servant, who had attended the unfortunate lady on her journey, and of whom, up to this time, she had been able to give no distinct account.

In less time than we can relate the fact, he was mounted in the young lady's complete riding attire, with a profusion of his own natural hair showing itself beneath the elegant feathered hat.

" There he is, and a beauty!" cried Clare, in an ecstasy. "Sure it's himself that has the light finger to guide the animal with a silken thread! Look at the seat of him; there's not a lady in the land that need be ashamed of it. But, by the same token," says he, " we must give the interesting creature a trinket or two to put in her bosom for her lover," handing Horseman, at the same time, a pair of loaded pistols, which he concealed under his riding-dress.

At first the animal bounded and swerved with every motion of the long habit, which flapped about in such a manner as apprised the horse that his present rider was not a real lady. But the man sat back with graceful ease in the saddle, and soon reconciled the steed to the substitute for his own fair rider.

" Here comes the coach!" exclaimed Strickland; " I hear the sound of heavy wheels."

The whole party were immediately in motion. Miss Plowden wrapped warmly around in the military cloak, mounted on the groom's horse, supported on one side by her father and on the other by her dear preserver and devoted friend, preceded by O'Brian Clare and her representative on horseback.

N 2

Slowly and carefully they picked their way, till they reached the high road, where they discovered one of his Majesty's carriages, which had been dispatched from Sittingbourne, with the necessary servants, on his Majesty's arrival there, according to a previous arrangement. Into this the father and the lover very silently and tenderly lifted their dear charge.

"Mary, dear, good night,"

> "Robert, the night is ill
>   That severs us it should unite ;
> To live and love together still,
>   That were indeed good night!"

were the last words of the two whose hearts were wedded, but whom the curse of civil strife divided.

The coach rolled off at full speed for the residence of Lord Winchelsea, followed by two of the royal servants on Mr. Plowden's horse and that of his groom's. The brother guardsmen, accompanied by the very image of Miss Plowden, as Clare called the groom, to the great annoyance of the lover, went on their way to Sittingbourne, chatting as they went.

"Never mind," says the man of the present, "we shall have a jolly good supper and the best drink that love or money will purchase ; and here we are at Sittingbourne."

They all alighted at the head inn, which was but a poor one. The lady, attended by the two gentlemen, was ushered into the house.

" The lady is fatigued after her long journey,"
says O'Brian, "maybe, you could entertain
herself and her horse till to-morrow morning,
and find her a private sitting-room. Business in
London admits not of our remaining." Saying
these words and calling for the best refreshment
the house afforded, which was a jugged hare,
poached from some neighbouring papist's park,
and some real brown October of the preceding
year, the young men thoroughly enjoyed themselves after the turmoil and awful events of the
day. Having imparted instruction and various
suggestions to the supposed lady, who regaled
herself in her private apartment, they flung
down a piece of gold to the landlord, who
engaged to pay every attention to the young lady.

"But," says mine host, "you ought to have
been here two hours earlier. The whole village
has been crowded,—great rejoicings, and great
doings and sayings. The Coldstream Life
Guards to the number of three hundred, commanded by Lord Feversham, and a great state
carriage for his Majesty honoured us with their
presence for a whole day. Every man in the
place stood bare-headed before his Majesty, as
he, the gay officers, and the handsome troopers
dazzled us with their splendour. The guard of
honour bringing up the rear was a sight I never
expected to witness. But, gentlemen, if I may
be so bold, I see your uniforms are the same as
those of the Horse Guards."

" Supposing we are what you seem to take
us for, would you be gratified to join us in drinking his Majesty's health ?" asked the young
men significantly.

"Yes," said the jovial landlord, " and I will
bring you up a bottle of wine for this purpose,
which has not seen the light since the king's
coronation.   He is the best customer I ever had,
and every inch a king," said he, returning with
the wine.   "Here then," standing uncovered,
says he, " I drink to his Majesty : long may he
reign over us, and soon may the royal guards
honour our town again."   As sworn friends and
loyalists, the young officers parted from their
hearty host ; but not before he had engaged to
supply the lady with a suitable attendant for the
journey, who was to wear the livery which Horseman had changed for the riding dress of his
young mistress.   They then sprang into their
saddles, and were in Rochester in time to prostrate themselves before the king, to explain all,
and renew their expressions of devotion and
gratitude to his Majesty for his generous indulgence and consideration in dispensing with their
services so long.

All retired to bed, some to sleep soundly,
some to sleep and dream, and the king to ponder
over the rapid and favourable reverses of his
fortune.   And now, since they are all so happily
reunited, we would just remark that these
hurried events were really crowded into a few

hours, though their recital occupies so much time.

We may as well also take this opportunity of glancing back at the earlier meetings and social intercourse between young Strickland and Mary Plowden, who had together grown up like two fair flowers, under the eye of Queen Mary Beatrice. The former had interest at Court, which soon introduced him to the notice of the queen. There was Mr. Robert Strickland, the queen's vice chamberlain, who headed the grand procession at the coronation, his cousin, whose name our hero bore; there was Lady Strickland, subgoverness to the Prince of Wales, the enthusiastic and devoted friend of the royal family, with her husband, the Vice-Admiral Sir Thomas Strickland, of Sizergh Castle, in Westmorland; among many others, with whom by relationship he was closely connected.

The young gentleman had been a favourite page some years to her Majesty, and was three or four years older than Miss Plowden, who had been a shorter period at the Court, though unusually young when admitted as a maid of honour, or indeed rather as a companion or younger sister to the queen, so tenderly did her Majesty regard her, both for the sake of the dear girl herself and on account of the undeviating and pious adherence of the Plowden family to the hereditary religion and royal succession. The easy engagements and light duties imposed by the sparing requirements of her Majesty, brought the young people often together in the palace of Whitehall, where they were both looked upon as children. They were seldom divided, even in their hours of study or recreation. They walked together, read together, and played together as two members of the same family. Mary especially was by disposition a child of nature. The flowery days of her girlhood were as sweet as we have seen they were transient.

She would wander alone in the park, and feed the water fowls with her hand, and watch them carefully building their nests amid enchanted and secluded little bowers of evergreens and underwood along the sloping banks. The graceful swans, only more snowy than herself, loved her well for her own sake; better still for the sake of the crumbs which she gave them. The wildest of birds gathered round her; they flocked to her on the margin of the lake. In each old tree she recognised a friend, and invested it with a character. To her every group of trees was an animated assembly, connected together by many tender associations; they had a language and speech, a look and a meaning, which some may have felt in their poetical youth, but which none can define. To her the first sunny smile of spring was heaven. Its breath the fragrance of paradise. Like all those who really enjoy true life, she was an early riser ; especially when invited from her couch by the blackbird's morning song in May :

" When opening leaves are bright,
And flowers are bathed in light."

The violet, the primrose, the bluebell, and the earliest, sweetest children of the spring, were her companions and her delight. That most touching of all melody, the song of the blackbird or the thrush, or the plaintive strain of the wood pigeon in the sequestered groves, while the morning gale of spring chants its holy matins amid the living temple of the arching woods, afforded her the liveliest pleasure. Hers was the bliss of childlike innocence and simple faith. The flowers and the birds breathed the fragrance and sang the song of Eden, as pure, as fair, as sweet and tuneful, as when they breathed and sang before man's fall. Relics and memorials to her they were of heaven on earth. Their silent lessons she loved to learn ; not that she was unendowed with science and art or unadorned with the accomplishments of her sex ; at least, according to her tender years, and the age in which she lived ; but to her clear intellect and fertile fancy all which she had attained by study and tuition was what landscape gardening is to natural scenery. They restrained not the majesty of freedom of thought.

Some happy, rural seat of various view was her favourite haunt. Beneath the snowy canopy of sweet scented hawthorn she loved to loiter.

In childhood's walks the flowers and shrubs were her companions; but not always they alone, for whether by accident or the guidance of congenial tastes, wherever 'she roamed Strickland was suddenly beside her, and his presence called forth from her no expression of surprise. They both only realised the idea of brother and sister; they walked together as friends, young and lovely in their lives, and happy, until they were parted. Long and often would they sit or saunter, as it were, by the shores of Romance, listening to some bubbling rill, trickling from its mossy bed, unheard by all but them. In their happiest hours of recreation, when the weather permitted, their little skiff, crowded with every sail which she could carry, her taper mast bending and springing like a reed, the rippling water of the breezy lake curling at the bow, and even rustling over the gunwale; tacking in every direction to make the most of their enchanted voyage; or, again, gently flapping her sails, like a swan her wings, might be seen gliding over the placid water, or, divested of her fluttering canvass, like a tree of its leaves, yielding to Strickland's well-timed oars, and skimming along like a duck. His manly form and her slight figure never, perhaps, appeared to greater advantage than when thus embarked together on a little sea of pleasure.

Her simple beauty was at such times varied by a look of deep thought, shading an arch and youthful playfulness which sparkled through it, like sunbeams through a light summer cloud. In every relation of her young life she not only was faithful to those with whom she dwelt; but amid her pleasures and her tasks she breathed from her soul devout aspirations to her Father who is in Heaven. She was an hereditary Catholic, but she was in one sense more: she was born a poet. Not that she wrote a line of poetry, or understood its mechanism, but she thought poetry. She enjoyed the communion of saints on earth and in heaven, of the unfallen angels, and all ministering spirits above and below, and all around her, who hymned their Maker's praise and sang His glory. Her poetry was happiness.

The dreary glare of the court, its plays and pageants, enacted by the noble and the royal, were only crowded loneliness to her, from which she often turned her weary eyes to the green earth and open sky, which were to her never so lovely as in the company of Strickland.

The queen, who was herself as free from suspicion of such meetings as she had been innocent and simple-minded as a girl, rather encouraged than denied them the happiness of each other's company, especially in hours of leisure; it never entered her mind that there would be anything more lasting in these meetings than the mutual passing pleasure of recreation which a boy and girl of the same

age, and in some degree of similar tastes and
congenial dispositions, naturally enjoy together.
What was, really, love, to the eye of Her Majesty was mere friendship, entitled to the mutual
privileges and pastimes of youth. When Strickland was promoted to the Guards, he still,
though not so frequently, continued to meet
Mary Plowden, especially in the home parks, and
even occasionally in their rides farther from the
palace. They gathered flowers together, and
often exchanged them with each other. In some
sequestered bower they sat for hours; read French
and Italian together. In the very autumn of the
year, only two months before the commencement
of our tale, they planted two oak trees, which
may still be in existence, calling each by the
name of the planter of the other.

In winter the most improbable chances and
unexpected accidents placed them side by side,
in riding parties, or even in the royal hunting
field. In fact their frequent rencontres at this
period of their intercourse was maturing their
early acquaintance into a feeling of very delicate,
perhaps unconscious attachment, which soon
began to wear the air of love rather than mere
friendship and accident.

For these happy companions, the real world
had as yet no spell. The bright world of visions
was their home.

The cast of Mary's beauty, as we have said,
was varying. Her temper had little of caprice,

yet it was at one time rejoicing in thanksgiving at another tinged with religious sorrow.

To the lover she was a creature of poetry, living in his imagination. She drew from the decay of the year food for pensive thoughts. The glory of noon—the repose of twilight—rosy sunset, its shadows and its hues, whispered peace to her heart. How little could men who beheld in Strickland the martial air of the young soldier tell how soft, how tender, and even subdued was his heart and sentiment in the presence of the girl who had blended her sorrows and her joys with his.

Love, indeed, was never named, but yet flowers, books, and pictures continued to be gifts of one fond heart to the other.

The court young lady's intimacy with the queen was closer than that of the young guardsman. Her talents and her accomplishments were rarely equalled in one and the same person, whether male or female. In her face were heavenly virtues, but the emotions of joy or grief passed over it too visibly and quickly to admit of perfect beauty. Her manners owed their enchantment to inward humility and Christian charity under religious training. Both were brought up very strictly in the Catholic faith, the most beautiful emblems of which were often exchanged between them, such as the crucifix, which Miss Plowden devoutly pressed to her lips on her recovery in the old church.

It had, indeed, a history and a deep meaning. Everything had combined to raise Miss Plowden so high in the estimation of all who knew her, that at times the cornet could not but dread that their separation might encourage some suitor, not, indeed, more favoured than he himself was by the lady who called him brother, but more importunate and more frequently in her presence; for our hero well knew, young as he was, that of all the advantages which a young lady can afford the suitor she intends to reject the greatest is nearness: it prevails when all other recommendations are vain.

There was at least one who might probably avail himself of Strickland's absence to endeavour to gain access to Miss Plowden and supply his place. Rumour, at least, with her thousand tongues, had raised up such a rival in Lord Spenser, whom birth, political influence, and splendid opportunities, marked out in the estimation of Colonel Sidney's relations, who played a double game, professing loyalty to James and secretly securing their interests with William, as a candidate for the hand of Miss Plowden, who, at the decease of her paternal uncles, was to succeed to property of great value.

The young nobleman, of whom the reader has already learnt something in a former chapter, was the son of Robert Spenser, Earl of Sunderland, who had acquired the highest ascendancy in the administration. He was, therefore, grandson to Lady Dorothy Sidney, celebrated by Waller under the name of Sacharissa. Evelyn, whom she consulted in all her difficulties, speaking of Lord Spenser, in the year in which our tale begins, and contrasting his character with that of his younger brother, Mr. Spenser, said, "Lord Spenser rambles about the world, dishonours his name and his family, adding sorrow to a mother who has taken all imaginable care of his education. From him one Mrs. Jane Fox had a fortunate escape, for he would have made her but a sorry husband." Such was the man who, under the shelter of his great name and distinguished relations, found access to court, and eventually to the presence of Miss Plowden. After this brief sketch of the man and his character, we need not be surprised that to him Strickland, in his own mind, ascribed the outrage, not to the nobleman personally, but to his bravoes, on whom our hero had taken such signal vengeance.

In our time were a nobleman to have recourse to hired bravoes for such a purpose he would justly be hunted out of society; but in the age of Charles II., and even James II., the chivalrous sense of honour seemed a wild and extravagant delusion, so barbarously had the civil wars left their traces of ferocity in the sentiments and manners even of the higher classes. Rencontres where the assailants took all the advantages of number and weapons were frequent, and held as honourable as evenhanded duels, and especially in affairs of gallantry, or enterprises which involved the capture or possession of a lady. "Spenser was a splendid sinner." In fact, he never pretended to a profession of religious principle, unless by his conversion to the Catholic faith. The gaming table, the turf, the cockpit, the ring, the theatres, the nightly haunts of revelry and vice absorbed his early manhood. It may easily be believed, after what Evelyn said so regretfully of him, that the young nobleman's friends soon cast him off, and would not recognise him until he thought fit to alter his course of conduct, and to redeem their opinion of his character. His father had succeeded Halifax as president of the council, and had obtained a pension from Louis XIV. for opposing an alliance against France. Spenser might naturally, therefore, look for promotion which would entitle him to the hand of a maid of honour of the first distinction.

In the July of this year the noble profligate had been dangerously wounded in a duel, and professed himself a Catholic about three months after; and about the same time the pretended conversion of his father to the faith of Rome, when he made his abjuration in the hands of Father Petre, took place.

This religious change, which confirmed the confidence of the king in the attachment and fidelity of the proselyte, might be supposed to recommend the converted and penitent son to the notice of the Catholic young lady.

Mary Plowden had too long and too fondly cherished Robert Strickland as a dear and early lover, to become the bride of any man by her own free choice, save Strickland. She could not, however, disguise from herself and those who were so amiably interested in her destiny, that very little encouragement on her part might realise in their minds their mere conjectures of Spenser's intentions. This was the more studiously to be avoided, because had Lord Spenser been suffered to make her a formal declaration, as a Catholic so highly connected, he had a fair chance of the encouragement of some of her court friends who wished her well. She determined, therefore, not to await his next visit, and left Whitehall some time earlier than she had intended, thus separating herself from those who could best protect her. But it is no part of our object here to dwell on the unmanly intrigues of my Lord Spenser, who had precipitated the flight of Mary Plowden.

Before her lover and the Irishman retired for the night they talked over many things in which both were mutually interested. The pleasant buzz of voices, enlivened and varied by wine and mirth, were heard around in different rooms of the hotel where the officers were assembled. The only emotions which the time and the occasion called up seemed some mere vague, visionary anticipation of an unfavourable change in the army or a stricter discipline, with a sigh for the disbanded troops and the distracted state of the degraded and wavering temper of their commanders. But each individual had his own personal interests and domestic concerns to affect him, and Strickland had his, which found words partly to himself and partly addressed to the Irish officer, who was alone with him.

Love—true, real love—merges all in the object of its affection. Far more terrible is the apprehension of danger to those we love than any death we can anticipate for ourselves. The heart whose pulse throbs not with a quicker beat at the presence of personal peril will flutter like a wild bird beating itself against its cage when death or danger comes near the one in whom all our love is centred. Out of the fulness of his heart, therefore, Strickland could but speak. To hold silence after the day's adventure had indeed been to him pain and grief.

" What passed this evening can never be forgotten," said Robert, with a sigh, " and your co-operation and ingenuity will often rise to my memory with gratitude. Oh! if you did but know her!—so intellectual, and yet so innocent, so noble-hearted, so amiable. Oh! that she were safe and happy!"

" She is, my dear fellow, all, all that your

fancy has made her," interrupted O'Brian. "In fact, what I would say, was a devilish fine slip of a girl."

Shocked at the profanation, Strickland was silent.

"Though the gay and gallant the Honourable O'Brian may not be sensible to the charms which he has never seen, he will not be indifferent to the feelings of one to whom they are endeared. An Irishman is never so absurd," continued Clare, "as when he is in earnest. In trouble or in love he is also too modest to be a rival in an affair of the heart with an Englishman. Though when his courage in the field, his counsel in the camp, or his natural genius against the world is challenged, he shrinks not from the contest."

His thoughtful friend made no reply, but fell into a reverie.

After gazing on him for a moment or two Clare added—

"Strickland, you worship her whom your imagination enshrines as a saint."

His friend, however, was still silent, and, changing the conversation, the young Irishman talked of indifferent things, and did not return to the subject of such tender interest.

There was enough, however, mutually interesting to both to keep them in close conversation till midnight, when both betook themselves to rest.

CHAPTER XXV.

A milk-white hind, immortal and unchanged,
Fed on the lawns and the forest ranged;
Without unspotted, innocent within,
She feared no danger, for she knew no sin:
Yet had she oft been chased with horn and hounds,
And Scythian shafts, and many-winged wounds
Aimed at her heart, was often forced to fly,
And doomed to death, though fated not to die.—*Dryden.*

WE must now change the scene and time. The scene is London. The time is the day after that which witnessed the events narrated in the last chapter.

In a house in Gerrard Street there was a large room lined with richly-carved oak panelling; one side presented three windows, with narrow-paned lattices in lead and iron frames, looking out upon Leicester House and gardens. In the centre of this room was a large square table, covered with plate and glass, rich viands and choice wines; and at each side of that table was seated a gentleman clothed in the costume of Charles II., but somewhat subdued and less flaunting, perhaps, than the glittering gold and gay silks of the period of our tale. Wit and revelry sparkled like the wines which enlivened their pleasures. The gentleman at that side of the table next the door was older than the other, and apparently the master of the house, for he it was who gracefully exercised the laws of hospitality, and gave his orders to a man older than any of the servants whom he directed, and who kept his place by a buffet richly laden with jars of silver, and gilt drinking cups, basins and salvers frosted and chased. There were four other guests, besides the most distinguished of the party already mentioned who sat opposite to the host, of various ages, but all younger than either of the other two gentlemen.

The master of the house was a married man; he had, however, evidently, in the absence of his better half, established for himself the independence of a bachelor. Many bumpers, even in that small party, had been drunk to the health of the great men of the day, not excepting the present company. The fun and frolic were rather cool and demure than riotous, and the easy dignity and lofty bearing of the elegant gentleman who seemed to occupy the place of honour was evidently a restraint upon excess of any sort. He directed the conversation to the opinions, events, manners, tastes, learning, but above all to the religion and politics of the day. He rapidly recited a few of the most remarkable incidents of his own long life, glancing through the civil wars against Charles I., the protectorate of Oliver Cromwell, the reign of King Charles II., making all the varied occurrences of James II. which he had recorded bear upon that busy, stirring day. "They all conduced," he said, "to the Revolution, which could not be averted, though the popular voice welcomed the king back again only to learn his error."

Monarchs, ministers, eminent men, were the themes on which he loved to dwell. A gentleman rather more gaily dressed than the rest began to talk freely of actors, actresses, poets, statesmen, philosophers, critics, divines; and was going on to pull them to pieces, not in malice but in mirth, when the last speaker drew up, seemingly somewhat shocked, and looked more gravely than wisely at their entertainer, saying, "Now Mr. Dryden, I have, as a tribute to your great genius, given you something of my experience and observation; pray favour us with a few of the recent events most familiarly connected with your present history, with reference to the literature of the day, and the probable effects of a revolution on the nation." Then casting a glance on the speaker, whom he had without offence cut short, he said, "Everybody knows Mr. Pepys is a wit, therefore we take his clever sayings as we take change from a banker, we rest satisfied with the coin he gives us, without much attention to it."

"Yes, but," retorted Dryden, on behalf of Pepys, "the value of all money, and especially paper money, depends on the estimate of the receiver."

Dryden :—" Truly my life, too, is part of the literature of England. Amid all its changes for nearly half a century, I have found that as when no king, no bishop,—no throne, no theatre. The Restoration naturally revived the taste for these elegant amusements, which during the Usurpation had been condemned or sentenced to punishment, as favourers of royalty."

"I have," said Evelyn, " seen your ' *Evening's Love; or, the Mock Astrologer.*' It certainly has that lively bustle which the taste of the age required when it first appeared, now exactly twenty years ago. The scenes are ably and well imitated from your great predecessor ; but to be candid, it affects me much to live in an age which demands profane plots and Popish intricacies."

" Do you, then," said Dryden, " take up the cudgels against me, in company with my Lord Rochester and his protegé Settle ?"

Evelyn—" You must write for the age, to see your play succeed. If you allude to the material cudgels of personal chastisement, I cannot see how one gentleman, either by his own hands or by those of his hired bravoes, can cudgel another without disgracing himself ; such brute force only reflects dishonour on him who has recourse to it. It is hard for you to make head against the tide into which you are launched."

"When learned scribblers," said Dryden, "dare to compare the author of 'Palamon and Arcites' with that shabby Shadwell."

"Were I," said St. Aubyn, "to compare our celebrated host with any writer of the age, it would be with Otway, not with his bitter foe, Shadwell."

"That reminds me," said Pepys, "of the report that Shadwell is to succeed you as poet laureate."

Dryden, who was amiable and kind to all who had access to him, coloured deeply, and replied, "For forty years of my life my character, personally and literary, has been the subject for every shabby scribbler, titled or untitled, crowned with laurels, or sitting in the pillory; and I shall not be surprised at any insult offered to me in the event of a new dynasty. Bishop Burnet already calls me a 'monster of immodesty and impurity of all sorts.'"

Mr. St. Aubyn, desirous to change the subject, looking at Dryden, said, "When I was last at Oxford I had the pleasure of meeting your second son, who then stood very high."

"He was," said Dryden, "a private pupil of the celebrated Obadiah Walker, master of University College. He, like myself, became a convert to the Roman Catholic faith. As to my boy, 'Othello's occupation's gone' in England at least, so he has followed his brother Charles to Rome, where he will officiate as his deputy some day in the Pope's household." Here Dryden tapped his silver snuff-box, after the manner of Prince George of Denmark, and was thoughtful and silent.

Morton then asked, " How is Lady Elizabeth ? I hope she can endure your cooling diet and preparation for a course of writing. Your absence from her and your devotion to your works are indeed a trial to her ladyship. I had the honour of meeting her at her father's, the Earl of Berkshire, at Charlton, while hunting in Wiltshire. And, pray, how is your youngest son ? I have also seen him there."

" Yes," answered his father, "his name is Erasmus Henry, he was educated at the Charter House, and, like his brothers, is gone to Rome. As for my wife, she loves town very much," said the poet, turning to Pepys, " indeed, as well as she loves me. The other day she wished to be a book that she might enjoy more of my company. ' Be an almanack then, my dear,' said I, ' that I may change you once a year.'"

" None but great men can afford to change their wives so often," cried Pepys. " Mr. Dryden may well be a great man : married to an Earl's daughter, honoured by Charles and James successively ; intimately connected with the great Duke of Ormond, and revered by three generations of some of the greatest men of our day. The Duke of Newcastle," he added,

turning to his host, "who sent you a play for
the stage; the witty Lord Buckhurst, afterwards
Earl of Dorset; Wilmot, Earl of Rochester;
and that witty rake, Sir Charles Sedley, are
all anxious to vindicate your writings, and
recommend them to the royal favour."

" The Duke of Newcastle and Rochester you
may have," said the poet, "they will give you
for your services a draft of gratitude on sight."

Here a very young gentleman, in whom we
recognise our friend Mr. Hough, said, timidly,
"How is it that such a well-known old writer
can produce such stuff as Duffray writes?"

" Fair young sir," replied Dryden, " you do
not know my friend as well as I do; I'll answer
for him, he can write worse yet."

" Young gentleman," said Pepys, " and that's
nothing to what Mr. Dryden can do.   The other
day when bowling with the Duke of Buckingham,
who offered to lay his soul to a turnip; ' give
me the odds,' says our great poet, ' and I'll take
the bet.' "   Whereupon our host, in repartee
to Pepys, asked him, ' whether he was as fond
of music as ever, and what was his last performance.'   At this instant the door flew open, and
Mr. Duffray was announced.   He looked time-
worn and out of spirits.   He was one of the
wits of the previous century, and therefore the
worse for wear.   Tom had been the companion
of Charles II., who had often leaned on the
shoulder of this genius of the lyre, while his

merry Majesty hummed a snatch of a song, or a new tune. But the monarch never supported his witty friend.

"We have just been speaking of your great ability, Mr. Duffray," said Dryden, blandly.

" To do what ?" quoth Tom.

" To write worse than your worst," replied the other.

" That is saying a good deal," says Pepys, " for our venerable friend has, I believe, composed thirty comedies."

" You are, gentlemen," retorted Tom, " as hard upon me as the refined and cool Congreve. But though my comical children may not long survive their parent, they have cost me less than the performance of our glorious John. If, sir, you had written worse you would, at least, have succeeded better, and have received more laureated honours than your unfavourable impression of my Lord Rochester's black devils."

" Well," rejoined Dryden, " the taste of the age is so bad, and the sense so affectedly sacrificed to silly conceits and play upon words, that I begin to think writing for the stage is no suitable employment for a gentleman."

" On my soul," cries Pepys, " this is rank heresy in you, worse than you ever harboured even in your Protestant days. You are as ungrateful to your muse and her entertainment as a man who abuses the woman who has conceded to him a husband's rights, and leaves her when she has bestowed her favours upon him. A fine play after all, with fun and frolic, and not too many intricacies in it, is the highest achievement of the human intellect."

Tom, looking down upon his thread-bare coat, cried—

"Oh, fie upon you, Mr. Dryden, to say so! —your patent of gentleman came to you by your birth—you have graduated in the college of politics, and have taken your degree of patriot; for my own part, I would not write a play again. Besides, my school is antiquated," said the old man, sorrowfully.

Evelyn, whose object in every visit, next to the delicate viands and wines themselves, was to learn tidings of people and events, speedily ran over a catalogue of mutual and former friends and acquaintances.

Steering clear of party quarrels and literary squabbles, by his noble bearing and courtesy to men of all politics and religions, he had gained the good will of all. He had all those gifts essential to the man who would influence society, whether in the literary circles or the larger spheres of active life.

Pepys, on the other hand, listened to the old man with that surprise with which successful men look upon their less fortunate schoolfellows or more advanced contemporaries, who had apparently the same or superior opportunities and advantages. Such is the feeling, perhaps,

with which some archbishop or distinguished
member of the bar, in our own time, looks down
from his lofty elevation on his contemporary
schoolfellows and college friends whom he has
left in the valley below, where they plod on still
and jog along their daily road of toil.

"Evelyn," said Dryden, "the wine stands
with you—pass it on."

No sooner had it come to Pepys' hand than
he swallowed off his twelfth glass and helped
himself to his thirteenth, and said, frankly
addressing himself to all present—

" Through every change of dynasty and phase
of government under which I have served, I
have reason to be thankful to the Giver of all
Good. Like my friend Evelyn, I keep a diary,
which I commenced the first year of my official
life," (here his voice arose to animation) "and
it is written in a peculiar short-hand or cypher;
so that should it fall into unfriendly hands it
cannot be easily published to the world. It was
almost death to me when blindness compelled
me to leave it off."

"But," said Tom Duffray, "you have seemed
to see your way pretty well ever since you groped
your way to a clerkship of the exchequer.'

"Thanks to Sir Edward Montague, I did
so," rejoined Pepys. "This was a great relief
to my poor wife, who, in our little room at Lord
Sandwich's, used to make coal fires, and wash
my foul clothes with her own hands."

"Then," says Tom, "your vision must have recovered mightily; for if my memory serves me, you found your way up the hill to the snug little thing called *Clerk of the Acts*."

"Thanks to my noble host, the Earl of Sand-•wich," said Pepys.

"You are not as short-sighted, Pepys, as you would have us imagine," said Dryden.

"We must do Mr. Pepys the justice to say," observed Evelyn, "that under trying circumstances he has been as upright as clearsighted. He boldly opposed the infamous system of selling places, giving them to Court favourites, who disgraced them. Some future age will improve upon his suggestion, and reject all candidates for offices under the State, without a proper examination for admission."

"If I may venture a word," said Mr. St. Aubyn, "in praise of a gentleman, whose worth is recorded in the history of the country which he has served, I would particularly advert to his calm, deliberate, self-devoted and charitable courage displayed during the Fire and the Plague in this city. Such is the rare courage of a great man. Higher and holier is it than the prodigies of valour to which the excitement of battle stimulates the conqueror."

"Yet, sir," says Pepys, looking at the last speaker seriously, "it was to such efforts as those I owed my promotion; for many poor Catholic priests and maligned nuns were ever present in the midst of misery, danger, loathsome disease and death. Such were those, who with our king, then Duke of York and Lord High Admiral, experienced all these calumnies, with which they never ceased to be loaded, during the infernal persecution, commonly called the ' Popish plot,' when that vertigo, as bad as the Plague and the Fire, seemed suddenly to seize the heads of the people of England, so that the blindness of hell came over them; nor could they see truth, or distinguish it from falsehood. The Earl of Shaftesbury was foster-father of the fiend which haunted us night and day."

" There will always be such in every age," said Evelyn. " His spirit is hereditary, and may probably descend to the sixth generation."

" These times," said Morton, " often call my mind back to Catholic England, and I almost feel that the very sufferings of my countrymen, whose faith my father had forsaken, must bring me back again to the old fold, to which my great ancestor, Dr. Nicholas Morton, Apostolical Penitentiary from Rome, was so deeply attached that he raised the northern counties, for the purpose of liberating Mary Queen of Scots from captivity; and this he did more for the sake of the Catholic religion than for herself. Your age, Mr. Pepys, must be nearly the same as mine."

" I am, says Pepys, " just turned fifty-six."

" I thought," said Mr. Morton, " you were older."

"You yourself suffered persecution, Mr. Pepys, I believe," observed Mr. St. Aubyn, quietly. "Did not the Protestant Earl implicate you in a charge of Catholicism?"

"He did me the honour to report that I had a crucifix in the house," said Pepys, "and had an altar, on which it was mounted."

"That was indeed suspicious," remarked St. Aubyn, in his own mild manner.

"Come, out with it," cried Tom, who was impatient at the grave turn which the conversation was taking. "Let us have the whole story. Were you not removed from the navy board to the Tower board, on the charge of being an aider and abetter of the plot?"

"Certainly; but in gratitude to him who has been charged with ingratitude, I must tell you, gentlemen, that Charles II. not only replaced me in my situation, but it was through him that I rose to the proud office which I now hold, as secretary to the Admiralty."

"But," cried Tom, "our host was asking the secretary something less serious than all this when I first entered the room. It semed more in my line of business."

"I have been so deeply absorbed in Pepys' short account of himself, or rather of his times, that I had forgotten all about it," rejoined Dryden.

"Oh! I have it, Pepys," said the elegant and accomplished gentleman, who adorned the

highest circles in Europe by his company. "You
and I have long been friends: we have much
sympathy with each other, and have much to
anticipate in common. Both of us know something of science and the fine arts. Our host
asked you whether you were as fond of music as
formerly, and I would ask if you cultivate it as
studiously as ever?"

"You know, Evelyn," says Pepys, "I was
always a lover of melody."

"Yes," cried Dryden, "it is the very essence
of music."

"But your d—d sonatas and solos," said
Pepys, "they are enough to give a fellow the
spleen. I have, however, a reasonable ear for
jigs."

"I compare a good melodist to a fine race-
horse beating time with his hoofs on the green
turf," said Evelyn.

At the close of this sentence Killigrew
was ushered into the room, bearing all the
marks of one of Charles's roués, rolling like one
of the King's Own, and as he took his seat he
cried on a high pitch, "A brave—à brave et
demi!" Upon which the Demi of Magdalen
College, who was unaccustomed to such a party
and so much wine, fancying that he had been
called on for an opinion, recited, scanning every
foot as he went into dactyls—

Quadrupedante putrem sonitu quatit ungula campum;

observing that the sounds represented the galloping of a horse as well as the melodist. This quotation reminded the company of Dryden's translation of Virgil and his opinion. Here they went off into a discussion not interesting to the general reader.

Evelyn, highly born, a cavalier, and one of the most dignified specimens of the fine old English gentleman, could scarcely conceal his annoyance at the admission of wild Harry Killigrew, one of the mad fellows about town, and a frequenter of Vauxhall."

"Pepys," says the new comer, "the last time I saw you was at the theatre. We both enjoyed the 'Maiden Queen' of our glorious Dryden. Ah, Mr. Dryden!" says he; "how prosper the 'Hind and the Panther?'"

"As well as can be expected, sir," was the quiet reply. "When the panther puts the hind to flight she will escape. The swallows, too, are ready for emigration."

"But," cried Killigrew, "was not pretty, witty Nelly charming, both as a mad girl and when she acts a young gallant?"

Old Tom Duffray, upon hearing a new voice, aroused himself from a doze.

"I fear, Master Thomas," continued the last speaker, "I have aroused you?"

"And so you have, you graceless dog, and broken a very amusing dream. I thought I saw behind the scenes in the women's 'shift room,' where pretty Nelly was dressing for her part, our

friend here the Secretary to the Admiralty, and
that there was no merry maid in the green-room
that he admired so much as the witty actress."

" She is certainly," assented Pepys, " a most
pretty woman who acted the part of Celia the
other day, very fine, and did it pretty well."

Killigrew.—" And you kissed her, Pepys."

Pepys.—" And so did my wife ; and a pretty
sort she is."

" Who?" asked Tom. " Mrs. Pepys or
Nelly?"

" My wife's picture will soon be finished,"
said Pepys, " and you shall see it," was the
answer, " and judge for yourself."

" And the portrait of Lady Castlemaine?"
said the gay Killigrew, slyly, casting a knowing
look at Evelyn, who was grave. " Come now,
Pepys, you are rather fond of frolicsome society,
and you used to love a concert."

This was a great relief, for all the company
desired to change the subject. Dryden hinted
that Pepys was also a poet.

" Pass the bottle," says he, " Mr. Evelyn."
And once more it came to Pepys' hand. He
was a man of business, but knew that " dulce
est desipere in loco." He filled his glass, as
did the rest. Then looking triumphantly at
Evelyn, whose high opinion he valued most,
he said—" I compose a song now and then,
and, as an amateur, I sing it to my own
music."

" But," says old Tom, " as solos give you the spleen, of course you require assistance?"

" Yes," says Killigrew—"female assistance."

Old Tom exclaimed, " Well to be sure, there is Mistress Mercer, Mistress Pepys' maid, who displays some talent for music."

" Oh!" said Pepys, "how I *do* wish Mrs. Pepys could sing!"

" Is there not," said Killigrew, "a syren called Knipp, an actress, only inferior to her comrade Nell Gynne?"

" Ah!" said Pepys, "I taught the baggage my song of 'Beauty Retire,' which she makes go most rarely."

" And a very fine song it seems to be," said Dryden, who felt that his inferior brother wanted a little praise.

" But you have not let me finish my dream," says Duffray.

" I saw this lady in my dream, and heard her in the dressing room tell you the whole practice of the playhouse."

" And she certainly is," says Mr. Pepys, " most excellent company. But how do you know my song is popular?"

" Because," chimed in both Tom and Killigrew, " Knipp says so, and praises it much moreover. She herself will soon be the best actress on the stage."

" But did she say so, the merry jade?" asked Pepys.

Evelyn could stand this no longer and shook his head.

"My dear friend, Mr. Evelyn," continued the last speaker, "you must remember that all this which our venerable friend was dreaming about happened, if ever it did happen, before I ascended to my present station. Early necessity and duty made me laborious and careful; but my natural propensities are those of a man of pleasure."

"Now, Mr. Pepys, you have passed through many changes: you have been a republican, a cavalier, a loyalist, and real promoter of your country's highest interest. When do you think you enjoyed yourself most, and were most happy?" asked Dryden.

"When with my wife," says Pepys, "I visited our friends, including Roger Pepys and others, the first time that ever I rode in my own coach, which did make my heart rejoice and praise God, and pray him to bless it to me and continue it."

"He would ride to heaven in his coach," interrupted Killigrew.

"Indeed," continued Pepys, "it was a mighty pleasure to go alone with my poor wife in a coach of our own to a play, and made us appear mighty great folk, I think, in the world, at least, greater than ever I could, or my friends for me, have once expected; and I think greater than ever any of my family who ever yet lived in my memory, but my cousin Pepys in Salisbury Court."

This expression of Mr. Pepys' greatest happiness left a smile on the faces of the company. Mr. Evelyn, however, said there was something to redeem our opinion of mankind in such candour. "And after all, our distinguished friend may not be more vain than the rest of us. He has attained wealth, and indeed renown, by his own exertions; and has been candid in expressing by words those very feelings which others by words seek to conceal. To ride in his own carriage with the same dignity with which he could order it was an indication of his success."

"And now," says Mr. Pepys, "since my avowal seems to afford our comical friend Killigrew so much amusement, I will ask him what may have been his greatest pleasure in life?"

"The death of tallow dips before the splendours of wax tapers, which, fresh from my hand, banished the inferior lights as the rising sun the fading stars. That is my answer, sir," said the dramatist.

"Since it jumps with the humour of the party to ascertain the happiest moment of the life of each of us," said Mr. Dryden, "and being, not a better, but an older soldier, I will venture to ask the erudite, accomplished, and affluent Mr. Evelyn to what event in his life he attaches the greatest pleasure?"

The calm and measured reply was—

" Since profane as well as sacred philosophers of all ages have decided that no man can really be pronounced happy before his death, I can scarcely speak with confidence of any time when I estimated myself as perfectly happy. The Restoration found me in my own place : I had with reference to this world nothing to repent of, nothing to solicit, nothing to fear from the resentment of my king or his minister. I was not, therefore, always obliged to wink at such vices as my conscience called on me to condemn —I felt grateful to providence and was tolerably happy. I was cheerful at the retrospect, through my own diary, embracing the time between the youth of Milton and the more advanced age of our celebrated friend here, Mr. Dryden, and his contemporaries, extending from the time of Charles I. down to the present, with its most stirring events, taking in more than half a century. In this I still find a fund of amusement, and live over my own life again. I feel proud, but cannot be certain that I am really happy."

" Is there no day in your long, useful, and peaceful life, sir," asked Mr. St. Aubyn, respectfully, " which you can mark as the happiest of all the rest ?"

" It was, sir, as far as happiness can fall to mortal, on that day when the completion of my great work, now in MS., crowned my labours ;

but which can scarcely be published during my life. I first called it Εὐσεβεία, but finally Θρησκεία, entitled in English the 'True Religion.' Nothing could exceed my delight when I came down with full force upon what I believed to be the worst of all the heresies, that which illogically arrogates to itself the title of Catholic. Comprehending the Papists, the Papalines, Anti-Christians, Image-worshippers, and Marians—I mean no offence to any present who may be of that erroneous persuasion—whose learning and piety, doubtless, will rescue them from the charge of superstition, which is brought so forcibly against the blind and misguided vulgar. But I was very happy when I refuted errors, which sooner or later must yield to truth. These (for courtesy we will say) *Roman Catholics*, adore and worship images; take away part of a moral and express commandment of the Table of the Decalogue, cutting the fragment into two to supply the number."

St. Aubyn here exchanged significant looks with Dryden, but was silent.

Evelyn then, having mentioned things too awfully sacred for our pages, went on to include under the worship of relics, St. Michael's sweat, when he fought with the Devil; a feather of Gabriel's wing; the parings of St. Edmund's nails. "I also showed," he said, "how they used enchantments, conjurations, exorcisms, crosses, lustrations, sufflations, rosaries, beads,

chaplets, agnuses, scapulars, amulets, conse-
crated pallia, censings, cursings—of salt, spittle,
oil, &c. &c.,—christening of bells, sanctifying
of candles, swords, children's clouts; such as I
believe were blessed by the Pope for our little
Prince of Wales—swaddling bands, and what
not. Repetitions, antic postures, cringes, shaved
crowns, and a hundred other impertinences.

"From the result of my reading I saw, and
set forth, that from the year 378 to 1428 the
true Catholic Church had been so miserably
clouded, that few, very few could discover where
she was, but in the grotts and crypts, such as
the antelucani cœtus: in a manner invisible, yet
existing in some place or in some persons, nay,
in whole countries; as Berengarius and his dis-
ciples, in the eleventh century, the Albigenses,
the Vaudois, the poor men of Lyons, the
Taborists in Bohemia, and others in the succeeding century, and so on to Luther, down to
our own days.

"A century or more, thought I, may pass
away before the seal which I place on this MS.
will be broken, and the truths which it contains
be disclosed. With a future age my heart may
hold a holier communion. To the 'True Religion' the eyes of some after generation may be
opened, to see that priests of all religions are the
same. I thought thereon, and when I thought
I was happy, most happy."

"Pray, sir, which religion might be the

true religion in your estimation?" cried Morton.

"The Church of England as by law established," said the great man of his age, without hesitation.

"May we not rather," asked Hough, with blushing diffidence, "say 'The branch of the Holy Catholic Church planted in these realms?'"

"You are, I think," said the other, "the nephew of a bold, good man who will doubtless be one of our bishops yet; you are entitled to my best reply. The name, my young friend, with which you, in common with about one in ten thousand of her members, desire to distinguish our most holy Church is spurned at this moment, particularly by the Church of England herself."

"Yes," says Mr. St. Aubyn, in soft, silvery accents, accompanied by a sweet smile; "the judgment of the indifferent world—the common sense of the nations—concurs so far in the decision of the Church of Rome."

"I must admit," says Mr. Morton, who knew something of the English history, "that the title is given up by most Protestant writers, and is most unequivocally repudiated by your hero Laud, who, when no disguise or earthly interest could lend him words, said, 'I die in the Protestant faith as by law established."

"To entitle my work 'Catholic' in the sense of

Christendom," said Evelyn, regretfully, " would be to give it a name which the world would deny, and which would rank me among the most silly of writers of the seventeenth century. And yet our Church is in fact Catholic, pure and primitive. 'Christianus mihi nomen, Catholicus cognomen.' 'The true Christian, the true Catholic,' was the old answer; but as for the term itself, of which some so highly vaunt, it does not appear to me indispensable. Our profession of faith, however, is Catholic, and we are in the only true sense Catholic."

CHAPTER XXVI.

The hapless Dryden of a shameless age.—Whitehead.

"It is easy to take up a name," said Tom Duffray, "and after all, what's in a name? But it is not so easy to get it recognised by the world or by competent authority."

"Just so," says Mr. St. Aubyn, in his own quiet way.

"Any one of us," cried Killigrew, "may call himself John Dryden, 'the glorious John.'"

"Yes," said Dryden, drily, "till I, the real 'glorious John,' denounce him, and prove him at best but a bad imitator. The question is, will the ancient monuments of England, her foundations, her traditions, her statutes, her universities, or the very last coronation service, though accommodated in a degree to a Protestant church, establish your claim to the title? Would any member of the ministry or the senate rise up and call the reformed Protestant church Catholic; and, if he did so, would he be understood, or would not the Lord Chancellor in his place treat the idea as a fiction too absurd for anything but ridicule ? To decide the matter, let us ask the first child of any religious persuasion whom we may meet in the street, which is the way to the Catholic church ? I will concede the title to that edifice to which he directs us."

Many sincere Catholics at this period had been taught by necessity to consider their religion as a secret, and from motives of policy to say little or nothing in its defence when assailed, lest they should draw on themselves the dreadful suspicion of being members of the exploded, feared, and detested Church. When persecuted in one city they fled to another, and rarely provoked controversy or answered it, unless those who sought the crown of martyrdom. In our day we may invariably observe this reluctance in the minds of the hereditary Catholics to encourage oral controversy. Conversion to the old faith, not the warfare of words is what they desire. Mr. St. Aubyn, therefore, who was a profound theologian and controversialist, suffered Mr. Evelyn and others to express their opinions without serious opposition.

" I am ignorant," says Pepys, " of church history, and you know, have not very long cast off my Roundhead principles. But I think the men who set up the reformed religion for a church, in opposition to Rome, proved themselves unequal to the execution of their grand design. She is like one of our craft that will not answer to the helm, but loses part of her crew in every squall."

"The Church of the Reformation is full, not empty; gathering from the right and from the left; full of deep, Catholic doctrine, all holy and evangelical truth—Primitive, Apostolic, Catholic, Scriptural, Reformed, Evangelical—it has eliminated nothing but error."

"Certainly, sir," said old Tom Duffray, "the Established Church may doubtless be truly said to be at least as full as any other Church, of the good things enumerated by Mr. Evelyn. Concretely regarded, it may with equal truth be said to be full, not empty; but the good things of which it is not empty but full, appear to partake rather of the nature of the good things of this world: bishops, deans and chapters, and a goodly company of rectors and vicars are full, and not empty, of the like good things with those which gladden the inner man of the mayor, the aldermen, and the officers of the royal establishment. If, indeed, the superior parsons were as richly endowed with benevolence as they are with the glebe and tithes of the ancient superstition or royal revenue, the deep Catholic doctrine would be more apparent to the untutored mind."

Evelyn rejoined, "Having proved all things, the Church holds fast that which is good, and that only."

"Just so," roared Killigrew. "The bishop

proves all things, and proves money to be that
which is good. He accordingly holds it fast to
a large amount, and leaves a goodly heritage to
his children, and those of his household; thus pro-
viding for them not like a heretic, but a Catholic
Christian : leaving the back settlements and
slums and rustic wilds to the inferior clergy.
Gold is the earthy Deity to whom the princes of
the establishment intrust their destinies. It is
power—it is happiness—it will buy gratitude.
What can a bishop bequeath to his children
better than wealth ? How can he bind the lover
and the loved with a stronger bond than a chain
of gold ?"

" Ay, more," said old Tom, with a demi-semi
sneer cast at Dryden, " Will not gold purchase
even salvation from the Holy Church ?"

Without any reference to these retorts, Mr.
Evelyn ascribed all the evils of the Established
Church to the assumption of the king, and to
the supremacy which he asserted.

" Because the king asserts a divine right, and
assumes the prerogative of the Pope," cried
Evelyn, " against the interests of the Protestant
Church." All present seemed to think such had
been the transfer of power at the Reformation.

But Morton, fearful of polemical discussion,
sang out, " To the question !"

" Before the gentleman usurps the authority
of the chair to call us to order," said the former
speaker, with warmth, " we would learn some-

thing of his ancestor, the Earl of Morton. Did
he not assist in Rizzio's murder ; and brought
with him the ' maiden of Halifax ?' "

" Who was she ?" asked Mr. Hough, in a
whisper to Morton.

" She was the beauty of her age," answered
he, " and would clasp a fellow round the neck
in a close embrace, and hold his head in her
arms."

Hough wondered at her audacity, when Mr.
St. Aubyn explained that it was an axe, which
came down like the sash of a window and
chopped off the head.

In the meanwhile, Morton had been explaining
to Evelyn that his name, not his title, was
Morton, and that his ancestor was not the regent
of Scotland. " Far from that," said he, " I am
of the family to which Dr. Nicholas Morton,
Apostolical Penitentiary of Rome belonged, as
I have before observed."

" Since you derive your authority from the
Holy See," says Evelyn, " we must submit to
such a decision. ' Roma locuta est, causa finita
est.' "

Old Tom, who had been snoring some time,
while Killigrew was helping himself copiously to
the wine, started up, exclaiming wildly that the
Hind had been hit too hard by the Panther, to
which all were ready to show fair play. Then,
as if transported back to youth, he recited, in
measured accents, a little impaired from loss of

voice and teeth, the following lines in defence of the panther—

> " Sure the noblest next the hind
> And fairest offspring of the spotted kind;
> Oh! could her inborn stains be washed away,
> She were too good to be a beast of prey—

" to the wolves, bears, boars, foxes, and the rest of the inferior animals," said St. Aubyn, with an arch smile.

Dryden had recourse once more to his snuff, which on this occasion he took in plentifully, then looked as if he wished to be in a position to relieve Evelyn from so much pleasantry, which that sedate man could not tolerate.

But Killigrew was again on his legs; and looking full in the face of old Tom, recited in his own droll way—

> " By long experience may Duffray, no doubt,
> Ensnare a gudgeon or sometimes a trout."

Before he could say more, Mr. Morton, seconded by Mr. St. Aubyn, desired to learn Mr. Dryden's happiest day.

" To realise our happiness it must be contrasted with our unhappiness. When, seven years ago, I published the satire of 'Absalom and Ahitophel,' I was, you know, poet laureate of the King, Charles II. Then Ormond, Halifax, and Hyde, Earl of Rochester, were among my patrons, but Shadwell and Settle settled upon me like wasps. I was satisfied with my portraits of Shaftesbury and Monmouth. The dissolution of the Oxford parliament, as paraphrased at the conclusion, gratified the king; but the animosity of living characters and of existing factions, the issue of whose contentions, then in the womb of time, I painfully anticipated, made me unhappy."

"When I condescended to notice the insects of Grub-street, who buzzed about me, I was more unhappy. When I suffered myself to write 'The Spanish Friar, Dominic,' and should the theatre ever be my resource for support I shall be grieved to see this play acted on the stage, in the person of Father Dominic I satirised the religion for which I would lay down my life. The very thought makes me most unhappy. My translation of Virgil tasked me heavily, but I claimed the licence of a translator. At moments I hoped to excel the original of the noble 'Æneid,' and was therefore happy."

Here Pepys broke in with a doubt whether Palinurus could have made his crew obey the order :

> " Tack to the larboard—and stand off to sea,
> Veer starboard, sea, and land."

" However this might be, were these words turned back into Latin," said the translator, " I shrewdly suspect the best pilot in the British navy with this command in his mouth would be unintelligible."

" Never mind, Mr. Dryden's ' Æneid ' will live for ever," observed Evelyn.

" I reflected the image of the original. ' The Hind and Panther,' cruelly brought the whole house of faction upon me, headed by buzzing Burnet, who vented his political animosity upon ' the papist Dryden' with attacks upon his translation of Varilla's ' History of Heresies.' "

" Such as Mr. Evelyn has given us ? " asked Morton, with a humourous roll of his eye.

Dryden went on : " The bishop assured me that ' The Hind and Panther ' was the worst poem of the age ; but I did not believe the impartial divine, and all which he said convinced me that however I might try to soothe the panther, the animal was untameable. When I wrote the ' Religio Laici,' I was sceptical about revealed religion, nor could I see any middle course between natural religion and the Church of Rome. My researches and inquiries brought me to the threshold of the House founded on the Rock of Ages. I began to see the necessity of some infallible judgment, which literally the great Head had promised to his church. I went further, and was happier ; nay, very happy."

" You *saw*, Great John, the convenience of such authority," cried Evelyn, " and *desired* it."

" Such an omniscient Church, we wish, indeed,
'Twere worth both Testaments, cast in the Creed."

" The wish was father of your faith," added the erudite journalist.

Taking no notice Dryden went on—"After many wanderings and doubts I feel at home in that old house which has survived every house under Heaven ; the destruction of which, if it be destroyed by the revelations of Evelyn's ' True Religion,' will be the destruction of Christianity itself. I am therefore happy, most happy !"

" Would," sighed Evelyn, "that our dear and valued friend could but come to the knowledge of the light ! Oh ! that the advisers of our misguided sovereign would convince him of the error of his ways and establish his throne in that righteousness which exalteth a nation, a great Protestant nation, whose religion is the Bible, whose strength is the Test! To encourage popery," he added, with animation, "is treason."

" That is very strong language," said Morton, looking stedfastly on Evelyn, whose irrevocable decision was recorded on his brow.

" Not stronger," rejoined the author of the " True Religion," " than that of Usher, primate of all Ireland, who scripturally denounced from the altar and the pulpit any counsel to the king to tolerate Catholics. Yes, denounced it as a deadly sin, amid murmurs of applause. According to Coke," continued he, " to cause the king to tolerate papists is treason."

" But," said St. Aubyn, " even popery itself is not, I apprehend, treason in the fountain of power—the king himself."

" However this may be," said Evelyn, more cautiously, " it is the opinion of all the great statesmen with whom I have recently conversed, that the time has not yet arrived to associate religious with civil liberty. We are still too near the Reformation—the great change of the religious polity of England. There is, perhaps, yet a lingering spirit of superstition hovering among the tombs and monuments of ancient days. The stream of time—the besom of destruction must first sweep away these vast monuments of the past on which are inscribed the false faith of our forefathers."

" Still," cried Pepys, " it was the king's fortune and not his fault to be born in a Protestant age and country. Every age has its peculiar enthusiasm. The excitement of the present hour has long been gaining strength. It arises, I think," said he, " out of modern notions of liberty. First of all, the unbridled torrent of religious controversy, which has carried us beyond the limits of the agitator's dream. To concede to each individual separately the choice of his religious or state policy, is to foster rebellion against legal supremacy. My former life," cries Pepys, " will rescue me from the imputation of popery, and yet, I have always believed that there must be a despotic power vested in the Church,—centred in the Pope or the king ; even this supremacy in the middle ages (' the darker, ' suggested Evelyn), was far more useful than its assailants now admit. But for its decrees, sir," said the quondam republican, " the very name of peace would not have been known in Europe."

"Just so," said Morton, delighted to have so much in favour of what his heart approved; " and mighty was the protection spread over the weak ; while monastic charity hourly ministered to poverty and suffering such voluntary relief as extorted poor-rates and legal enactments have never supplied."

" At the same time," said Evelyn, who seemed startled almost out of his aristocratic serenity, "we must all allow that this vast authority was often directed to evil; and that so far as it had been assumed by James, has gone some way to undo the great work of nearly two centuries." Then, as if he had said too much, he checked himself, saying, blandly, " But what human authority has not been abused ? And as you all well know, the Roman Church was a human institution, growing out of human circumstances and human exigencies."

" Such, for instance," hinted Morton, with a droll look and serious voice, " as the marriage of Henry with Anne Boleyn."

" Or," put in Dryden, very archly, " the marriage of some of the persecuted nuns with some of their liberators, the monks, such as Luther and others."

Without heeding what might be considered an

irrelevant jest, Evelyn continued, " The moment the supremacy of Rome was no longer needed, that moment it was impugned. The intelligence of the age would not submit the mind to the tyranny of Rome. The authority was not required, and it fell before the liberal faith which suits the present period. It is no longer suited to the people or the age."

Dryden observed that, " The faith, like Him in whom it centred, was the same yesterday, to-day, and for ever."

But the company took no note.

" The great body of the English people," said Evelyn, " will never support the establishment of the Stuarts on that throne for which varied experience has proved their house to be so unfitted."

" I have long shared their fortunes and their patronage," said Pepys, " and I may say their reverses. For the exiled prince I felt the deepest sympathy; but now, as an expatriated monarch, cast upon the charity of France—for such I fear he will be, I pity him; I mourn for him as one deprived of his just heritage. And, yet," added he, in a spirit of reconciliation, " I know not that a crown, like an estate, ought to be transmitted to a prodigal heir."

" The monarch's faults and follies take a wider range, and involve the happiness of thousands," said Evelyn, " but, should James be restored to his heritage and his power, to him I will swear fealty."

" Oh !" added Dryden, " William has waited for the tide of opinion, which he has laboured to direct, and will ride into power, if it be over the dead body of his uncle," cried he with poetic enthusiasm. " I cannot but see in poor James, distracted and demented as he is, the Lear of modern history—betrayed, delivered by his two most guilty"—but before he could complete the parallel in the play, or even finish his sentence, tumultuous sounds of mingled voices rent the air, and drew the party to the windows. Above the uproar might be heard one clear loud shout, as from one mouth, which reverberated along Gerrard-street, " The king !—the king !"

CHAPTER XXVII.

The heroic soul, amidst its bliss and woe,
Is never swell'd too high, nor sunk too low;
Stands like its origin above the skies,
Ever the same great self, sedately wise;
Collected and prepared in every stage
To scorn a courting world, or bear its rage.—*Henley.*

THE passions of the people had subsided. The raving of rebellion was fast sinking down into a sullen calm. Public confidence had been in some measure restored. Business was reviving, but was not generally resumed. Once more the shop windows here and there were glittering with their rich and wonted display of inviting goods. During the pleasant entertainment at Dryden's a proclamation made by the council, announcing the king's expected return to White-hall, had penetrated every lane and alley, and at the moment when Dryden's accommodation of King Lear to King James had commenced, the cry had awakened the echoes of Gerrard Street.

The tidings of their returning monarch, whom the multitude had but so recently rejected and reviled, now turned the tide which had been surging to and fro into one channel. It was setting in everywhere in favour of him now apparently in the ascendant. Every class was already impatient to welcome back again with the liveliest expressions of joy him whom they had but yesterday condemned.

Groups of lads and lasses, with red ribbons flaunting from their breasts and button holes, in their best attire, were in raptures at the change, and the holiday and the parade which it delights the sight-seer to behold. The more aged of both sexes, if not more thoughtful, were more tardy, only issuing from their houses, and meeting at different points, some, to witness the spectacle, and some to fall in with the royal procession, which all desired, but knew not why. Such was the aspect of affairs when the sights and sounds in front of the house broke up the conversation of our party.

Pepys declared, if there was ever an occasion when his new coach and its pomp could be called into requisition, that glorious occasion had now arrived. He left Dryden's with these words in his mouth and Evelyn on his arm. Morton and young Hough returned to their inn, and were soon mounted, and on their way to join the cavalcade. Dryden and St. Aubyn quietly and unostentatiously fell back upon the palace to wait the grand event, to note the revulsion of feeling in the populace, and to contemplate the practical result to which this afterthought of the Privy Council might lead. Old Tom Duffray, supported by his comical friend Killigrew, freely mingled with the pedestrians and trudged along on foot, to form a part and parcel of the undistinguished masses. To see and hear, not be heard or seen, was their object and their convenience.

From Faversham, as we have seen, the fugitive monarch, acceding to the request of the noblemen who waited on him, and to the counsel of his friends, set out on his journey. At Sittingbourne he was met by his guards and equipage, and joined by some of his adherents. He slept that night at Rochester, whence we omitted to state he dispatched Feversham with a letter to the Prince of Orange, inviting him to come to London for the purpose of an amicable treaty. The next day, December 16th, from Rochester James proceeded in royal guise to London. As he approached the city his progress resembled a triumphant procession. Greetings of affection and demonstrations of loyalty welcomed him at every step. A body of gentlemen, forming a volunteer guard of honour, preceded him, with their heads uncovered. Immense crowds at every point received him with acclamations. These manifestations, the spontaneous free-will offerings of sympathy, were more grateful, perhaps, to his Majesty's heart than a decisive victory on the battle field over the Dutch invader.

Every art which cunning treachery could devise had been used to keep up and encourage those incendiary cries, which set churches and mansions in flames, but in vain. History does not inform us that the violence of a hired mob obstructed the grand procession. There is, however, no subject, perhaps, on which contemporaneous writers differ more materially than on the reception which awaited James through the city, and on his arrival at Whitehall. That a vast crowd followed the grand procession into Southwark to meet and, to welcome the king, we may believe. His passage over London bridge, then the only one across the Thames, was choked up by the crowd. Meanwhile, acclamations rose louder and still more loud. As he advanced under the gateway of the bridge, the royal standard was hoisted above it; this was the signal for a royal salute from the Tower guns.

The appearance of the King in the royal carriage, drawn by eight snow-white horses, each attended by a groom, and surrounded by the yeomen of the guard, besides a guard of honour bringing up the rear, called forth from the spectators the most enthusiastic exclamations of joy. One long, loud, heart-thrilling shout burst from the throng, and drowned a struggling screech of "No popery!" which could find no echo. A resistless torrent of enthusiasts, such as we have in our own day seen rushing on with the royal carriage, pressed on either side, waving their hats and deafening the king with their tremendous huzzas. In this manner the procession forced its way towards the end of the bridge next the city. Here a scene of confusion ensued, for the masses were so dense that all came to a dead lock.

For a moment the king in some alarm aroused himself, and signed to Strickland, who rode up close to the left window, as O'Brian did to the opposite, warding off the thickest of the masses from the king's immediate presence by sundry well-timed kicks and plunges, merely accidental of course, but peculiar to the horses of the Life Guards.

" Tell the commander-in-chief that I desire a word with him instantly," said the king.

Clare perceiving, with the instinctive quickness of his country, the feelings of his Majesty and the real state of the case, bent gracefully and uncovered, deeply bowing, until his obeisance brought his head close to that of his royal master, and said with a rich brogue, but a really soft, soothing voice—

" May it please your Majesty, Lord Feversham has not yet rejoined the guards ; but, my liege, sure it's your Majesty that's safe and supreme in the hearts of your people. Com-mand us, my liege, your royal self in person, and we will make a sham charge and scatter the crowd like leaves in autumn."

" Curb your zeal, young man," cried the

king; "nothing can be effected till Lord Feversham resumes his place at the head of the main body."

"But," observed Strickland, "I see a company of horse coming in this direction at full speed from Cheapside, an escort of honour or some special commissioner."

"It is Lord Feversham with a guard of honour from the Prince," cried James. "We must halt by word of command, not of this rude necessity."

"That were death to the populace," said Hales, who was seated beside the King; "for in such a case many who are on foot must be trampled to death in the pressure behind."

The royal grooms were therefore ordered to make the best way they could gently and perseveringly. They all had not cleared the bridge when the horsemen met the royal party. They escorted, however, not Feversham, but, to the king's unutterable horror, Zulestein, from whom they learnt the news of Lord Feversham's arrest at Windsor Castle, which the Prince now occupied.

Every gleam of hope was extinguished in the troubled mind of the king—his worst fears were realised. But the measure of his afflictions was not full, till Zulestein on the spot presented him with a letter, of which he was the bearer, from William, requesting his uncle, whom it had been intended to reach at Rochester, not to advance nearer the capital than that place. While James was reading the letter, and giving an audience to the unwelcome messenger of evil, the yellow light, or rather gloom, even then peculiar to London, was already borrowing a darker shade from the approach of evening; through this, to the west, another scene presented itself, more lively, and to many more striking.

The assembled multitudes in London, who are easily brought together by some tragic or comic prodigious attraction of any sort, are always greedy to feed their curiosity and fill up the interval of suspense by the entertainment of an interlude, an episode, a bye-play, or diversion —whether it is a king to be beheaded on the scaffold or to be restored to the throne, a common criminal to be hanged or to be gibbetted. And such a diversion at this stage of the royal progress soothed their impetuosity and gratified their tastes. It was over such a scene as this that the eyes of grave and loyal subjects now wandered; and it seemed to afford greater attraction than all the rest, especially to the two young guardsmen, Strickland and Clare.

The actors in this scene were about fifty paces on the city side of the bridge, apparently making for Whitehall, in advance of the royal cortège. In the midst of the throng appeared two human figures, richly attired, and splendidly mounted on two horses gaily caparisoned, which raised their riders above the multitude that surrounded them. One of these was a lady in a green riding habit, and wearing a most becoming hat, surmounted with a feather; from beneath this a profusion of glossy auburn hair escaped in rich natural curls. The other was a young gallant, in the height of the fashion of the day, unattended by his servant, whom intervening masses had probably cut off from his master. The groom in attendance on the lady was about eighty paces behind her on a lofty steed, and evidently addressing a knot of attentive hearers, who increased every moment, and seemed enchanted with his discourse. Among the crowd Cornet Clare caught a sight of his Oxford friend, Mr. Hough, riding beside Mr. Morton, but impeded by the motley group around the servant; Clare relieved by another officer, hastened towards him, greeting him most cordially, but with difficulty keeping down a laugh, which was breaking forth in spite of his efforts.

On a platform erected just beyond the bridge, away from the thoroughfare, were many spectators looking down, now upon the grand sight on the bridge, and now on the sea of heads and upturned faces below. In front stood an old man bowed down rather by years than care, judging from his merry face, leaning on a young and more comical, but not a more jovial fellow; they seemed unconscious of everything and everybody but the subject of their mirth. The wit

and fun of the senior seemed as fresh and spark-
ling as his shabby-genteel black-brown coat was
bare and thread-worn.

" Fire and faggots ! what have we got here ?"
cried the younger.

" An appendage of aristocracy," answered the
elder.

" Here's proper gear to entertain a king,"
said the younger ; and there was something so
theatrical and attractive in his gesture and voice,
that they caught the notice of Hough, who immediately recognised Killigrew.

" See, the lady avoids him, and like a pageant
queen motions him away." The tone and accents
of the words reminded Hough and Morton of old
Tom Duffray, and sure enough there he was in
all his glory.

" But hark to the noble lady on horseback,"
observed Morton quietly to Hough.

They heard distinctly the words, " Away !—
leave me !—go ! approach me on your proper
peril !" There was a strange tone and defiant
manner of rebuff, which seemed intended for the
ears of the bystanders, and which, if heard by him
whom they warned, were not heeded.

" My dear girl, I have waited for you long. I
have watched your movements night and day ;
sought you everywhere, and followed you all the
way from Rochester, where I hoped to find you
last night. But, my dear, we are at home here
in London, and unobserved in the crowd. 1

have found you at last, and I cannot leave you till you say you will be mine—my sweet, sweet Mary! Providence has brought us together!" He raised his voice, forgetful, in his passionate admiration, of those within hearing, "Come, come to my bower. Take wealth, rank and power."

With a motion of the rein and whip she made her well-trained steed bound away from him, making what is called a semivolt, and clearing a space between them; but still he persisted with no faint heart.

"Listen to me, fair lady; but why do you shrink from my touch?"

"Because," said she, coldly, contemptuously, and with a withering look of loathing, "it would profane a woman."

Morton, who was a noble minded gentleman, was disposed to interfere; but Clare cried: "No, sir, by no means, the procession will move on directly; there is no time," and rode back to his place in the king's escort, passing by Strickland, with whom he exchanged a word.

Many were the soft things which the gay gallant said to the lady that could not be heard by any but herself; but at times the eloquence of his disinterested affection passed all bounds, and his exclamations were heard by all around.

"I love you, dear lady, more than honour, fortune, life, Heaven; on my salvation I do."

The lady made no sign, but a look of scorn

mingled with horror, overspread her features.
To mark her feelings she pulled a veil over her
face to screen her from the intruder's gaze.

The passionate cast of his countenance gave
way to a cold, stony, stern expression of resentment ; and muttering something like vengeance,
he bit his lip, and tried to look as if ' he never
told his love.'

All remarked the angry spot upon his cheek.
" I am ready to die for you!" he exclaimed.
She turned her head from him, and looking at
the gentlemen, raised her voice for their ears,
not for her suitor's, and retorted, " It were better
to live and serve your country like your noble
father, my Lord, than to persecute a damsel who
has nothing to give you in return for your
devotion but scorn."

" How proudly she tosses her head aloft; with
what state she carries herself; and yet," cried
Killigrew, " her voice is as sweet as syrup."

" Rather," rejoined old Tom, " as soft as a
zephyr."

Her lordly admirer, like some other persons
who rank high in their own opinion, would brook
no refusal, and affected more gaiety than he
really felt. Overwhelmed and confounded with
the variety and contrasts of character, and the
conflicting attributes which the damsel seemed
to include in her person and demeanour, it
appeared to Morton and Hough, whose active
duties in the procession left them but little time

for reflection, and less for any observation which even for a moment took them from his Majesty, that had the attachment of the lover been as pure as it seemed desperate, he might have made the discovery which they made, and, perhaps, our readers may already have made, that the face and form before him, though pretty enough for any girl, were different from those of her whom he professed to adore. Of her voice she gave him less opportunity of judging; her veil, too, on his nearer approach had possibly concealed her countenance from his too eager gaze. Anger and mortification smarted him more bitterly than any wound which he had ever received, and there is a tradition that he received many in single combat.

But how could he be mistaken in the fair equestrian? Had he not seen her often, and within a few hours the preceding day, and in various places? Her habit, her jennet, the precise livery of her father's house, all declared that he could not possibly be mistaken.

"No, no," says the confident gallant; "I could swear to that rich cluster of ringlets which escapes from under thy hat, sweetheart."

She still kept aloof, and said,—

"Speak to me no more, my lord; for your own sake go, for our conversation is evidently attracting more notice than will be gratifying to your lordship. Look, my man is drawing near, and the crowd, who is hanging on his words."

"Since, then, my fairest, dearest, you will not listen to me," said the gallant, "in this wilderness of the multitude, let me follow you to some sequestered spot. What care we for the king! You are the queen supremely enthroned in my heart!" He put spurs to his horse, and was instantly by her side. "Nay, nay, by my faith, my pretty papist, we must not part thus. I am indeed converted to your creed—one we are in faith and love. Oh, Mary!—believe me true gospel light never beamed with a lovelier lustre from Anne Boleyn's eyes than from those heavenly but disdainful orbs of thine, fair girl, on which I love to gaze, and could gaze for ever."

He was peering almost under the maiden's hat, with his head close to hers. Indeed his own ambrosial locks presumed to mingle a raven tress with a fair auburn curl.

"By heaven!" cried Killigrew, at the very top of his most lyrical voice, and in an ecstasy of comedy which shook the very platform with a roar of laughter; "Nelly herself could not have done it better!"

Before this tumultuous outburst of laughter had subsided, a grand carriage-and-four rolled majestically from the city side towards the bridge, preceded by outriders in splendid liveries and displaying all but royal magnificence. Less like a gilded caravan it was than the moving, or rather, just now, stopping mansion of his majesty, and certainly more gorgeous, but less tawdry than the gingerbread concern of the Lord Mayor. "Make way for the Secretary of the Admiralty!" cried several shipbuilders and tradesmen; but nothing less than a broadside could have moved the dense masses, who seemed so edified by the little duet which we have vainly attempted to describe.

Through the open window of the coach appeared the dignified head and broad shoulders of a gentleman, who, notwithstanding his aristocratic gravity, was by no means indifferent to the beauty of the fair sex. He seemed astonished at the sight of an elegant lady hedged in by such a motley assembly, and was curiously penetrating every avenue of vision for some clue to this riddle, when, as if startled out of courtly and august propriety, he most involuntarily exclaimed—

"As I live, it is Spenser! What will his poor, dear mother say?" And Evelyn, for he it was, shrunk back from the vulgar fray, which he had so painfully witnessed.

"The Devil!" cried the old play-writer on the stage; "Nelly is a child to her."

Killigrew, seeing the secretary's carriage, screamed out from his stage most theatrically, so as to be heard by all around, "Pepys, what think you of that? She is the very image of her you wot of. I have seen her in the circus and on the stage but she is not fit to hold one of my wax candles to the lady who is figuring before us."

Pepys, only less proud of the company of Evelyn than of the coach which conveyed them both, laughed violently, but made no reply. Evelyn, who felt as much degraded by his position in the rabble as he was convenienced by the coach, fell back out of sight, deeply afflicted at the plight of the son of his dear friend Lady Sunderland.

For the interests of truth, we must acknowledge that Pepys, who had an hereditary taste for a fashionable cut of male or female attire, was more deeply delighted with the well-dressed horseman and lady rider, and the convulsive mirth which they excited, than he cared to confess to his grave and correct companion.

Pepys himself, born and bred a Londoner, with all the peculiar acuteness and address, and even audacity belonging to an experienced citizen, felt equally at home in a public crowd and in a private circle, thoroughly enjoyed this diversion ; nor was he, or indeed any of the company who had partaken of the hospitality of Dryden, less jovially inclined to public mirth than to stern loyalty.

The cause of the tremendous explosion of laughter which has tempted us into this digression, was apparent to the eye and ear of Pepys. Scarcely had the noble proselyte made that most blasphemous allusion to the conver-

sion of Henry VIII., who certainly was not
less sincere than his lordship, who had brought
to aid his love Anne Boleyn's eyes, and mentioned his own, in which the fair rider's soul,
he said, " was imaged," when, availing herself
of the opportunity, the graceful horsewoman with
inimitable dexterity and precision, slashed her
whip across his lordship's eyes, through which
flashed fire, and at the same time conviction.
Those eyes, which but a moment ago had been
impressed with the lady's beauty, were now in
an instant filled with tears that streamed down
his noble cheeks.

" If," said the fair equestrian, " you have
abandoned the Protestant faith, for the sake of a
girl of whom you have for the first time received
a most indelible impression, you are a traitor to
your religion. You are merely bribed by the
hope of a woman's fortune, not her heart. You
are a coward, aspiring to knighthood and a noble
name—you disgrace both."

The nobleman drew his hat over his brow.
He really endured the terrible chastisement like
a hero ; merely saying in a stifled voice, " Your
big, bullying words, lady, are unbecoming your
usual gentle bearing. I would that you were a
man for one moment," said the afflicted culprit ;
" then, Mistress Mary, by all the saints and
images you ever worship, the offensive words
you uttered were your last. Who ever dared to
call me coward?" And endeavouring as a

matter of honour, to possess himself of that hand which inflicted the blow—whether to kiss it or to squeeze it in a close embrace, tradition declareth not.

The damsel, still inexorable to his endearments, sang in sweet and monotonous accents:

"And now from these same eyeballs, blind with rage,
Wash out those tears and thus thy griefs assuage."

And with this touching admonition, quicker than lightning her well-directed whip came down upon the knuckles of his left hand.

"Well done, lady in green!" broke in some voices.

The reins fell from the peer's grasp, and the liberated animal he had so long held back made one frantic dash into the heart of the people—rushing against the fair defender with a shock which nearly brought both horses to the ground, and shook the hat and feather from her head. An indignant yell, almost like the mingled voices arising from a menagerie of wild beasts, burst forth from those around him, with cries of "Too bad! too bad!"

The lady's servant was by her side in a moment, respectfully presenting her with her fallen hat, so that the vast multitude could see the feather waving.

"The cowardly varmint has hit the lady," cried many voices. "He has hit the girl with his whip and knocked her hat off," cried one. "May I never shoot a papist," cried another, "if I don't lick your lordship before the day is much older."

Evelyn, whose object was not to embroil himself with the people felt much, but said little, simply remarking to Pepys, that he was certain the nobleman had not assaulted the woman on horseback, whose violence exceeded anything he had ever seen in such a lady-like looking person.

"Let us drive on, Pepys," says he; "the procession is in motion."

"What a devil of a hurry you are in!" cried Pepys impatiently, forgetting the virtuous dignity of his companion.

"I don't see what right that big carriage and those fine tall fellows have to push us out of our places," says a sturdy pugilist.

"We must pass, in the king's name," said Evelyn, sternly; but no breach in the rampart of humanity could be effected.

"Non possumus," was Pepys' only reply.

That no gentleman would have struck the girl was the opinion of one and all.

"Well done, Bill," cried fifty voices, as a fellow with a bludgeon aimed a blow at the nobleman, whose horse seemed possessed by a demon, so furiously did he scare all before him. His master, however, displayed more than his usual discretion; and though the cry of vengeance had been taken up successively by the assailants, he was soon out of the reach of the threatened blows, and the mob oratory, which sent a volley of oaths after him, urging each spectator to pitch into him.

" Have at him ! Down with the noble ruffian !" " He has been chastised enough," said a man who could not get near him, " let him pass.' " He is only gone down to the river to wash the tears out of his eyes," said another.

"But not the cut of the whip," screamed a fishwoman, who was in ecstacies at the victory of her sex.

CHAPTER XXVIII.

O perilous mouths
That bear in them one and the self-same tongue
Either of condemnation or approof!
Bidding the law make curtsy to their will—
Hooking both right and wrong to th' appetite,
To follow as it draws !—*Shakespeare.*

ALL the little affair, recorded in the last chapter, lasted perhaps about ten minutes ; but before the enchanted, surprised, and excited crowd could pursue the entertainment any further, from the side of the crowd next the bridge, in a voice of authority and command was heard, "Make room for the King and his guards ! Room for his most gracious Majesty !"

And prancing through the midst of the people, was O'Brian, in his own element of action. It so chanced that he rode against Hough and Morton, and utterly astounded them by the inexplicable expression of sly drollery on his countenance. "Ah ! Hough, my dear fellow, I hope I haven't hurt you." Then looking at Morton, said with a low bow, "I beg your pardon, sir ;" then hastily shaking Hough's hand, said in his ear, "That girl is a man ; but just watch how I will scatter the ruffians of the rabble," and off he went into the heart of the crowd.

Strickland's object was to conciliate, to smile the people into good humour, and to use only gentle violence: each officer in his own way with his respective followers soon cleared the thoroughfare, so that the dense masses were speedily divided into two parts, and stood like a living wall at each side of the widening passage, or fell back into every outlet that would receive the overflowing of the multitude. Nothing more was seen or heard of the lady or her aggressive and defeated lover.

Having at length emerged from the bridge, the procession fell into regular order. Five hundred yeomen rode bareheaded in the van, followed by the aldermen in their state robes on horseback, while two heralds in ancient armour, and a band of trumpeters mounted on stout horses preceded the lord mayor, sheriffs, and their officers: next to these followed a troop of horse guards, then came the members of the council arrayed in court dresses, on large horses gorgeously caparisoned. The guard of honour resumed its position, and closing brought up the rear. Flags were streaming from the windows; ladies showered down laurel wreaths studded with flowers. The advancing tide of loyalists rushed on in a resistless torrent, until arrested in its course at Temple Bar. As the procession came on the barricade flew open, and they passed through it; while deputations from the rich and various City companies joined the procession, which after some delay resumed its course, amidst the ringing of bells, the firing of cannon, and the acclamations of the people.

But the king's spirits had not revived from the shock of the unexpected and arbitrary message which greeted his return to his own metropolis. Indeed, the officers and loyal friends who immediately surrounded their kingly master began to participate in the apprehension which disturbed the royal mind. The huzzas of to-day might give place to the execrations of to-morrow.

The Strand at this time was less crowded with buildings than it is now. Stately mansions of the nobility, with gardens behind them sloping down to the Thames, and stairs for the purpose of stepping into the boats, occupied the chief part of the river side. To the titles of the owners of these mansions some of the streets leading from the Strand to the Thames still owe their names.

It was along this course which now forms the regular street, uniting the Court end of the town with the city of London, that the progress of the king was most imposing. He next passed Charing-cross, which on this grand occasion was indeed the artery through which poured the full tide of London population that swelled the procession.

At last Whitehall received once more its
royal hereditary owner and his immediate
friends and officers of the household. Passing
through the chief noble gateway, they entered
the spacious precincts of the palace. A hundred
guns thundered the salute which greeted his
return, and the royal standard was unfolded and
proclaimed the welcome tidings.

While the lord-chamberlain and officers of
state in their royal costumes are falling on their
knees and raising their monarch's extended
hand to their lips, doing him a thousand
honours, which it would take a volume to
describe, we cannot but send our thoughts to
one whom we have met before, and who had but
a glimpse of the procession, in which there was
an unattached spectator very dear to her heart.

A window in one of those mansions to which
we have alluded, on the south side of the open
road called the Strand, commanded a view of
the whole scene of the royal procession, and at
that window a lady had been seated for hours.

During the preceding night the retrospect of
the recent events and the anticipation of the day
which we here commemorate had chased sleep
from the eyes of Lily Penderel. With the
sanction of her uncle Morton and her guardian,
Mr. St. Aubyn, and under the personal protection of the latter, she had taken a step on which
she had long resolved, but from which she had
as often withdrawn.

The exaggerated accounts of the assault on Lady Place, of the part which she, as a passive object of attraction, bore in the affair, and the whole of the information that Mr. Faircloth conveyed the next morning to his master, Lord Lovelace, had incurred the bitter resentment of her noble host, and threatened her with all those calamities from which she saw no escape short of her instant departure from the scene of her annoyance and the sphere of her senior guardian's influence. Accident had apprised her of deep designs against her person and her fortune. With Mr. St. Aubyn, therefore, she had repaired to London to consult with him and her uncle on her future destination.

That over-mastering energy of urgent exertion which carries woman through every emergency had now no more stimulus for Lily and therefore died. Her indignation, too, which urged her to action was passing away, so that a sense of solitude and desolation came over her spirit. During the short unavoidable absence of her two friends, she more especially felt the loneliness of her situation, and sighed for the presence of a third, dearer than either, of whom she had only caught one slight glimpse as the procession passed by. And the painful but necessary results of the resolution which she had put into practice, made her unhappy, before the peaceful effects of her independent position could be experienced. Many

of the vicissitudes of her life had been so crowded
into a few days, that they had almost overwhelmed her. Her sorrow was indeed great, for
it was unmixed with selfishness. Her grief was
for others—for the king, for her uncle, for St.
Aubyn, and even for Lord Lovelace, who at that
very moment was taking steps to make her a
ward under the crown of William, who she
believed would soon openly usurp the throne.
Nor through all the conflict of her emotions did
there mingle a single thought of the ruin which
the Revolution might bring upon herself. That
dull heaviness which denies the relief of tears,
depressed her naturally joyous, nay, buoyant
spirits. She had just gazed on all that pomp
and royal display which at a happier hour would
have filled her fancy with pleasant prophecies,
but from which she now drew only sad images.
For a moment her life seemed aimless, she had
no real object. Without her mind's consent, her
thoughts turned fondly to the interest of a dream :
the dream of love. But that had ended ere it
had well begun. To her the world and all its
pomps, London and its joyous pageant, with
the countless multitude which passed so near
her, seemed but a desert, and the most lonely
waste of the great wilderness. One only, lately,
truly loved, yet forbidden to share her heart
caught her eye, exchanged with her fond looks,
and was then swept away in the inevitable tide
which bore him from her.

In all that passing crowd, was there, she asked herself, one single heart, that loved her alone ; then she wished that she did not love or care for one.

Thus she sat in meditation, endeavouring to drive from her memory and her heart, the being of only a few days' acquaintance; and whom her faith, her own firm purpose, and circum- stances separated from her destiny for ever. Her reverie had been but too long unbroken ; for her maid Di, whom she had brought with her, enjoyed the scene so much, and, at least in imagination, so fondly exchanged a sign of re- cognition with Hubert, who seemed to her the handsomest fellow in the procession, that she was long before she interrupted her lady's train of thought. She came at length, as she said, to take her mistress's orders, but really to talk of the grandeur of the sight, and to see what effect the whole thing had on Miss Penderel's spirits. She hoped, she said, her mistress had enjoyed a good view.

" It was mighty fine," says she, " sublime like."

But a sorrowful look, was the lady's only reply.

" What makes you so uneasy ?" asked Di. " You are now as free as a bird—as rich as a queen—and your own mistress."

" Were I even all you mention, Diana, I should not be happy," answered Lily ; " but you cannot understand that. I hope you never may understand it as I do, my good girl."

" Oh, lord ! my goodness, ma'am !" said the faithful Di ; " what's the good in taking on so about anything ? It will all come right at last : mark my words !"

" God grant it !" answered Lily. " But go, my good girl, and let Mrs. Warner know that I expect Mr. Morton and her nephew, Mr. St. Aubyn, here this evening, or to-morrow early !"

Mrs. Warner was the lady of the mansion, and to her care Mr. St. Aubyn had committed his ward for the night.

The girl hastened to obey, and soon returned, and brought to her mistress a letter, which had just come to the hand of the venerable hostess from Mr. St. Aubyn. Lily eagerly opened it, looked over it, and said, " They will be here to-night. I will go and join Mrs. Warner below."

The old lady happened to be a Catholic, and therefore talked freely of the religious affairs of the nation to her young guest, whose appre- hensions she tenderly endeavoured to relieve. The time passed away more agreeably and lightly than Lily had expected.

There was much which she longed to say to some lady in whom she could confide. Madam Warner was of all others the very person with whom she was at home. That venerable lady sympathized with her feelings and treated her like her own grandchild. Such an evening of calm conversation she had not known for years —indeed, she could scarcely ever remember one.

The thickening shades of a December evening in London were now gathering over the Strand, and while the kind lady of the good old time cheered the fair stranger with her anecdotes of Worcester and all the associations of the Royal Oak, the forbidden object of Lily Penderel's interest had retired from the royal splendours of the crowded court, with Morton, Dryden, St. Aubyn, and Evelyn, to the sanctuary of quietness and repose which the picture-gallery in the Palace of Whitehall afforded.

This noble apartment was originally constructed for Prince Henry, eldest son of James I., by Inigo Jones, and completed under the auspices of the prince's brother, Charles I. The picture gallery of Whitehall was situated about the middle of the palace, running across from the Thames towards the banqueting house and fronting to the west the privy gardens.

It was resolved by the Parliament, during the civil war in 1645, that "all such pictures and statues at Whitehall as were without any superstition should be forthwith sold for the benefit of Ireland and the north, and all such pictures there as have representations of the second person in the Trinity or of the Virgin Mary should be forthwith burnt."

On his accession to the Protectorate, Cromwell re-purchased and restored many of those pictures. The collection at the date of our story had been enriched by choice gems, added by the genius of Lely and Kneller, and ranked among the first picture-galleries of Europe.

Here and there a lamp was already revealing the wondrous works of some great master, but the gallery as a whole was obscured in twilight gloom. The ranges of statues delighted Hough and transported him back to Athens and Rome. Among the pictures, too, there were a few that rivetted his classic attention. One a picture of Queen Dido's death. The unfortunate queen resting on a pile of wood, with a sword piercing through her body, looked upwards in agony. Æneas had left her—the barque in the distance was about to leave the shore. Dido's act of self-destruction was a striking subject for a picture. The expression of her beautiful face was triumphant in agony. As a school-boy of the present day would describe it—

When she found Æneas would not come,
She wept in silence, and was Di, do, dum!

Above one of the fire-places was a curious picture by Peter Lely of Dorothea Sidney, celebrated as we have before mentioned by Waller, as Sacharissa. This was the peculiar attraction for Evelyn, who in her, read, no doubt, the history of her great son, and admired her for the sake of her extraordinary beauty. Then,

as if in a monologue, he sighed, "How unworthy such a grandame, is that spendthrift,
silly Spenser!" Then turning to Pepys, who
was admiring the portraits of the most celebrated beauties of Charles II., he asked him
whether Sunderland had left the country, and
whether he was aware of his eldest son's ex-
ploits.

Pepys said he believed that Sunderland was
in Holland, and too much concerned for his
own future interests, to think much about his
son. Dryden, who had just entered from an
adjoining cabinet, with St. Aubyn, reminded
the party of Barillon's report of Sunderland
and his profligate son:—"Cela est regardé
comme une chose concertée entre milord
Sonderland et lui, ce qu'il y a de certaine c'est,
qu'il profitera auprès du roi, son maitre de
conversion de son fils."

Evelyn remarked that such an enlightened
statesman could not be sincere in submitting
his great intellect to the tyranny of Rome. St.
Aubyn mildly concurred with Barillon, and
feared that the conversion of the son was not
suggested by holier motives than those which
influenced the father.

Whereupon Evelyn declared that Sunderland
did not dance in a net, and that he would soon
return to the church of his baptism, using
the same arguments as any high church Protestant of the present day would urge.

"Those," cried he, "who are lured away from their father's church by the boasted profession that they will thus leave discord for unity, are the victims of the shallowest imposture. The differences which distract the English church are the mere differences of the mind of man, and must exist wherever free thought is not stamped to death by the foot of arrogant assumption. The policy of Rome may cover these differences under the cloak of authority, and throw around them such a halo of devotion, that they are lost in the cloud of sacred incense; but they are present beneath the veil, and woe to him who stumbles into the folds of that mist. He who quits the liberty of the English Communion for that rest which his weary spirit seeks, unless he can stoop to the supremacy of impostors requiring him to believe with equal faith the lying legends of saints, and the miracles of our Lord, will be miserably deceived. He shelters himself from the wind, and is tossed about by the whirlwind; or, in the words of the prophet, 'it will be to him as if a man did flee from a lion and a bear met him; or he went into the house, and leaned his head against the wall, and a serpent bit him.'"

"Or rather," said St. Aubyn, looking archly at Dryden, "as if running away from the panther a man should be met by the hind."

Evelyn, taking the allusion to Dryden's poem as a challenge, was just about to launch forth into a polemical discussion, when the sudden, unmeasured footsteps of a rough party, demanding, rather than craving admission to the palace, excited their fears, and brought them down stairs to examine the cause of alarm.

CHAPTER XXIX.

The higher guests approach a room of state,
Where tissued couches all around were set,
Labour'd with art; o'er ivory tables thrown,
Embroider'd carpets fell in folds adown.—*Henley.*

At the feast of the Centaurs they ate with one hand, and had their
drawn swords in the other.—*Clarendon.*

It was the arrival of a deputation from the
freebooters of Faversham that disturbed the
company in the picture gallery, unceremoniously
pressing forward for an audience with his
Majesty to crave his pardon for their late
outrage, and to proffer the restitution of the
gold of which they had rifled him. The good
disposition which the relenting ruffians evinced
towards James filled him with generosity; he
first of all formally received back his property,
and returned to the plunderers their receipt,—
looked sternly, but soon melting into his wonted
good nature, gave back the pelf, adding to it
ten guineas to drink his health. Strickland had
been summoned by his royal master to witness
this second act in the performance of his
Kentish acquaintances. It was with great
tact and difficulty that he could make them

desist from their boisterous loyalty and huzzas
in the sacred presence of the monarch. He
was assisted by O'Brian Clare who introduced
him to Hough, and thus they fell in with
Dryden's party.

Refreshed from bodily fatigue and sustained
by the apparent reaction in his favour, the king
prepared himself to hold his court, and to sup
as on grand occasions in full state.

The metropolis was already illuminated, the
streets and even the parks were lighted up with
brilliant bonfires, which now shed a glowing
influence around Whitehall.

Fires precipitated the king's flight ; and now,
the evening of his return is ushered in by fires.
To those who knew him best, particularly to
Hales, the outward unconcern which he put on
was but a thin mask for his heart's misgiving.
Not a week had passed since the roar of the
mighty multitude which now bellowed out his
welcome had stunned the monarch with their
thundering desecrations. Mischief was their
element, and love of change their impulse.
" Down with the tyrant !"—" Hurrah for the
king !" might be played on one and the same
instrument, differently tuned : all depended on
the skill of the master hand which touched the
chord. The masses themselves, like any other
machine, are religiously and politically set going
by the mainspring, unseen by the body whom
it regulates and directs ; the mere organ equally

unconscious of its object and the influence of its
moving power. The vox humana stop of the
organ this evening might be changed for the
trumpet sound of rebellion before to-morrow.
The red glare, the burning houses and churches,
made the dismal horrors of that awful night
which witnessed the sovereign's flight to him
more hideously distinct ; the black rolling
masses of smoke, shrouding from his view
the delight of his eyes, now lingered round
his vision and still haunted his thoughts. The
mad cheers that tore the very atmosphere and
rent the night air, were still to his fancy urging
on the mob ; their fiendish yells seemed to issue
from the ill-omened region of that darkness
which in a dense volume hung suspended over
the devoted temples and smouldering mansions.

An oppressive sensation had then overwhelmed his majesty and tinged his melancholy
mind with a touch of sad prophecy. The dis-
sonant sounds, like the exultations of demons,
had scarcely died away from his ears—the red
flames, which leaped and flashed towards the
sky, had hardly faded away from his sight—the
restless fire-flood once more arose to his imagination. Even while designing the banquet and
the great doings and sayings of the evening, on
which the royal existence of the king might
mainly depend, and with which, in the annals of
the country, it is intimately associated, his
stupified mind sat, as it were, a passive spec-

tator of the pageant and the scene; there was little or perhaps no active operation in his intellect, and no mental arrangement of his future plans. To him not only "sufficient unto the day was the evil thereof," but he was doing nothing to avert the coming calamity. He was leaving the event to God, but was doing nothing for himself. In a word, Memory had usurped the throne of Hope.

Pepys and Lord Dartmouth stood by his majesty during the supper, which was worthy of the most palmy prosperity in Whitehall.

"He told me," says Lord Dartmouth, "all that had happened to him at Faversham with as much unconcernedness as if they had been the adventures of some other person, and directed a great deal of his discourse to me."

To Pepys the king turned familiarly, and drawing from his robes his portrait, he presented it to the secretary of the admiralty, saying, "I was sitting for this picture for you when I first heard of the landing of the invader upon our shores. I ordered the painter to finish it before I stirred, and here it is, my colleague and assistant in all naval improvements. Keep it, and value it for the sake of your Sovereign and your friend."

We are not aware that Evelyn himself has left us a record of what part he took at this splendid entertainment, or whether he cared to claim acquaintance with Pepys; but we know that he liked good suppers as well as good dinners, and good society better, if possible, than both. Pepys had struggled uphill by the dusty, hard roadside of life. The other was born in the sphere of life which he so gracefully adorned. Evelyn might have been more at home; his contemporary felt himself a greater man : both were in their element. On the one, the effect of rank and state was too legitimate to be apparent; on the other, the consciousness of earned distinction and rewarded worth, especially when conversing with his Majesty, spoke in the secretary's countenance, and inspired him with self-possession and self-respect. Among the numerous and conflicting candidates for royal favour, none, perhaps, was more devoted to the good of his country than Pepys ; than Dryden, there was not one more sincerely disinterested in his policy, and more constant to the faith to which the convictions of his heart had turned him. The rest of our little party, though personally attached to James, were as independent of court favour as they were loyal. To Mr. Hough, as well as many others who found admission into the palace, the grandeur of the court was dazzling. The impression naturally made on the mind of an inexperienced youth by the magnificence of the scene was deep and vivid. The splendid apartments through which he passed, the gorgeous apparel of the grooms in waiting, the rich uniform of the guards, the

glittering livery of the domestics, but above all
the imposing ceremonial which met him at every
step, was almost alarming to one who went
through such forms for the first time. As for
Strickland and O'Brian, they had been admitted
even into the ante-chamber of the presence
court in right of the posts they held in the
household, and by the particular grant of the
king; though O'Brian, whenever he had an
opportunity, preferred his place in the guards on
duty. To save his young Oxford friend from
any embarrassment he supplied him with the
necessary passwords to the warders, ushers,
and men in waiting, or whatever these gentlemen
were called, so that he went on without interrup-
tion. It was in this manner, as he was passing
through one of the ante-rooms, filled with the
attendants of the court and their acquaintances,
that he fell in with O'Brian redeeming his
promise to the deputy doctor of the king, to
whom, no doubt, he imparted the " ulterior result " of the contrivance.

To James the deliberations of his statesmen
seemed as desultory and unstable as his own
purpose was undecided. Utterly exhausted by
the contending emotions which he had laboured
to reconcile or to suppress; and surprised by
the revulsion in the minds of the populace, he
could, as the evening advanced, say but little,
and do less. " Such devotion," cried he, at
length, with great effort and feeling, " as I have

this day experienced, and the affectionate
loyalty of the friends whom I once more see
around me, compensate me for the treachery of
some men, and the enmity of others." The
natural tenderness of the man was too much for
the severe dignity of the monarch. His feelings
of gratitude were mingled with an indefinable
presentiment of evil.

An indication of his Majesty's desire to seek
quietness and rest soon cleared the palace of all
who were not immediately attached to the household. The glorious gallery, or chief saloon,
soon ceased to blaze with its brilliant lights,
multiplied by reflecting mirrors ; the choice
paintings and delicate tracery in panelled oak
were indistinct ; the beautiful frescoes of the
ceiling no longer glowed in splendour ; and the
statues, now cast in deeper shade, looked like
the living dead,—one by one these pale images
of mortality came within the melancholy influence of the lingering lamps ; each marble
figure wore a more ghastly hue and more dismal
brow than that which first so sadly met the eye.
The cold groups of carved marble seemed ready
to start from their pedestals into awful if not
living reality.

Attended by Lord Mulgrave and Sir Edward
Hales, his Majesty was retiring to his chamber,
when at the foot of the staircase which he was
about to ascend, the apparition of a huge staghound drabbled with mud and lank from hunger

arrested the monarch's startled eye. The place, the hour, the sad thoughts which were sinking on his heart, all conspired to call up wild and goblin shapes on every side, peopling the shadowy space with flickering spectres, and to his fancy metamorphosed the poor weary animal before him into a spectre dog. Mulgrave also seemed of the same opinion, for he declared that no such creature belonged to the canine establishment of Whitehall. Strickland, who was close at hand, perceiving that there was something wrong, approached the king with profound silence and respect, until accosted by James when he answered, "May it please your Majesty, it is only Topham that defended Sir Edward Hales so loyally at Faversham."

" It by no means pleases us, Mr. Strickland," answered the king, severely, "to be dogged by Topham."

Strickland, in order to convince his Majesty that there was nothing to fear, called out in his most sporting tone, " Here boy! Topham." The only reply was a low savage growl, curling up his nose, and gathering up his lips into a grin from over his teeth, which were as white as they were sharp, he let the cornet see what a powerful friend or foe he might prove himself.

Observing with pain the annoyance of the king, Hales, who had experienced the timely protection and friendship of the noble animal, at the Hotel of Edwards, fearlessly advanced

to the surly brute, saying, "Good dog." Attracted by the gesture, but still more by the
voice of Hales, the poor hound crouched at his
feet—rose—fawned upon him—wagged his tail
—then licked his hands, and pressed his fine
noble head against them. Hales evinced great
emotion—shrunk from the dog's caresses for a
moment, recollected himself, then exclaimed
"Lion!" The magic name brought the dog's
head close to that of his master, for such Hales
really was. The ecstasy of the half-famished
staghound knew no bounds. The mutual confidence and recognition of the baronet and his
long-lost dog was even affecting. The faithful
animal raised his noble head and lofty crest,
and looking up into the face of his owner, as
much as to say, "What can I again do for you
to prove my attachment to so good a master?"
kept his speaking eye still upon Sir Edward.

"Alas!" sighed the astonished monarch,
"the love and faithfulness which this poor dog
has displayed so sagaciously is of a higher quality
than that which many of my professing followers
and statesmen have evinced towards their master
and their monarch—but, after all, there is one
loyal, if not Catholic dog, to defend us. Let the
poor fellow that is sharing our hardships enjoy
our good cheer. Let him be fed and cared for,"
said his majesty, as he closed his chamber door
upon himself, as he thought for the night.

While the dog was bolting down his delicious

meal, Hales explained to Strickland that amid
the confusion of the scenes which had taken
place at his country residence and during his
absence from home, Lion had been missed—that
the robbers of the deer park had probably
enticed him away to avoid his attacks. In the
hurry and confusion at Faversham he did not
recollect the dog. It seemed certain that the
instinct of the animal had led him to London—
probably in the company of the ruffian who had
stolen him, and from whom he had no doubt
made his escape on his arrival in the metropolis.
Lion resisted every attempt to separate him
from his recovered master, and whining and
pawing, licking his hands and rubbing against
him, slept at the bed-room door of Hales.

All at length separated for the night and
betook themselves to sleep. We must not,
however, limit our view entirely to one side of
the picture; we shall, therefore, during the lull
at Whitehall, change the scene and introduce
the statesmen of a rival court.

CHAPTER XXX.

Thy forests, Windsor! and thy green retreats,
At once the monarch's and the muse's seats;
Here hills and vales, the woodland and the plain,
Here earth and water seem to strive again.—*Ode to Windsor.*

Well had he learned to curb the crowd,
By arts that veil, and oft preserve the proud.—*Byron.*

ON a gloomy evening in December sat William and his Court elect in Windsor Castle.

It was then, and is still, a proud old pile; full of poetical interests and storied romance. Time, which spares the more material memorials of man's little greatness, has matured and immortalised the local scenes of Windsor, and hallowed its retreats.

While the illustrious deeds of the warrior and the everchanging laws of the legislator are obliterated by the ceaseless wave of time, the unfading flowers, and the sweet undying spirit of the song of poetry breathe their fragrance and their melody along our daily paths—above our heads, amid our earthly pilgrimage, and soothe our sorrows.

Centuries have gone by, and many records of Windsor's antiquity have been swept away; yet there the gardens continue to flourish; many

T 2

shrubs and flowers in perennial and hereditary succession live on, and on for ever. And what though modern walls now sever kindred spots inseparable in recollection, yet still are there living arbours, sequestered shades, and secluded walks. As sheltered and retired are they now as they were four hundred years ago. Its sylvan situation and pleasant retreat have made Windsor a favourite residence of our monarchs from the time of William the Conqueror.

Charles II. confirmed the inhabitants in their former privileges. Some restrictions had, however, been imposed upon them a little previously to the period of our tale; but at the Revolution, the original provisions of the charter were taken under consideration, and have since that time remained unaltered.

The noble avenue, which only ages could produce, is nearly three miles in length, shaded by a double row of lofty elms at each side. The grand Town-hall had only been erected two years before the events which we commemorate. Among the portraits which adorn the hall are those of James II. and William III.

Soon after the Restoration Charles II. adopted Windsor Castle as his favourite residence, and commenced a series of alterations.

Between the two wards of the Castle stands the Keep, or round tower, which is built on the summit of a lofty artificial mound.

The Long Parliament and Oliver Cromwell

frequently confined several of the Royalist party within these walls. Here the Earls of Lindsay and Lauderdale suffered captivity for several years, and were not liberated till the Restoration. Twelve counties are said to be visible from one of the battlements.

The sun was going down in clouds, and seemed to mourn the sad necessities of the times; yet sweet and soothing to the anxious traveller was this hour of calm, amid the dim and solitary shade. The mute and melancholy footfalls of evening—the thickening darkness brooding over the woods—all outside was throwing the magic of romance, of sylvan solemnity about the old, old castle keep. It stands on a mound, as we have observed, which lifts it above other parts of the building; just as the ascent of public opinion had lifted the Prince of Orange above the king, James II.

The entire majestic edifice, even stript of its romantic associations, in the sylvan twilight was impressive and grand. There it stood raising its irregular walls and massive towers, a crown of adamant encircling the brow of an elevated ridge, hoisting its dubious and wavering banner in the dusky clouds, as expressive of the still undecided fortunes of its august and thoughtful inmate. The castle looked down with the air of an hereditary monarch upon the leafless woods; and the short-lived glories of the surrounding world.

As the intelligence of the capture of his son, afterwards James I. of Scotland, broke the heart of Robert III., when he heard of the young prince's imprisonment in the grey Round Tower of Windsor, by Henry IV. of England, so now, though not so fatally, the news of William's unwarrantable confinement of Lord Feversham, in that same keep, overwhelmed our unhappy sovereign, James II., with grief; for the arrest of the commander of his forces convinced him of what he ought to have understood long before from the very conduct and counsel of the surprised captive himself,—that William was already acting as King of England, invested only with that authority by foreign troops and English deserters.

The language of the letter, and of its bearer, Zulestein, which we have already noticed, was quite enough to show that William was assuming the supremacy of a conqueror; and no longer, even in semblance, treated his uncle as the sovereign. And one only wonders how, under all the circumstances, James could have been sufficiently master of himself to hold a court, meet his ministers in counsel, and sup in public state. While we contemplate for a moment the outside of the old grey tower which has stood the brunt of ages, our thoughts flow backwards and forwards with a natural and touching pathos, and are, perhaps, tinged with a hue of greater romance by the solemnity of the dark winter woods and the harmony of the dying year than by the trains of poetical recollections which the history of Windsor awakes. However this may be, such thoughts contrast strongly with the scene within those ancient walls.

It was twilight : in a state chamber, decorated for the occasion, sat the Prince of Orange, surrounded by an ostentatious display of regal pomp, for which he usually affected indifference, or even contempt. He was attended by his confidential servants, Schomberg, Sidney, Bentinck, who remained near his person ; while, at a greater distance, were Lord Halifax, perhaps Godolphin, and a host of expectant traitors.

William was dressed in a military costume, studiously fashioned to conceal the defects of his person. He was under the middle stature, slight, round shouldered, singularly awkward and shuffling in his gait, sharp visaged, stern browed and eagle nosed. He was of all men the most thick-skinned and reserved. His eyes were sharp and keen, but like his words, unexpressive of his meaning. They shed almost an unnatural light, over a cold stony face, and impassive countenance. He was son of William II., of the house of Orange, and of Mary Stuart, daughter of Charles I. Having under many advantages attained to distinguished manhood, he took the field, against the vast armies of France, and forced them to retire. Raised to the dignity of Stadholder of Holland,

William in a short time compelled France
and England to conclude a peace with the
States. He visited the English court, afterwards
espoused the Princess Mary, eldest daughter of
James, then Duke of York. From the moment
of this marriage, he designed his own ascent
to, and the exclusion of his father-in-law from
the throne of England.

Being well aware of his conduct and bravery
in Holland, Sweden, and France, the Prince of
Orange had invited his present companion,
Marshal Armand de Schomberg to join him in
his expedition to England. Not open battle, but
cunning intrigue, was the game of these two
great generals; now surrounded by the nobles
who had deserted from James.

When Feversham arrived, he found the prince
and his advisers perfectly confounded. It was
on the assumption that James had left the
kingdom that William had assumed the supremacy, and issued orders to the royal army and
the officers of government in the style of a
victorious potentate; and, as Lingard says, they
had parcelled out among themselves the great
offices of state and the rewards to which they
were entitled for their services. In Feversham
the prince saw a formidable and powerful enemy
—in his person as commander-in-chief was
centred the strength of England's lawful king.
The message he bore to William was only less
stunning than the impertinent order of William,

through Zulestein, to James. Besides he never forgave the loyalist for disbanding the royal troops, which might have been organized as they were, and transferred to the invader.

To the general reader it may not be irksome to give him a brief account of the man on whose liberty of action the fortunes of either potentate were suspended—the accredited messenger on an embassy of peace.

The army, by detachments from Ireland and Scotland, had been raised to 40,000 men. The command was taken by Lord Feversham, aided by his brother the Count de Roye, against the Duke of Monmouth. The Count de Roye was an officer of greater talent and longer experience to whom, as we have before noticed, on the tenth of this month King James, before he retired to rest, handed a letter for his brother Lord Feversham. Lewis de Duras, Earl of Feversham, was a native of France, and the son of the Duke de Duras, and brother of the Duke de Lorge. His mother was a member of the noble house of Bouillon, and sister of the great Turenne. At the Restoration he bore the French title of Marquis of Blancfort, and accompanied Charles II. to England. Having married Mary, eldest daughter of Sir George Sondes, of Lees Court, Kent, created Earl of Feversham, the same title was conferred on the Marquis of Blancfort on the death of his father-in-law. This was the man who defeated the Duke of

Monmouth, and who, had he been allowed fair play, would have utterly vanquished and repulsed William.

Such a staunch adherent to the royal cause, therefore, it was the interest of William to throw into a dungeon. But whatever was •the motive of the Prince, according to the testimony of Clarendon, Barillon, and Lingard, the arrest of the commander shook the confidence even of the adherents of William.

No sooner had Feversham respectfully delivered the message with which he was charged, in the spirit of a courtier as well as of a general, and was taking his departure, than to his horror and disgust, he found the passage through which he had approached the Prince occupied by a Dutch guard. One of whom, stepping up to him, said coolly, " I am quite sorry to interrupt you, my lord; but I must see your passport."

" Surely no such credential could be expected by the Prince of Orange from the King of England," answered the commander-in-chief.

" Your pardon, my lord, but the prince has commanded me to place this paper in your hands."

Feversham glanced his eye over the paper. "I see it all," says the ill-used officer, contemptuously; " I am your prisoner, and must submit."

He was, in violation of the law of nations,

conducted to the keep associated with such romantic memories.

Bentinck was the first to remonstrate gently against this measure.

" What think you, who are my countrymen, of the prince ?" asked Clarendon, timidly.

" Alas ! my lord," said Halifax, with a shrug, " this proceeding startles me."

The English deserters and traitorous noblemen and ministers who were present began to feel very uneasy with their new patron.

" We sent for the prince," observed Churchill, aside to Halifax, " to protect our liberties, and the very first use he makes of his power is to imprison a peer of the realm, without any adequate cause, or even the form of any legal proceeding."

" He is not quite so prompt," cried Cornbury, " in assigning to each of us the precise reward to which we are entitled by our services."

" And yet," exclaimed Trelawny, " he acts as if he were sure of success."

Of all the party, Bentinck seemed the most composed, and exhibited no expression of annoyance ; his phlegmatic disposition, or intimate knowledge of his master's cunning policy, assured him of its success and satisfied his mind.

" Do you not perceive," cried Sidney, addressing his countrymen generally, " that this bold stroke will stun chickenhearted Jimmy out of his senses, and frighten him out of his kingdom? He will thus play the game into our own hands."

Schomberg exchanged some words with the prince, which did not reach the ears of the assembly.

"Without a free parliament," said the Prince, "the king can now do nothing;—a parliament of any sort he cannot have while he feels the force of our arms. We shall be able at this rate of proceeding to return half the members ourselves."

Churchill, as if to gain ground in the estimation of Marshal Schomberg, said gruffly, "His Mightiness has no greater opponents in England than the prisoner Feversham and his brother De Roye, nor any so competent to give advice concerning the army."

Major-general Keith and Colonel Trelawney confirmed this observation. "Yes, may it please Your Mightiness," said Keith, "had it not been for Feversham and Roye, James Stuart would not have been in your way at Whitehall this night."

"And though Keith is too modest to acknowledge his merits," says the Duke of Grafton, "he was arrested on suspicion by your guest Lord Feversham."

"Every dog has his day," cried the reckless Sidney.

"If such merits are the test of true worth," said Schomberg dryly, and looking as cool as a cucumber, " what must be the prize in store for the gallant lieutenant-general, who has sacrificed his colours, and secured to our interests Prince George of Denmark and his royal Princess Anne ?"

" To effect the deposition of the king, if he will not of his own accord abdicate, your Highness has only to call a legal parliament of your own," said Halifax blandly to the prince.

William, without addressing any individual in particular, regretted the king's return to Whitehall ; and added that he would gladly avail himself of any delicate suggestion, with reference to the royal person, which the statesmen present might desire to make privately. He listened to what each had to say with great consideration, as if everything depended upon it, then followed his own counsel, probably the result of the conflicting opinions. He concurred really in no measure: but resolved to work on the king's fears of death, or what he dreaded more, imprisonment ; and thus to banish him from England : so that the cunning invader might represent the escape of the king as his own voluntary act—in short, abdication.

Clarendon, so far as he dared to presume, said that the difficulties which James had brought upon himself, and the chastisement which he had already received, might call forth all his good qualities, or even create them ; and at the worst restrain his encouragement of Popery.

"I believe the love of liberty," said William, as a passing remark, "is innate in these men who, in communion with and like all protestants, possess it, but that the willing slave will never be taught to appreciate freedom."

"Step by step the people's liberties have been taken from them, and when a monarch, as James, has done away with the legitimate means of moral resistance in the senate," cried Halifax, with energy, "he flings them back on their only resource—physical force. To this force we are now reduced."

"It appears to me, gentlemen," said Schomberg, "that the right of resistance cannot be established till the voice of the people decides that their liberties can only be secured by an appeal to arms."

"Or in other words," said Churchill, "resistance is only justified by a certain prospect of success."

"Not exactly so," said the Marshal, "for seldom or ever is the numerical majority of a people successful in maintaining their rights or repelling their enemy—all the great revolutions in the world have been effected by individuals."

"Just so," said Halifax. "The masses are the tools with which the political tradesman works, and unless they be skilfully handled they will cut his hands, or their power may be worse than useless."

Then followed a desultory conversation on

the subject of political affairs, not very interesting to the general reader.   At the close of which Halifax spoke to the following effect: Assuming the powers of parliament, dispensing with constitutional authority, reposing in divine rights, James has forfeited his crowns.   The popular leaders had then only to ascertain the amount of foreign support on which they might rely. The voice of the people is omnipotent, and it has been heard.   The avowed intention, however now, it may be modified or denied; to monopolise the prerogative of the parliament, is a breach of contract between the monarch and the people.

"His attempts to corrupt our representation and to stifle the voice of freedom," cried Sidney, "have cancelled his title to the throne.   These are the acts," cried he, more impetuously, "which call for resistance; nay, more, such are the offences which cry for vengeance: offences, far less than these, have, in my opinion, brought a king's head to the scaffold, and may again cry for the blood of the tyrant who has dared to touch our charters, the great seals to Magna Charta—the guarantees of our freedom and our strength."

William smiled, so far as it were possible for his cold immoveable face to smile, and said, "Colonel Sidney displays his sentiments; not to conceal them from ourselves and our friends is, perhaps, at this crisis enough.   Everyone that loves liberty will range himself on our side. On the other hand, that the unhappy and misguided king still has a will of his own, and that an obstinate one, is certain. I will, therefore, despatch to him, with your concurrence and co-operation, my lords and gentlemen, a message which will bring him to a better state of mind, and prevent those dreadful consequences to which our friend, Colonel Sidney, has but too boldly challenged our attention. Your counsel in this emergency, my noble friends," continued William, thoughtfully, " affords me every advantage, and is worthy of our grave consideration," fixing, while he spoke, his searching eye on the men whom in his heart he despised ; then, making one of his well known signs to Count Solms, he retired with him to the recess of a window. Slowly, and inaudibly to the noble deserters, he said, " Count, we understand each other. Get four battalions of our Dutch guards and a squadron of horse in readiness ; you will march them into Westminster and co-operate with the trustworthy statesmen, the quondam servants of the late king, and watch their movements closely. Get the men under arms, and lose not a moment."

No sooner had Solms left the chamber, to put the order in execution, than the Prince entered into conversation with the English noblemen, but addressed himself particularly to Halifax, of whose faithfulness to either party he doubted.

He reminded that nobleman of his unbounded confidence in his judgment and integrity. " To prove my reliance on you," said the Prince, " I dispatch you in close concert with Lords Shrewsbury and Delamere to Sion House, where you will find further orders." William was absolute for their departure, for he suspected the sincerity of Halifax's conversion, as he had done Clarendon's, and desired proof of his devotion.

The question which Clarendon had proposed on a former occasion, was now again renewed by that nobleman in the presence of the prince. He asked Churchill and Halifax to obtain better terms for the king. " Might not King James," asked his relenting brother-in-law, " be escorted to one of his own palaces ?"

" The king !" exclaimed Delamere, asking with his eyes for an approving glance from his new master, " we no longer look upon him as a king."

"He is the late king," cried Sydney, " and no more ; he is royally and politically dead."

" What business," resumed Delamere, still anxious for approval from one master, at the sacrifice of the other, " has the self-deposed and abdicating king in any of the royal dwellings, as if he were a king ? For my own part," cried he, in a voice which made the ancient hall re-echo the declaration, " James Stuart shall never more by me be obeyed as a king."

So reiterated the fears of the rest of the

English State deserters; but so re-echoed not their hearts.

The noble triumviri departed on their honourable mission. The sounds of their retreating footsteps along the echoing corridor were welcome music to the ear of their silently exulting master; but to the English noble patriots left behind them, the death knell of their independence.

The Windsor Conference is ended; its object is attained. The scene which exhibits the invader to our view, and connects him with our story, has come to a close. The curtain falls— the private play of the actors is concealed from our sight.

CHAPTER XXXI.

Full many a storm on this grey head has beat;
And now on my high station do I stand,
Like the tired watchman in his air-rock'd tower,
Who looketh for the hour of his release,
I'm sick of worldly broils, and fain would rest
With those who war no more.—*Johanna Baillie.*

THE next morning the king sent a message to
Stamps and Lewis, two of the aldermen, that
convinced them and all of his sincerity. He
was willing, he said, if the civic authorities
would guarantee his personal safety, to place
himself in their hands, till full security for the
religion and liberties of the nation had been
established by Parliament.

" Had the offer been accepted," says Lingard,
" it would have thrown a most perplexing obstacle
in the way of the prince." It was, however,
declined, through the influence of Sir Robert
Clayton. In the meantime no answer had been
returned to the king's message by Zulestein;
but the only outrage that elicited an expression
of anger from the king was the imprisonment
of his accredited ambassador, Lord Feversham.
He indignantly demanded his release, but without any practical result. Were anything

U 2

wanting to show the reckless improvidence of James at this extremity, it would be his destitution of ready money, on which his own personal safety might depend. It is, indeed, within the field of probability that a regard for the integrity of the purse removed from the royal presence not a few of the courtiers of yesterday. In the hour of his greatest need, two noble and generous-hearted Scotch adherents, Colin, Earl of Balcarres, and the gallant Viscount Dundee presented themselves with offers of service from his privy council in Scotland. They were affectionately received by the king, but seemed concerned that none were with him but some of the gentlemen of the bedchamber. Scarcely had they made their loyal announcement to the king, than one of the generals of the disbanded army entered the presence chamber, and, after the first loyal greetings, assured his Majesty that the most efficient part of the disbanded army was either in London or near it, and only waited the sound of the royal drum to rally round their sovereign to the number of 20,000 men. " With your Majesty's command, we can get the men together before the close of the day."

" I know you to be my sincere friend," said the king, " but the men who sent you are not so, and I expect nothing from them. It is a fine day, my lords," said the king, turning to to the noblemen ; " let us walk ; and, attended by none but these two faithful adherents, he was soon with them on the Mall.

For some time he was silent and abstracted; then stopping suddenly, as if some new thought had come to his relief, he exclaimed, "How is it, my dear lords, that you are with me, when all the world, even my own children, have forsaken me, and gone to the Prince of Orange?"

"We have nothing to do with the Prince of Orange," cried Colin; "our fidelity to our own royal master is unshaken by the treachery of others."

"Will you then," sobbed the king, "as two gentlemen, give me your hands upon it?"

"We will before God," answered they, falling on their knees, and respectfully extending their hands to his Majesty, who grasped them in his own.

"Well then," said he, "you are the men I always took you to be. From you, at least, I will not conceal my intentions. In England, I can only be a cipher, or a prisoner to the Prince of Orange; and you know there is but a step between the prison and the grave of a king; the dungeon and the scaffold are in store for me here—the fate of my royal father. William is preparing both. I go, therefore, to France. You, Lord Balcarres, shall have a commission to manage my civil affairs; and you, Lord Dundee, to command my troops in Scotland. I think it unwise," resumed the king, "to incur any present danger, which might prevent my effecting my object. My people have been imposed upon by the specious pretence of religion and property." Then he ran on—"And I appeal to all men, who have had experience, whether anything can make this nation so great and flourishing as liberty of conscience? Some of our neighbours dread it, but sooner or later it will pervade England. I could say much more, and confirm it, but now is not the proper time."

"No man," answered the Viscount, "should be persecuted for his religion."

"Nor, indeed, for attacks upon the popular faith," said James.

"If religion," cried Colin, "be, as I believe it, true, it has nothing to fear from any such assaults."

"Just so," says James; "it may be injured, but can never be destroyed by secular interference. Truth is mighty, and will eventually prevail. Whether in England, Ireland, or Scotland, I would put all on the same footing. An attempt to put down a creed by the secular arm of the law is an argument in favour of the persecuted religion."

"Force," said the Viscount, "may make a man a hypocrite, but never a sincere believer."

A Scotch colonel here joined the little party, and heartily congratulated the king and his two countrymen on the universal joy of the city at the king's return ; he also reiterated the assurance of the general of the disbanded forces.

" I am aware of your honour and noble conduct, Colonel Gordon," said the king; "if my knowledge of your family is correct, you are descended through the female line from Robert II. of Scotland, and by the male side from the Duke of Gordon, through the great Duke's son, Captain Gordon, who married the heiress of Abergeldie. You demand our attention."

By the law of the narrative the persons first introduced only re-appear when the course of events bring them to our view and disappear when they have no immediate connection with the circumstances detailed. Each expresses his own sentiments independently of any other, and the political and religious opinions, nay, even the representation of facts in the mouth of one party differ materially from that of the other, as the conflicting historians of the period, or the various portraits of the same original accord to the colouring of the hand which drew the picture.

The character of William, for instance, is lauded by his admirers, while it is portrayed by others with the darkest shades which can blacken humanity.

According to Sir W. Temple, he was silent and thoughtful, given to hear and to inquire; of a sound understanding ; of much firmness in what he once resolves or once denies: with this testimony many entirely concur; but that he was a prince of many virtues, without any appearing or mixture of vice, few impartial writers, perhaps, will grant.

The union of the Whigs, which placed the Prince of Orange at the head of the party opposed to the Court, gave authority to the representations of Colonel Sydney and the testimony of Doctor Gilbert Burnet, which the successful event of their endeavours allowed them to reiterate and to strengthen. On the other hand William's artful conduct and affected zeal for the Protestant religion, as by law established, of which he was not himself even a member; his cunning fomentation of disagreement between the States and James; and his treachery to him, his uncle and father-in-law, can be denied by none. Of all the great men whom the world ever produced and magnified into a demigod, William was the most unamiable. In his diminutive form there resided a master mind. His eagle countenance spoke of aspirations to a lofty height, and in spite of his ungainly figure, he was formed to command. His Court at . the Hague is said to have rivalled that of Whitehall in licentiousness. "Neither in great things nor small," says the Duchess of Marlborough, "had he the manners of a gentleman." He was a deep drinker, a deep gamer, illiterate and silent.

Before we return to the king at Whitehall, there is only one person more whom we need notice.

Churchill, the celebrated Duke of Marlborough, was the second son of Sir Winstone Churchill, of high Tory principles, who was devoted to Charles I. Soon after the Restoration, his son at the age of twelve was removed from St. Paul's school, and made page of honour to the Duke of York; next, he was made an ensign in the foot guards. He first fought against the Moors, and further perfected himself in the art of war, under the celebrated Marshal Turenne, in the early part of the Dutch invasion, when Charles II. had been induced to lend support to Louis. When very young he married the beautiful Sarah Jennings, who had been brought up with and afterwards appointed maid of honour to the Princess Anne. On the accession of James II. to the throne, he was raised to the peerage, and subsequently, for his services at the time of the Duke of Monmouth's rebellion, rewarded with a colonelcy of a troop of horse guards. That he continued, up to the very time of his joining the Prince of Orange to retain the king's confidence and regard, appears undoubted by any party. That Churchill's conduct on this occasion "was dictated by a sense of duty above every temporal and selfish object" an Oxford writer of the present day is willing to hope. Charity surely could go no further. Surely Churchill should have been off with "the old love before he was on with the new." He should in common honesty have resigned his place near

the king, and openly have followed the fortunes
of his new master! Where was his honour?
The influence which the Churchills exercised
over the minds of the Princess Anne of Denmark
and her comfortable spouse, " Est il possible,"
was supreme. Churchill's previous engagements,
eighteen months before the date of our tale, to
the Prince of Orange; his perfidious designs
towards James, and his power in the battle field,
exhibit him most prominently to our notice, not
only, however, as a politician, but as a commander, whose victories extend over three reigns,
and cover England with glories and himself with
laurels, such as no commander-in-chief had worn
since the days of Agincourt. The military
renown which crowned him with the Dukedom
of Marlborough, was the highest military honour
which had been attained by any British subject.

Doubtless the loss and hostility of such a
commander and the imprisonment of his most
intimate General, Feversham, must have deeply
affected the king's mind, and suggested that
decision of present despair, which he had just
communicated to his Scotch friends. In them
he had the most unreserved confidence, and it
was not misplaced ; for Scotland, amid the
Highland clans, still grasped the standard of
King James, and evinced the brave spirit of
that very noble Dundee, who comforted the
forsaken king, and who soon after at the moment
of victory fell in the pass of Killicrankie. As

for Ireland, she neither desired nor recognised the new dynasty. In Irishmen was the monarch's strength, and of them none did it delight him to honour more than O'Brian Clare and his dashing son, whose fiery spirit chafed at the king's forbearance and inaction.

After his walk with his noble Scotch friends, James took it into his head to devote a part of this, his last day of regal sway in England, to the ceremony of "touching for the evil." To obtain the pieces of gold indispensable to the display of the "divine right," and which must be bound round the arm of the patient by the sovereign, was his difficulty, which Lord Godolphin goodnaturedly removed by lending the king one hundred guineas for the purpose. This generous act seems to throw a doubt on the presence of Lord Godolphin at Windsor later in the day. Such an occupation at such a time seems very strange, and whether it proceeded from charity or the last lingering wish to exercise the royal privilege we know not.

To his religious convictions, miracles of mercy or of power had been by no means limited to the days of the Apostles. In his estimation the Church, in priority of time, came before the Bible, and in authority, informed and guided by the same infallible spirit, was not less truly the voice and power of the eternal God. To tell him that miracles did not exist in his time was assumption. His religious sentiments, too, were deeply tinged with recollections of Edward the Confessor, whose coronation service had crowned him.

The patient's faith in the health giving cross, or holy well, to which he resorts for recovery, is his cure. His belief in the virtues of his medicine and the skill of his physician, whether of a spiritual or material character, is the healer of maladies. Recourse to such gifts of healing and miraculous remedies only ceases with the belief in their efficacy.

Late in the evening of this day Solms, in execution of the order recorded in the last chapter, which he had received at Windsor, arrived in London, occupied the palace of St. James's, and was advancing at the head of three battalions, with their matches lighted, and in order of battle, to demand possession of White- hall. The Coldstream Guards were on duty at the palace, under the command of William Earl of Craven, an aged man, who more than fifty years before had distinguished himself in war and in love. To lead a forlorn hope, and cap- tivate a lady's heart, had been to him equal triumphs. He is said to have won from a thousand rivals the heart of the unfortunate Queen of Bohemia. Craven was now in his eightieth year, but time had not tamed his manly spirit. His courage and his loyalty were aroused to action.

That night the poor king was about to retire

to bed, in his own royal house, when Lord Craven approached him with the usual ceremony, saying, "It is my painful duty—a duty which I never thought I should live to fulfil—to apprise your Majesty that the Dutch guards, horse and foot, are marching through the park in complete order of battle to take possession of your ancestral palace of Whitehall. But never, my liege," cried the old man, rising to an upright posture, and colouring with indignation, "never, sire, so long as breath remains in my body, shall a foreign force of Dutch dogs make the king of England prisoner in his own palace."

James hesitated to reply; but after a moment's reflection, with deep feeling, thus remonstrated; "Our resistance against such superior numbers can only lead to bloodshed as unnecessary as it must be unavailing."

The old hero, with tears on the brink of his eyelids, supplicated the king,—"May it please your Majesty, do not command me to desist; my sword will not rest in its scabbard here." The soldier's hand involuntarily grasped the hilt of his sword, and he was taking a solemn oath to repulse the insolent usurper or die, when the king, affectionately putting his hand on his shoulder, soothed the rising resentment of his ancient soldier.

"Forbear, my dear and faithful old friend," said the sovereign, "I entreat,—nay, I command you." At this instant the door opened, young Clare entered, and, falling at his Majesty's feet, declared the Dutch troops were close at hand, and the king's guards were only waiting for their commander to give the word. " What may I do for your Majesty before the engagement ?" cried the energetic guardsman.

" Summon Cornet Strickland to my presence," answered the king. In the meantime he held Craven by the arm, begging him to have patience. " There must be some mistake, which mutual forbearance will rectify," said James.

"Suffer us, my liege," besought the old veteran, " to be cut to pieces, and to die like men, rather than resign our posts around your Majesty, to the invader."

Before he could say more Strickland was in deep obeisance before the king.

" Go," says the king, " and summon Count Solms, the Dutch commander, to my presence."

This order allayed the impatience of Craven. No sooner had the Dutch commander made his appearance, than James, with great self-possession and dignity, said,

" Why surely, Count, there is some mistake. The Prince of Orange could not intend to order the King of England to surrender himself a prisoner, or resign his palace to your guards. Were not his orders for St. James's ?"

The count was silent, but with a profound bow produced his orders and authority to occupy the

palace of Whitehall. Craven cast a withering
look of defiance at Solms, and the king with
great difficulty restrained him from any word or
act of hostility.

" Withdraw your men, Lord Craven," was the
final command of the king. Nothing but loyalty
itself could have compelled the commander to
give way; and as for Clare, it was the discipline of the army and obedience to orders that
kept him from rushing single-handed upon the
Dutch. Indeed, the whole of the English guards
reluctantly gave place to the foreigners, by whom
they were superseded.

The king thus a prisoner in his own palace,
with a misboding mind retired to rest a little
before midnight. He felt as if he were a prophet
of evil to himself, to his family, and to his kingdom. His mournful mind foretold, that terrible
and troublous times were coming and that it
was his fate to bear a deep and painful part in
them. In his calamities he longed for the
counsel and support of his queen.

CHAPTER XXXII.

" The crowd are gone, the revellers at rest ;
    The courteous host, and all-approving guest,
    Again to that accustomed couch must creep,
    Where joy subsides, and sorrow sighs to sleep.
    Glad for awhile to heave unconscious breath,
    Yet wake to wrestle with the dread of death."--*Byron.*

THE excitement of the preceding day, with its momentary triumph and its pageant were gone ; the lassitude that succeeded was followed by lowness of fever, which the startling insolence of his nephew was exciting into an approach to delirium. It seemed to James as if his sun had set for ever.

Worn out by the fitful vicissitudes and almost sleepless vigils of the last dreadful week, he fell into a deep and heavy sleep, from which he was suddenly awakened by the Earl of Middleton.

His Majesty's dreams harmonized but too well with his melancholy thoughts, and with a violent effort he aroused himself. He felt that he was at home, but that home was in the hands of the enemy. In the confused alarm of the moment he could only fancy that he heard a noise, and was raising himself to listen, when the curtains were drawn back, as the Earl of

Middleton, kneeling by the king, presented himself with profound respect, saying, "I crave your pardon, my liege, for thus invading your repose ; but, alas ! necessity is my apology. I grieve to say that at this unreasonable hour, three lords, in the service of the Prince of Orange, demand an immediate audience with your Majesty."

"Their business must indeed be urgent to desecrate the sanctity of the hour and the privacy of our chamber," replied the king. "Methinks the dead of night is an unusual time for an audience ; but who may these courteous visitors be, and what is their nocturnal object ?"

"Your Majesty's commissioner, Lord Halifax, is one; the other two I cannot fully recognise, as they are muffled up ; but the second, by his voice, I take to be Lord Shrewsbury; who the third is I cannot even conjecture. I was disturbed," continued Lord Middleton, "by a loud, rude knocking at the door of the antechamber where I slept, to be in attendance on your Majesty ; they insisted on admittance to your royal presence."

From such a gross intrusion in the dead of the night, when suspicion itself had been hushed to sleep, it is probable that the king, forced from his death-like slumber, anticipated some darker design even than that of William and his commissioners.

The king's suspense would brook no delay. "Admit them," cried James, affecting a firmness which he successfully assumed.

The inner door opened: Lord Halifax, followed by two others, entered.

"Ah! my Lord Halifax," said the King, "to what generous purpose are we indebted for your loyal homage at the sacrifice of your comfort and repose, in the dead of winter and in the dead of night?"

"I am charged with a commission from the Prince of Orange, Sire," says the statesman.

"Your commissions do you an honour, which can only be exceeded by your gratitude, my lord," said the King. "Your distinguished negociations afford you a splendid opportunity of deceiving and betraying both parties who intrust you with their reciprocal interests; but," added James, with desperate bitterness, "you are, my lord, I perceive, accompanied by one of my open enemies, if not two, who will protect your new master from the intrigues of a false friend. There was a time, my lord, when you had more reason to dread the royal resentment."

"When I opposed the bill of exclusion?" said Halifax.

James interrupting him, replied, "That one redeeming measure, living in the grateful memory of your Sovereign, with your expressions of penitence for grievous sins against him, found pardon for you, Lord Halifax." Then before

Halifax could answer, turning to Lord Shrewsbury James said, " It is long, my lord, since you
have graced our Court with your presence, but at
length you return as a gentleman of our chamber ;
but we require not your attentions, since on your
return to England you must doubtless require
repose yourself. Would not the munificent offer
of your loyal sword and £40,000 on mortgage
purchase from his High Mightiness less servile
drudgery than this night's employment ?"

" I crave your Majesty's pardon," cried Halifax, impatiently, " but the prince's message
admits of no delay. His commission is more
cogent than that with which another potentate
favoured his ambassadors in their mission to
Hungerford," retorted the offended minister,
approaching nearer to the bedside.

" Your third colleague, that noble gentleman
who is so closely muffled from the cold chill of
night, I know not," said the King inquiringly,
darting a suspicious glance at the figure to whom
he alluded.

" We only wait your Majesty's perusal of the
presents," said Halifax, handing the king a letter
from the prince.

" Yes, his Majesty," urged the unknown
person, " must read it at once."

Looking up from the paper before him, startled
by this rude remark—" I should know that voice,"
murmured James, partly to himself.

" Your Majesty is aware," said Halifax, softly,

" that the palace is invested by the Dutch troops, and in spite of my mediation. You may be treated as a prisoner, then trust me your only safety is not in the capital." Then approaching close to the king, whispered, " I am anxious to preserve your life ; but, as you implied, I am watched. But see who it is that is already too near you."

The king's eye fell on Lord Delamere, who stood now undisguised and terribly revealed at the foot of the bed, glaring upon the monarch whom he hated. James turned pale ; a sickening horror for a moment came over him. Monmouth's rebellion and its alarms arose to the monarch's memory, with all its painful associations.

Lord Delamere had been associated in arms with the duke. He objected to the jurisdiction of the court of peers before which he was arraigned, but his claim to be tried in parliament was overruled. James attended in person, and, though Delamere was acquitted, there was little doubt of his guilt. At his hands James naturally dreaded retribution ; but soon discovered more sympathy in the face of the nobleman who had lately raised the standard of insurrection in Cheshire than the mean traitor Halifax could bring to his countenance. That faithless friend and pretended servant of James treated his king in the hour of his sorrow and his fall with mean insolence and insult.

Steadily fixing his eyes on his noble tormentors, James exclaimed, "Methinks your talents claim a better employment than this night's dark work. The iron barons of old were scarcely hard enough to intrude themselves into the chamber of King John, even to extort a Magna Charta, granting the liberties of the church and the protection of the people. ' Et tu Brute,' " sadly said the king to Halifax, as he folded up the paper, which he had carefully perused. "Then must I leave my capital, to which I am welcomed by my subjects ?   And, Lord Halifax, would you still persuade me you are my friend ?"

"Indeed, my liege," replied the minister, with as much emotion as he could feign, " at no period was I more devoted to your highest interests.   I advise you at once to retire from London : your further delay will cause that bloodshed which your Majesty would be the first to avert or to deplore.   Should there be a collision between the Coldstream Guards and the Dutch troops I dare not answer for your Majesty's life."

There were two points James would stipulate for if he could bring himself to leave London.   First, that his temporary residence should be at Rochester ; to this William's commissioners finally agreed.   But the second urged by James, that he should depart publicly through the city, was rudely and harshly overruled by Halifax, who declared loudly that such an exhibition would breed disorder and move compassion."

His words were so high, that Hales, with Strickland and others, who were now in one of the anterooms adjoining the royal chamber, feeling alarmed for the king, hastened to his Majesty, and met the three departing lords, whose task it was to expel their sovereign from his palace, and expose him to the inclemency of the weather on the swollen river.

All the three had passed Hales but Halifax, who, either by accident or intention, jostled him in the door; Lion at the same instant flew at the great statesman's throat, and to the ineffable delight of Strickland and O'Brian, who had been attracted by the scuffle, had nearly pulled him to the ground, when his master cried, "Down, Lion! down, good dog! down!" and made the animal relinquish his grip.

The extricated traitor was too glad to make his retreat without a word of remonstrance.

The young men were quite vexed at the necessity which induced Hales to make the dog desist from his loyal purpose, for Halifax had been wantonly morose and unnecessarily severe, either to show his zeal as a recent convert, or his revenge for what he considered unfair treatment; while Shrewsbury, the king's open opponent, with great deference to the unfortunate monarch, laboured to soothe his afflictions, by gratifying him in every request.

The next morning was wet and stormy ; black with clouds, cold and dreary; yet, the banks of the Thames were crowded with spectators, who poured down from all quarters, to take a parting look at their unhappy king.

About twelve o'clock the king bade adieu to the lords and gentlemen and foreign ministers who had gathered round him to give him this last proof of their respect. Amongst them might be noticed Evelyn, as a mere observer of the scene. Pepys, St. Aubyn, and Dryden, stood still nearer to the royal person, Cornets Strickland and Clare were followed by Morton and Hough, all of whom were among the sorrowing number who burst into tears. To these, as well as to the thousands present, this inglorious spectacle of insulted royalty was a mournful humiliation. They could not behold, without the burning blush of shame, the King of England hemmed in by a convoy of Dutchmen, like a base criminal on his way to the dungeon or the scaffold.

Unprotected from the drenching rain and from the obtrusive gaze of a vulgar throng, whose very sympathy at such a time is painful, James, hastening to the river, went on board the royal barge, which with such surroundings was a mere mockery of majesty. He was attended by the Lords Arran, Dumbarton, Lichfield, Aylesbury, and Dundee. At length, after an hour's delay, in an open boat and exposed to the soaking rain, at a signal the royal captive was proceeding down the river. It was only at the express command of the king that Strickland could be restrained from placing himself near his Majesty; as for Clare, whose blood had been boiling to fight, and whose spirit had been chafed by the morbid inactivity and passive submission of his royal master to such an intolerable outrage, his feelings were like those of an insulted lion, vainly lashing his sides against the iron bars of his cage. Consternation at seeing his king tamely made prisoner without a single stroke stunned him so terribly, that it was not till the barge was under weigh that, in the absence of his orders, he knew what to do. But now, as if by an irresistible impulse, he plunged into the dark river, and by dint of swimming was soon at his sovereign's feet. The next moment a splash was heard, and the assembled crowd cried, "There goes a dog!" "A popish dog," cried the rabble, "to bark about the king!" And many a bet was made that he could not make even the last of the boats; but he stoutly breasted the rough river and was, contrary to all expectation, after five minutes' desperate swimming, in the royal barge : and the inference is that Sir Edward Hales was in the king's little British court.

"This is, indeed, a sad sight," said Evelyn to Dryden. "We have seen the king take barge for Gravesend; but never will he return, unless as a competitor in arms for his abandoned throne, and steeped in the blood of Englishmen."

" Why may he not be recalled by the voice of the populace, if we embalm him in their memories and affections by loyal songs and patriotic appeals ?" rejoined Dryden.

" Never !" again said the great journalist. " The prince is on his way to St. James's, and takes as firm possession of Whitehall with his troops, as the lethargy of despair has taken possession of the king's mind."

" The worst offence after all," broke in Pepys, "that James ever gave to his navy and army and the country, and for which, on reflection, he will never be forgiven, is, that he suffers himself to be driven away from his ancestral palaces and hereditary realms, and, that, without a struggle. While there was a shot in the locker he ought to have held his own."

" The energy of manhood has been slain," cried Dryden, " by the hand of those whom he trusted and loved."

" In his present state of mind and body," rejoined Evelyn, " he could not grapple with the storm, because he does not feel he is equal to victory."

Many and affecting were the regrets and fears, the significant looks rather than words of loyal sympathy, mingled with silent reflections on the poor king's apathy and passive subjection, exchanged between the noble adherents of James on that dismal voyage.

Clare's feelings mastered his judgment and defied etiquette. "By the Lord," cried he, without directing his remark to any one in particular, "'tisn't here I'd be, if the brave old general had only given the word. On my sacred word of honour, if Dutch Billy had put his foot on the Isle of St. Patrick, Tyrconnel, ay, and every man, woman and child, barrin' a few d—d heretics, would have sent the Dutch boor after Pharaoh and his host into the Red Sea of their own blood. But sure the king, God help him! though 'twas himself that held the trump card, he played the game into the hands of the Devil's own, and lost the honours."

The noblemen and gentlemen who attended their king to the water side, sorrowed most of all at their own sad forebodings, which said, "We shall see his face no more." Even the most zealous friends of William could scarcely have seen unmoved the sad and ignominious close, for such it now seemed to all parties, of a dynasty which promised to be so great.

Among those who remained behind, there were none, perhaps, more sincerely and unaffectedly sorry for James than the little group who now watched the receding boats, and gazed regretfully on the departure of the captive monarch. This group consisted of St. Aubyn, Morton, Hough and Strickland. They watched

the louring heavens and dark undulating waters,
with unquiet eyes.   Their hearts had gone back
to the past, and rested on scenes which never
could return—they had probably looked their
last on their banished Sovereign.   Strickland
stood silent, and hid his face with his hands.
Morton suddenly addressed him, knowing he
was deep in the confidence of the king, and
asked, " Will he ever return to London ?"

Strickland replied, " If the king's efforts are
as effectual as his hopes are sanguine he will."

Hough marked his sympathy with the king,
and possibly also with Lily Penderel, by a silence
as deep, though less thoughtful, perhaps, than
that of St. Aubyn.

Mr. Hough, who had made a voyage up the
Thames to witness, though not to share in the
fortunes of James, was not subject to such
restraint as Miss Penderel, and was, therefore,
only less unwilling to offend Mr. St. Aubyn, than
to see her whose happiness Mr. St. Aubyn by
no means identified with Hough's meeting her
in London.

The whole of Dryden's party had separated,
each bent upon his own pursuit.   Strickland
had been that very day directed to proceed to
Scotland.   Morton was obliged to return to his
pressing affairs in Berks, before he could consider the request, or, accede to Hough's wish to
visit Miss Penderel.   Scarcely had Hough
returned to his inn when he found a letter from

the great Doctor Hough, dated the fifteenth of December, commanding his return to Oxford without a moment's delay. " The Revolution," says he in his epistle, "is no longer doubtful, and whatever may be our loyalty to the exiled king, ' the powers that be are ordained of God ;' and he, therefore, that resisteth the power, resisteth the ordinance of God.' But William's government will be the power, therefore we must not resist it. On this very day," adds the valiant Doctor, " the Princess Ann is making an entry into Oxford to meet her husband, Prince George, and her progress is as grand as that of her poor deluded father, whose short-lived honours you will probably witness in London. The Earl of Northampton, with five hundred horse, is leading the van. Her Royal Highness is preceded by the Bishop of London, at the head of a noble troop of gentlemen : his lordship riding in a purple cloak, martial habit, pistols before him, and his sword drawn,—not merely the sword of the spirit, but a real, material, not to say a carnal weapon. Never, it is said, was the church militant and the future Queen of England, as the head of the Church, more faithfully represented. The rear was brought up by a body of militia troops.

"But I had almost forgotten to tell you what comes home most forcibly to us, the President, fellows, and demies of Magdalen College. As though it had reference to our own statutes in

particular as well as those of England, the
Bishop's cornet bore a glorious standard, inscribed with golden letters, the constitutional
words, ' Nolumus leges Angliæ mutare.' " No
sooner had St. Aubyn, to whom Hough read
the letter, heard the inscription, than he quietly
declared ; this could scarcely be a guarantee
against a change in the laws ; though it was very
well selected for the moment. " These imposing
words," said he, " were used by the barons of
England at Merton College, 1258, in rejection
of the petitions of the clergy. Simon de Mont-
fort, Earl of Leicester, soon after the session of
the ' *Mad Parliament*' at Oxford, presided over
a committee of nobles, and throwing himself into
the popular cause, took the governing power out
of the hands of Henry III. Thus he became
the darling, if not the saviour of his country.
He assumed the power of a dictator, and origi-
nated that great change of the laws which ended
in the institution of parliament and the House of
Commons. The Protector, Cromwell, had recourse
to the same inscription or motto, and effected a
similar change in the very form of our government ; on the standard of a new dynasty, it is
simply an indication of the popular mind ; yet,"
added Mr. St. Aubyn, " since our young friend,
Miss Penderel, sailed last night for Ireland, and
since your worthy uncle's orders are peremptory,
I would advise your instant return to Oxford. I
have weighed well all you have confided to me :

you are indulging in a vision which never can be realised. Your young mind cannot calculate the evils that would attend the fulfilment of your dream. The obstacles to your union with Miss Penderel are insuperable."

"Why? My dear sir," replied Hough with a sad smile; "You seem to be a prophet as well as a teacher. You divine my thoughts, and see results, which rest with God alone." "Out of the fulness of your heart you have spoken to me," said St. Aubyn, "and it needs no prophet's tongue to tell the rest. The results are, as you say, in the hands of God. But all the probabilities are against what you now think would make you happy. There is always bitterness, even in the most affectionate words of counsel, which casts a shadow on the bright promise of the youth to whom it is addressed. As Miss Penderel's deliverer from death, you must feel that the life which you have saved should be devoted to your happiness—you would claim her hand—her heart. That you love her deeply is but too evident; that she regards your happiness and her own too tenderly to afford you more than gratitude, is equally certain."

"Then," cried Hough, desperately, "since on your assurance, she does not return my love, I will fly from her at once and for ever." And with a melancholy smile, he said, "To-morrow's sunset, if possible, shall find me in Magdalen

College. Farewell. Tell her at least to think of her promise, if she forgets him to whom she made it. Farewell, my friend, farewell!"

That very day he was on his way to Oxford; and the same hour of the evening which witnessed his departure from London, saw the arrival of James and his small, though noble escort, at Gravesend.

END OF VOL. II.

www.ingramcontent.com/pod-product-compliance
Lightning Source LLC
Chambersburg PA
CBHW060529030726
47498CB00004B/1124